Ian' Revenge

Payback

Jeffrey R. Crimmel

A Murder Mystery

Sequel to Brain Bleed

ISBN:-10: 0985223286

ISBN-13: 978-0-9852232-81

DEDICATION

I would like to thank my writers group who have helped me with editing and many other duties writers hate to do in the process of finishing a book. It takes a thick skin to survive these groups and I've grown a few layers in the process. The group members are valuable and at the same time I want to kill one or two every other week. Good thing I write fiction, murder mysteries and can play out my fantasies on paper.

ACKNOWLEDGMENTS

I would like to acknowledge the people who are playing the game of life as fairly as they can. I especially want to thank teachers who give back so much of their lives to prepare the next generation in their adventures ahead. Also my wife, Suzanne, from whom I gained inspiration for Leslie. Our bantering has given me material for the dialogues that appears in the story.

Also by Jeffrey R. Crimmel

Living Beneath the Radar

Learning to Love the Peso

Centavo; A Dog From Mexico

The 60's; If You Remember It You Didn't Live It

Brain Bleed

Nab Yoga

Chapter One

How did this happen? Ian asked himself. His father had recently died and he was CEO of a company that had been reduced to a shell of its former self. Somehow an insurgent had scaled the walls of the *castle* and dealt him and his family a devastating blow. He was not completely ruined, but he was still in the dark as to who the enemy was.

Ian made a call. "Anything turn up, Smith?"

Smith was the head of Ian's investigation and *special jobs* team. Ian gave the pictures of each Company member to Smith before he left for his father's funeral in Ireland, to see if the team could determine who took them. Ian had just returned home from the meeting with the members who voted to close the clinic in Mexico.

"There should be a full report on your desk, Mr. McClure. I put it there this morning. Try the upper left corner."

"Oh yes, I see it. I'll call you back after I read it."

Ian spent the next thirty minutes reading the report. It stated that all the pictures were taken at the memorial service from a distance. Strong telephoto lenses were used from two different angles. Most of the pictures came from directly across the street as Company members left the church. A few came from the apartment building next to the church as people got out of their cars. From the angles of the headshots the team determined the roof of the office building across the street was the first location and the third or fourth floor of the apartment complex next to the church was the other spot.

Included in the report were the results of the interviews of office members and apartment occupants. The team asked if anyone, not a member of the office staff or occupant of the apartments, was noticed walking around either building.

Ian called Smith back. "Smith, it says in the report that two suspects turned up and facial sketches were made. I can't find them in the report."

"We are using them right now to see if we can get a match. So far we believe there are two women involved because neither description matches the other. Both women were seen carrying their own camera bag. One was spotted in the office building near the elevator and the other was noticed leaving the apartment complex. We still don't have a lot of detail yet. Mostly hair color, height, and a few basic features, but it's a start."

Ian now had a lead. "It says in the report you contacted a few cab companies and discovered that two women were dropped off during the same time frame as the memorial ceremony."

"Yes," Smith added. "According to the cab drivers, each woman was dropped off a block away from the church in the same location. The pickup locations were different. One woman came from the front of a coffee shop downtown and the other was picked up near a department store in the Village. No apartment buildings were within a block of the two locations. It seemed the women covered their tracks leading to their homes."

"Anything else?" Ian asked.

"The sketch artists are in the process of getting detailed descriptions of each woman from the cab drivers and the result should be in your hands within the hour. Matching a sketch to a real person isn't easy but it's possible."

Ian knew he was on his own in the investigation to find the people who hurt his family and business. No one else knew what he and his private research team were up to.

*****

Julia woke before Robert. She slipped out of bed without disturbing him. Wanting her life back was a priority and being cut off from New York was difficult. She had to change her identity while helping Robert take down the Company and their corrupt practices with the NYSE. She made the move to Albuquerque because she was in love with Robert, but she was born and raised in New York. You can take a New Yorker out of the City but you can't take the City out of a New Yorker.

Ten minutes later, Robert woke up and reached over for Julia. They usually greeted the morning with lovemaking, but not today. After a shower, Robert dressed and went into the living room. He found Julia drinking a cup of coffee.

"I made a pot for us. Come join me on the couch."

Robert could sense something was bothering her. He poured a cup of coffee and added his usual soy creamer.

"Is everything all right, Julia? You seem a little withdrawn."

"I miss New York, but not to live there. I really love being here with you, but I need to visit the City. I was thinking, since I have a new ID, a quick trip would do us both good. We could fly there, take in a Broadway play, have dinner, and fly back the next morning. How about seeing *The Book of Mormon?* You might get a kick out of it since you were one of them a few years back. What do you think?"

"Wow, you caught me off guard. I've never been a big city boy and seldom go to New York, but if this is what you need, I think we can pull it off. When do you want to go?" Robert asked.

"How about tonight? We could get tickets online, stay at the Hilton, and fly back tomorrow."

"All that traveling for only one night? Why not two nights? Then you could go shopping. We both need a break." Robert loved Julia and wanted to keep her happy. He was sure they could fly into the city without being spotted. Even though the Company was no longer conducting business as usual, he and Julia would not be completely safe as long as Ian McClure was still alive.

"Really? Two days? Robert, you're the best. Put down your coffee and come here."

Robert put down his coffee. He knew from her voice tone what would come next. Sex on the couch was not as good as pool sex, but it was a close second. This made up for missed lovemaking in bed.

Chapter Two

Three days later, Robert and Julia returned from their short trip to New York City. They were able to see *The Book of Mormon* on Broadway and enjoy a wonderful meal at Sardis in Manhattan. Julia lit up with the energy of the City. After a day of shopping the two were back in New Mexico without being detected.

Alan, Robert's computer assistant from the university, watched the activity of the clinic in Mexico for the past three days, from the satellite surveillance monitor in the home office. The building still appeared to be in shutdown mode. Furniture and boxes were removed and the new clinic director was observed showing the building to real estate agents. The two clinical nurses disappeared in the footage entering or leaving the building. Dr. Gupta put suitcases into a limo the day before and drove away.

"Are you sure Dr. Gupta hasn't resurfaced?" Robert asked Alan as he walked into the office. "His absence is a good indication this shutdown is really happening. I suspect they'll go underground in some used war bunker if they ever set up shop again." Robert still had a hard time believing he had forced the clinic to close.

"I'm sure that building's being evacuated. The new director is conducting this whole process. A moving truck pulled out about an hour ago with all the furniture." Alan sat back in his chair. He felt great and thought this case would look good on his job resume. *Instrumental in forcing a group of billionaires to stop conducting shady business practices on Wall Street.* This was his idea of humor in the workforce.

Julia came into the room after overhearing the conversation from the kitchen. "This calls for a celebration. I think we should have a party to honor everyone who played a part."

Robert was excited about the closure but remained cautious. Rich people didn't like to lose. The best way to make sure they didn't regroup was to keep tabs on each one. He continued his routine investigation cases because he had bills to pay. Having a party to celebrate was a great idea. The team needed to feel they'd accomplished something and be rewarded for their effort.

"What'd you have in mind, Julia? I'm sure you'll come up with something wonderful. Who should we invite?"

"Jason and Rosa, William and Leslie, and Cathy. You'd like that wouldn't you, Alan?" Alan nodded his head. "I know she wants to meet you in person. Let's keep the celebration small. Too many outside names may not be a good idea."

Alan didn't say anything, but meeting the woman he'd had several conversations with over the phone perked his interest.

"How do you see this happening?" Robert asked. "We can't have the party here. We still have to hide where we live. I'm positive Ian McClure will not let this situation go. The Irish have a reputation for revenge."

"The only person that has to travel a long way is Cathy. William and Leslie can drive from Arizona, so let's rent a meeting hall and have a meal catered. We can even invite the CAT scan tech if you want or even Laura."

"We better not spread ourselves too thin," Robert added. "Let's leave Megan and Laura out. If either one is ever tied in with us they could be in danger."

"I understand, sweetheart. I'll set the whole thing up. I need to call Cathy on your phone after we decide on a date and place. Do you want me to call Jason as well?"

"Sure. Hopefully, Rosa can come too."

Julia agreed and started to make the arrangements for the dinner party. An Elks Lodge was available to rent for next Saturday. Cathy was available to fly out for the weekend. William and Leslie could also come and would drive from Tucson. Jason and Rosa did not think they were being followed anymore so they planned to stay the night. Alan said he'd be there for sure. Meeting Cathy was of utmost importance to him.

*****

Saturday night arrived and everything was in order. Julia and Robert met Alan and Cathy at the Elks Lodge. Alan picked Cathy up at the airport. He had only talked to her on the phone when she was hired to photograph the memorial service for Ian's father. He had a picture Julia gave him when the two women were roommates in New York. Jason and William were e-mailed messages to their cars, while in route, as to where the dinner location was. Julia made sure the celebration remained as clandestine as the investigation.

Once inside the lodge, the couples greeted each other with hugs and high fives. It was a relief to know that the case appeared to be over. Everyone was seated with drinks in their hands when Robert rose to made the first toast.

"Here's to a job well done," he said. "We have accomplished what none of us thought possible. The clinic in Mexico has shut down. It looks like our demands have been met, and we can go on with our lives. Thank you all."

Glasses were raised and excitement filled each person.

"I now want to turn this over to William who has a few words to say regarding how we got to this point in the investigation," Robert said.

William stood up to express his feelings and give a little of the history as to how they all met. "A little over a year ago I developed a blood clot in my left leg. Due to a freak accident with the treatment, a brain bleed occurred, which enabled me to see into the future. The journey took me to Nevada and eventually to Albuquerque where I met Jason and Robert. After agreeing to work for the Company under the management of Jason I also joined Robert's investigation of the same organization. I became a mole for Robert. Italy and Peru were side trips and we were able to retrieve information about the research clinic and the formula used to recreate the blood thinner to foresee the stock market numbers."

Leslie rolled her eyes, but let her husband tell his story. She was thankful he was giving everyone the short version.

"The Company carried out evil deeds. Robert lost Karl who was murdered by this group. Several previous clients also died in the Italian clinic. An undisclosed number of homeless people, used in the experiments, were also killed in the testing phase. Through Robert's continued investigation with the help of Alan and Cathy, the names and faces of the Company are now known. We have enough information to make their lives difficult. Instead of trying to put these men in jail, we've decided to force them to stop their activities and reduce their stock market trading to a level playing field. Taking on billionaires and trying to defeat them in the court might prove next to impossible. At this moment, their illegal investment activities are terminated. We did it."

William paused and took a drink of his beer. He stood for a moment, reflecting on the past, and then continued.

"Today we have the compound, I mentioned earlier. Our job is to make sure Ian does not continue activating clients in another location. We have no control over that at this time. We can only threaten him with exposure and legal prosecutions. We are at a stalemate, but we seem to have the upper hand. We know who they are but they do not know who we are. Keeping it this way is a priority. Secrecy will enable us to live our lives and continue to monitor the previous Company members. I've said enough. I'd like Robert to fill us in with the next move."

William sat down and Robert stood to speak.

"My dear friends, we have come a long way. This case has been my most rewarding so far. It may be over but we won't know for a while. Alan, my computer genius, has done a fantastic job hacking through firewalls and retrieving information about each Company member. Many of these men gained their wealth through devious methods. Their quest for power seems to have enveloped their entire beings. Money is no longer their goal." Robert paused and looked around the room.

"A number of them invested in desalination plants around the world. Their plan is to control the world through drinking water. I have a plan to stop them, but I'm not ready to reveal it at this time. What I want to add to William's speech is this. I couldn't have done any of this without you."

Robert looked over at Julia, then continued. "Through this journey, Julia and I have formed a team and a partnership. Jason and Rosa are creating a new life in Santa Fe. William and Leslie moved to Arizona from Mexico and are living comfortably in their retirement. Alan is starting an Internet business so geeks can meet each other online. Cathy is here representing our New York team. Because of her and Laura who is till in New York, we have the pictures and names of all the Company members. Their work was the final thrust into the heart of this group of men, and they are no longer invisible."

Robert was starting to wind down.

"My hope is the case is closed. My suspicion, we may see more activity down the road, but right now is a time of celebration. That is why we are here. Let's raise our glasses as a toast. We have earned it and hopefully made the world a better place."

Everyone stood up and raised their glasses. Leslie could have had a V-8 so she did. The rest were drinking beer and wine. A sigh of relief seemed to come from each person as they toasted to a job well done. Luck had been on their side as well as hard work. They were all ready for this special time together.

During the meal, Alan and Cathy were deep into conversations to learn more about each other. Cathy told Alan all about the classes she was taking and what she had learned so far. Alan was surprised as to how comfortable he felt around her. She was easy to be with and didn't talk to him as though he was some kind of computer nerd.

Alan told her about the Geek Mingle site he had been working on and what it involved. He knew there were others like him looking for partners to share their lives with.

Cathy was impressed with Alan and was attracted to him right away. She had a good feeling about Alan even though he was several years younger. He did not try to impress her with conquests and material goods he'd accumulated. Alan was honest and easy to be with in all aspects. She wanted to explore where this connection might take them.

The dinner came to an end with farewells and more hugs. Jason and Rosa, as well as William, and Leslie departed to Hotel Albuquerque in Old Town. Robert and Julia exited after saying goodbye to Cathy and Alan.

Alan drove Cathy to her hotel near the river. She invited him up to her room for another glass of wine. He did his best to play it cool and accepted. At the same time, he was somewhat intimidated by this older woman taking an interest in him. He had a feeling as to where this visit to her room might lead. He was right. Alan never made it home. He spent the night trying things with Cathy he never knew the human body could do. She was a wild woman and Alan loved every minute of it.

*****

The phone rang at Ian's home. No one called Ian at home unless it was of utmost importance.

"Mr. McClure, we may have a lead. We were able to make a 70% match of the sketch of one of the women at the memorial service to a person at LaGuardia airport. The woman took a noon flight to Albuquerque via Atlanta on Saturday. We checked the arrival tapes and identified her getting off the flight. Some man in Albuquerque picked her up. We did a trace on each of their faces. Both identities have a firewall blocking any information connected with IDs. This is unusual and only someone with expert computer abilities could have placed a firewall around this file. We can't break through the wall. We feel confident this is one of the photographers at the service because she matches the sketch from the office building."

"Good work, Smith. Take the picture of the woman and show it to the office workers in the building across from the church. If they say it's the same woman then we may have caught a break. Also, show it to the cab driver that drove her to the service. If both parties say the picture is the same woman, then we have her."

"Shall I call you at home or at the office if we find anything else?"

"Call me on this line. I want to know right away. Again, good job."

McClure hung up and heaved a sigh. He had been warned not to search for members of the group investigating him. If he did take anybody out it had to look like an accident. First, he needed to find the woman. Was she from New York or New Mexico? If she lived in New York, she'd be flying back. Ian placed another call to his team.

"Smith, Ian McClure again. Keep checking the tapes of the same airlines with all their flights back to LaGuardia. More than likely she had a round trip ticket. If she does return then there should be a tape showing her leaving Albuquerque."

The flight back to New York would give his men time to get into position. The return flight went through Atlanta so it added more time for his team to get ready. He would make these people pay for what they did to him and his family. The game of the spider and the fly had begun.

*****

Alan and Cathy were having breakfast in the hotel dining room. It was Sunday morning and the restaurant was quiet. Most of the hotel residents were either sleeping in or going to mass at the Catholic Church a block away.

"How did you sleep, Alan? I know I slept well."

Alan had a glow about him. Both woke up several times during the night and continued what they had started the minute they got into the hotel room. Cathy had more experience with sex and guided Alan into trying different positions that satisfied her needs. The night passed with several replays.

"I slept really well. My appetite is at a ten. I could eat two meals right now," Alan said.

Cathy smiled. She liked this cute geek and found his humor to be enough to keep her laughing. She knew he was smart and probably spent a lot of time in his head. Any time with her would help to balance him out.

"I don't have a set schedule," Cathy said. "My flight is open and I can fly back anytime. How's your schedule?"

"No classes on Sunday. I'd love to spend the day with you. Have you ever visited Old Town in Albuquerque? There's plenty to see and walking around the plaza can be fun."

"That'd be great, Alan. I really like the weather here. New York is already freezing and 60 degrees here in December is fantastic."

"When do you have to be back?" Alan knew Cathy worked in New York and this weekend fling would eventually end.

"I probably should take a flight back on Monday night. I've got a job on Tuesday afternoon. I do different things and fill in for all kinds of work. I'm basically a freelancer. When Julia called me regarding this last gig I was excited to talk to you on the phone. My computer classes are in the evenings so I'm able to work days and study during the night."

"I was happy to finally meet you too. I usually stay busy with school and working for Robert. I don't date much."

"Tell me about the site you're starting up," Cathy said. She was interested in Alan and his project and wanted him to feel at ease with her.

"The idea of the Geek Mingle site came from Julia, or at least she started me thinking about it. It's ready to launch in about a month. It took a lot of work and research but it's close to having a start date."

"I think you may be onto something, Alan. There are probably a lot of shy, smart people like you who don't want to go to bars and other silly places to meet superficial women or men with gold chains around their necks. Besides coffee houses, where else do they meet?"

"Some go with their friends to Star Trek conventions. I think the idea may catch on because geeks are now accepted in society. There is a TV show called *The Big Bang Theory*. That pretty girl from across the hall fell for one of the geeks and they seemed to hit it off."

"Well Alan, you have a point there. I was attracted to you when we first talked on the phone. I'm really glad I made the effort to come to this dinner and meet you in person. What do you say we finish up here and go to Old Town for the morning? Then we can come back to my room have more fun together. I really like making love with you and would like spending rest of the afternoon in bed. What do you say?"

Alan could already feel himself getting hard. He was ready to go back to the bedroom right now, but he knew Cathy would like a trip to Old Town.

"Sounds like a plan. You're really an amazing woman, Cathy. I had no idea we'd have such a connection."

"Alan, I hoped I'd meet a man like you someday. I believe we have a lot to teach each other. Computers are what I want to learn about and I could teach you a few things under the sheets. How do you feel about that as a fair exchange?"

"You're a wild woman and I'd like that a lot. Let's visit Old Town, have lunch, and take up where we left off," Alan said trying to contain his excitement.

Cathy leaned over and gave Alan a kiss on his lips. "Okay, let's get out of here. Albuquerque, here we come."

*****

Robert and Julia woke up on Sunday, a little hung-over. Coffee was perking and a fire blazing in the fireplace. Sitting in their robes and drinking a dark roast of some Jamaican brew was a celebration in itself. Feelings of accomplishment filled both of them.

"What is on our schedule, sweetheart?" Pet names were now a part of their lover's vocabulary. They were a team in all respects and basked in the afterglow of their accomplishments.

"I think we need a break. I'll call Alan and tell him to take the day off on Monday. I've got a feeling he and Cathy might have hit it off from the way they left the dinner last night. Your roommate really seemed interested in Alan and he seemed to enjoy the attention."

"Knowing Cathy, I bet they're still with each other," Julia agreed. "Maybe we should call Alan this evening so we don't mess up any plans they may have today. It's Sunday so we can go somewhere or just hang out at home."

"I think you should decide what to do today. We both have earned some downtime and I'm ready to do what you want."

"All right, let's do a movie marathon day. We were so busy the last month we couldn't go to any theaters. Just you and me and Netflix."

"Sounds like a plan. I'll cook breakfast and then we can start the movie day in an hour. I only need to check the tapes of the clinic in Mexico to make sure everything is still closing down."

"Okay, but no other business. We can catch up with work

tomorrow. I think Cathy has to be at work on Tuesday. I'll call her tonight and say goodbye."

Julia made contact with Cathy that evening and was not surprised she was still with Alan. She told Cathy to let Alan know he was not needed on Monday. She then said her goodbyes to Cathy and demanded a full report of her time with Alan the next time they spoke.

Chapter Three

Ian was back at work downsizing the office space of The Company and giving severance pay to the remaining employees. Only his private assistant and the investigation team remained. Jack Wear, the clinic director, would remain in Mexico for another week until the sale of the research lab was finalized.

Ian still reeled from the impact of what the Company had just experienced. He still had no word of the mystery woman who flew from New York to New Mexico. His team was in place but any surveillance tapes could only be accessed with a twenty-minute delay. If she caught a flight back to the City, Ian's men would be waiting for her.

Monday evening, Ian received a call from Smith. "Mr. McClure, our suspect boarded a flight back to New York. I sent a team to LaGuardia to wait for her. They should be there in half an hour. Her connecting flight from Atlanta lands in an hour."

"Good work, Smith. Tell the team to only follow and don't interact in any way. Where she lives is all I need. Is that clear?"

"Yes, sir. They'll report back to me as soon as they have any information and I'll call you."

"We'll talk later." Ian hung up.

Hurting or killing the girl was of no value to Ian. She could be one of the two women spotted with a camera bag on the day of the memorial service but probably not the mastermind of this operation. He was now one step closer to finding the person in charge.

*****

Cathy departed from her flight and walked to the exit. She only had a carry-on bag because she only needed clothing for the weekend. The taxi line was short and she boarded the third cab in line.

"Where to Miss?"

"Have you ever been to a bar called Leggs? It's located in the Village."

"Is that the all-women's bar?" The driver rolled his eyes as he asked the question.

"Yes, you know it?"

"Dropped off a few women there. Must be a popular place for the ladies who want to get away from men?"

"Yes, that's it. I need a drink before going home."

The driver drove without making any conversation. Cathy wondered if the driver thought she was going to a Lesbian bar and that she was gay. She finally broke the silence. "Have you been driving for a long time? I see your name is Carlos on your taxi ID. Are you from New York?"

"Driving for ten years now. I was a teacher in Chile for five years but couldn't get a teaching job in the U.S. By the way miss, we have a car that's been following us since the airport and it's still behind us. I don't think it is a coincidence that two people are going to the same location in the Village, all the way from the airport. We're only a few blocks away, so should I drive to the bar or go somewhere else?"

Cathy turned around in her seat. She hadn't noticed anyone

following her at the airport, and yet there was a car right on her tail. She had to think fast.

"Drop me off at the bar, and thank you for noticing. I'm in your debt." Cathy got out at Leggs and gave the driver a pile of bills. As he drove away, she thought, Carlos might have just saved my life.

Cathy proceeded to the bar entrance and turned, just as the mystery car passed. She memorized the license plate and wrote it down after she was seated inside. The windows of the car were tinted so no one was visible. She watched from the bar window as the black Lincoln Town Car parked a block up the street from Leggs. She made a call to Robert on his secure line.

"Robert, this is Cathy."

"Hi, Cathy, are you home?"

"Not quite. I took a cab to a bar for a drink and was followed by a car from the airport and now it's parked outside. I got the license plate number. Someone is interested in me, Robert."

"Give me the number and I'll get Alan to trace it tomorrow. Can you get home safely without being followed?"

"Yes, I think so. I'll call Laura and see if she can pick me up. I can change my appearance enough to get out without being detected. I'll call tomorrow and let you know what happened."

"No, Cathy. Call tonight. Julia and I won't sleep until we know you're safe."

"All right, I'll call later. Bye, Robert, and love to Julia."

Cathy gave Laura a call and explained the situation. Laura would be there in twenty minutes. Cathy also told Laura to change her appearance so she couldn't be identified.

During the time Laura drove to the bar, Cathy went into the ladies room, put on sunglasses, tied up her hair and changed into different clothes. She was dressed and returned to the bar just as Laura arrived. They greeted each other with a hug and a kiss.

Cathy left her suitcase with Mae, the bartender, and told her she would pick it up in a few days. She gave Mae a twenty to ensure its safety. Cathy also asked Mae to deny she had seen her or Laura if anyone asked. The two women walked out of the bar, arm in arm, pretending to be a little drunk, and got into Laura's VW. They passed the Lincoln a block away, and it didn't follow them. The escape was successful.

When they reached her neighborhood, Cathy thanked Laura and gave her a kiss on the cheek. "You may have saved my life, Laura. I'll call you later and tell you about the weekend. Robert is following up on this incident in case we are identified by The Company."

"Good. I want to hear everything," Laura said.

Cathy had Laura drop her off a block away from her apartment to make sure she was not followed. She called Robert as soon as she was inside. Her body was covered in sweat due to the tension she had just experienced.

"Robert, I'm home."

"Are you all right?"

"Yes, I believe so. That was exciting. Let me know what you find out from the license plate."

"I will. Are you sure you weren't followed? We need to know you're safe."

"I changed my clothes in the bar and left my suitcase. I'll send someone to pick it up tomorrow. Also, I walked a block to my apartment to make sure I was not followed."

"Good. I'll let Julia know, and she'll call you tomorrow. We're both relieved you're safe."

Cathy hung up and flopped on the bed. She'd call Alan in the morning. Right now, she wanted to remember the great time they had together. Alan was a good student and responded to her in every way. Alan is one brainy nerd, she thought, who really turns me on. The best part is, I really like him.

*****

Ian got the call around seven the next morning, and Smith reported the bad news.

"We lost her. She took a cab from the airport and went to a bar in the Village. The team parked on the street and waited till the bar closed, but she never came out. One of the team went inside just as the bar closed and showed the picture of the woman to the manager. She said she didn't recognize her. The bar was empty so she must have slipped out the back or disguised herself and left earlier."

Ian was back to square one. He didn't know where the mystery woman lived or her name. She must have known we were following her. How else would she have known to escape? She was smarter than he expected.

The only information Ian had was that Albuquerque might be in play in his investigation. Now that the mystery woman knew she was being followed she'd change her appearance whenever she traveled. She was gone.

*****

Robert gave Alan the license number of the car, and the story of Cathy's adventure, the next morning at the office. A ten-minute search by Alan turned up a private company called Dexus, which owned the black Lincoln. With a little more research, he also came across the name, McClure.

"The Company owns Dexus," Alan told Robert. "Ian has the car title in his name.

"Ian didn't take my message seriously about trying to find us," Robert said. "I've got another project for you, Alan. We have to make Ian believe we can hurt him, so we're going to do just that."

"I'm looking forward to sticking it to that asshole," Alan said.

"Me too, but we have to have a cool head when we do the sticking. Remember the saying. *Don't get angry, get even.* We have to make our next move hurt."

Alan was much more invested now in damaging The Company because they attempted to go after someone he cared about. *The Revenge of the Nerds* had shifted into second gear.

*****

Peter Marks, Paul Orbit, and Thomas Raptor were the three Company names Robert gave Alan. They would be the first sacrificial lambs.

"These are the names of The Company members who we're going to send to three different government agencies. The information contains past activities and how they made money through the Company. We'll include their investment records and show the agencies that these men knew which stocks to sell and when."

"We're only going after three?" Alan asked.

"We'll start small and work up. The rest of the Company is our bluff card. Matching their records and showing their buying and selling practices will give the agencies enough reason to start investigating. They'll probably lose their trading licenses on the NYSE, serve time, and pay some stiff fines"

"Do you really think they'll serve time?" Alan asked. "I don't think they will. They'll buy their way out of jail."

"You're probably right, Alan, but they'll pay fines for sure. After the investigation is under way, we'll send a note to McClure. All it will say is this. *We warned you. Stop trying to find out who we are. You will be next if you continue.* I think that should get our point across."

"I think we should get this together right away, Robert. I don't want them to find Cathy. She had a close call and got lucky. Next time might be different. She'll have to fly out of a different airport from now on and make an appearance change. I made a new ID for her already. The sooner McClure knows we're onto him the better."

"You're right, Alan. We need to get this out today. A swift kick in the balls usually wakes up a bad guy or any guy for that matter."

Robert and Alan spent the rest of the afternoon getting the packages together and finding the right agencies to send them to. The NYSE had an oversight group. They'd get one package. The Federal District Attorney and his team would also be interested in the business practices of the men. The State of New York had a group who investigated illegal business practices as well. They'd also be a thorn in the side of the Company.

The parcels were ready by evening, along with a letter explaining the contents. Robert addressed the packages and put them in express delivery boxes. Robert contacted his special courier to deliver mail from another state so the postmarks were not traced back to Albuquerque. Julia and Robert drove into town that evening to drop off the boxes and have dinner. During the meal, Robert and Julia discussed the activities of the day.

"Do you think this will stop Ian?" Julia asked. "I talked to Cathy and she wants to come back to visit Alan. She said she'd wait for the new ID to arrive in a day or two."

"I hope so. Time will tell. I had a feeling Ian wouldn't stop trying to find us. His death may be our only guarantee the war is over," Robert added.

"When Cathy does come, Cathy's going to use JFK and change her appearance. She may be forced to move here. From what I can tell, she's not against that at all. She and Alan have talked about doing the Geek Mingle website together."

"If that dating website takes off, we could be losing a contact in New York and the best computer hacker I've ever had. I can always get another office worker but probably not as good as Alan. In a way, I hope it does work. They both deserve to have something together. Sort of like us," Robert grinned.

"All I can tell you is she really likes Alan. She thinks about him all the time and that's unusual for her. She's had many boyfriends, but this one might be the real deal."

"You're right. The next time you call her, let her know she can stay with us when she visits. We have plenty of room and Alan is here almost every day anyway. This will be a safe place to stay until we find out how Ian is going to react. We can pick her up in town after she takes a taxi from the airport. That way we can be sure she's not followed. We still need to make sure our home is safe. If Ian ever found out where we live, he'd call a drone strike and wipe us off the map. I believe he has that much power."

"I'll call her tomorrow and let her know," Julia answered. "She's never been here so this will make Cathy a part of our family. I'll love spending time with her when Alan's busy. We can go do girl stuff and get out of your hair for a while."

"I love having you around but I know what you mean. Women enjoy being together and having a break from their partners."

"That's what I love about you, Robert. You have more understanding of women than most men. Thank you for being you."

*****

A week passed before Cathy was ready to travel. She had to tie up a few loose ends and put items in storage. Preparation for the move to New Mexico needed time.

Alan sent Cathy the new ID she would need. He was excited about having a permanent girlfriend and a business partner. They spent hours on the phone making plans for the future.

By the time Cathy made the flight to Albuquerque, Ian had received news that three of the Company members were under investigation by the Federal Government. Two days later the message from Robert arrived, warning Ian to stop any further attempts at finding them.

The other members, involved in the building of the desalinization plants, called a meeting the next day. Ian's presence was mandatory. The message to Ian was brief. They voted him out as the head of The Company or whatever was left of it. They were clearly upset that their colleagues were being investigated. The NYSE had banned the three men for any further trading until the Federal Government completed their investigation. The remaining members were scrambling to block any ties they had with the three members under indictment. The Company was in shambles and the remaining members put the blame on Ian.

Ian was finished, as far a having any leadership role. Whoever was spying on him seemed to know what he was doing at every turn. Any more searching for the women or leader was dangerous. He'd bide his time and wait. He knew he was not finished yet. The Irish never give up.

Chapter Four

Revenge was always on Ian's and his health was deteriorating because of it. During the next six months, his blood pressure climbed higher and several stints were placed in two arteries.

His son graduated from Notre Dame and decided to move to Ireland and learn the whiskey business from his uncle, Sean. He wanted to open a distributorship in New York and supply the East coast with the family product, staying out of the NYSE altogether. Ian Jr. wanted no part in the revenge game.

During this period another blow to The Company unfolded. The countries that had desalinization plants, decided to nationalize them. Robert sent information to the U.S. government explaining the intent of the men financing the plants. The Attorney General forwarded the information to each country and strongly suggested they take over the plants themselves. The U.S. promised financial gifts if these governments followed through with the takeover. National security was always a good excuse for governments to do whatever they wanted and in this case, it worked. The information to the U.S. Government, regarding the plants, was sent via Arizona so nothing could be traced back to Robert.

The world was looking safe, at least for the rest of the week. This group of rich and powerful men had been stopped for now. Other means of controlling the world would have to be found. Ian still had his ace in the hole but then again so did Robert. The formula for the compound was still in play and both men waited to see who'd blink first. It was a stalemate for now. Ian's health continued to worsen so he needed to make a move soon. Just what he'd do was still unknown, but the wheels in Ian's head were turning.

*****

Robert and Julia planned a trip to Tibet and China.

"How do we even dress for Tibet and China? The elevation is high and all the people seem to be in warm clothes all the time. At least that's what I've seen in films and National Geographic pictures," Robert said.

Robert was reluctant to go to this far location in the world. What would he do when they arrived? Take a few pictures was all he could think of. Food, clothing and government control of the people had him a little on edge. He was comfortable in Albuquerque and travel made him uneasy.

"We're going to be out of our element for sure," Julia said. "The Chinese seem to be eliminating the culture of Tibet one monk at a time. We'll have to tread lightly and act like the perfect tourist while we're there."

Julia had read up on the history of Tibet and rented several movies regarding the Chinese takeover of the country.

"I hope we know what we're doing. Getting arrested in Tibet could be a permanent thing and we might never see the cacti of New Mexico again," Robert added. He felt he was losing control going on this trip.

"I have never seen you as worried as you are about this vacation."

"I'll be fine but probably not until we get back." Robert still sounded concerned.

"What'll Alan do while we're gone?" Julia asked.

"How about we give him a break as well. I know he and Cathy

are making progress with their geek site and are really busy." Robert thought for a moment. "If his site goes public he'll have more money than I ever made in all my cases."

"I also think having Cathy with him has helped get them this far. She does a lot with the recruiting, and he handles more of the technical stuff," Julia said.

"I'll send an application for an assistant tomorrow. I can tell Alan is a little distracted with all the work he has to do when he gets home. He stopped taking classes at the university months ago."

"Let's get this done before we leave for China," Julia said. "We need to interview and screen someone first. The stuff we do is borderline legal and we wouldn't want a whistle-blower working for us."

"I'll contact Dr. Mallory and have him interview a few students. He's the head of the Computer Department. I'll miss Alan but he has to live his life. We might be neighbors in the future. He's been looking at a prime lot about a quarter mile down the road from us."

"Having him and Cathy close would really make my day," Julia said with a big smile.

"Let's wrap up this last job and shut down the business before we're gone. If we find someone to replace Alan, we can start him or her after we return. We'll have a new case and a fresh start."

"Fine with me," Julia agreed.

Robert was ready for a break. He still kept an eye on McClure and any unusual activity made by the remaining members of The Company. Remaining in the shadows was his goal for now.

*****

A year had passed since Ian buried his father in Ireland. During the funeral, Sean, Ian's cousin, promised to help him with the problem in America. Sean took care of things the old-fashioned way. People disappeared if they could not be paid off. Ian was now a man without a company and he needed the help of his Irish relatives to restore honor to the McClure name.

A plan began to emerge. The past year Ian poured money into leads in hopes of finding those responsible for his family's shame. All clues so far led to Albuquerque. The woman, who had something to do with Mark Jones, disappeared in New Mexico. One of two women identified videotaping the memorial service in New York, flew to Albuquerque and returning to the Big Apple. Someone in that state had played a part in his demise. He made a call to Ireland.

"Hi, Sean, Ian here."

"I see things haven't improved for you, Ian. Is this why you are calling?" Sean asked.

"Yes, it has finally come to that," Ian said.

"I told you last year if you needed our help we'd arrive and clean up any mess."

"Thanks again for the offer, Sean. Here is the situation. The location of this group is narrowed to one city, but the people I'm looking for are still invisible. We've been following a previous employee in Santa Fe but so far, he's clean. My team thinks he may have a connection with the mastermind of the operation but we know nothing for sure."

"We could make him talk," Sean said. "I assure you, he'll tell us everything he knows when we're through."

Ian paused for a moment before reminding Sean what he told him a year ago. "Problem is if he has a connection to the group and is roughed up, then the rest of the Company members will have their name sent to the government. This includes my family. They've already taken out three members when we followed one of the woman photographers. She got away but three Company members are banned from trading and had to pay millions in fines. Any more activity on our side and the rest go down."

"How in the hell do you plan on stopping them? It sounds like your hands are tied." Even though Sean was willing to help, he was glad he had nothing to do with the stock market. Whiskey is what he knew and he was glad Ian's son was learning the business.

"If I locate the main people, I'm not concerned about anyone else. Other ex-Company members are on their own. I've covered my tracks and no longer trade because I have other investments. Clearing the McClure name will be my final act. You might call it revenge, but I call it payback."

"I get it, Ian, but you seem to be walking on thin ice. One false move and in you go. Do you have a plan or is it still a 'wait and see' situation?"

"A plan is developing but I may have to use people not associated with me. It seems this person knows all my employees or at least recognizes their faces. That's why I may need your help. None of your people are recognizable over here. That could be valuable."

"Say the word and we'll be there. The McClure name in America is important in Ireland as well. When you're ready, call me back."

"I will, Sean. Right now, tell me how my son's doing. Does he know enough about the whiskey business to strike out on his own?"

"He's getting close," Sean said. "He wants to set up a major distribution center in the States for Ireland and really push the McClure brand. He's a good student and not afraid of work. We started him in the production of the whiskey so he would know all the steps it takes to make the product. He seems to have his great grandfather's passion for this business."

"If there anything I can do to help him get started over here, just let me know, Sean. If this gets going in the States you may have to crank up production again just like during prohibition. The only difference is you can ship directly to America and not have to go through Canada." Ian reflected on how his life would have been different if his family remained in whiskey.

"The Kennedy and the McClure families did well for themselves. Joseph Kennedy even got one of his sons elected president. Money can buy just about anything," Sean added.

Sean could tell Ian was not in the best of health. His cousin's voice was weak and the last time he visited Ireland his color was almost white. He would help his cousin but he did not expect to see him alive by the next family reunion in three years. When Ian died, Sean would be the senior clan member.

"Just call when you're ready Ian. I'll get a crew ready and get them to you quickly."

Ian knew he could count on Sean. He'd talk to his investigation team and see if any leads had turned up. He now needed to rest.

Chapter Five

Alan and Cathy worked twelve hours a day on the Geek Mingle dating site, as advertising requests poured into their office. They were about to enter the world of millionaires when they went public, and have to make adjustments in every area of their life.

"I'm overloaded lining up these companies who want to advertise, Alan. They're throwing money at us and I don't know if I can handle it alone for much longer. I hope Robert can find a replacement for you soon. We both have a huge job just keeping up with the demand."

"I know, Cathy. I'm also looking for someone to replace me at Robert's house."

"I love you, Alan, and I love Robert, but we need to focus on us. We have to hire a few more programmers just to keep up. Let Robert find your replacement."

"I owe Robert a lot, but you're right. We've grown really fast, and I could use four more people. Lucky we bought that warehouse office downtown where we have room for more employees. There's plenty of room for us to expand in that location."

"Just give Robert a final date," Cathy added. "He and Julia are leaving for China in a few days. Geek Mingle is at a critical point, and being split between two jobs is not working. I'm really stressed when you're gone."

Alan was handling the programmers but could tell he needed to be around more to support Cathy. She was the best thing that happened to him, and her ability in dealing with companies wanting to advertise was invaluable. She could communicate well with the business heads and screen out the ones she didn't feel were a fit for Geek Mingle. It was obvious this site was taking off because of the thousands of users signing up on a daily basis. It was a changing world, and the geeks were taking over.

"I think Robert will have someone new before he leaves for China. We now have a date for going public, October 19th. Are you ready for more news?" Alan asked.

"What now?" Cathy asked. "Good news I hope?"

"I bought the house about a mile from Robert and Julia. We both liked it and building our own would take too long. You said it was a suitable possibility when you saw it, and we need to get out of our apartment now. There's no room there."

"Really? You bought it? When can we move? This is fantastic news."

"Since I paid cash, and didn't have to finance it, we can move in right away. We might be in before Robert and Julie get back from the Far East."

Cathy was ecstatic. She now would have room to really express herself with Alan and not only in the bedroom. She needed the pool that came with the house, and the large living room and den. Right now was a good time to prove her point. Alan's shirt was removed in one pull. Buttons popped off, but she knew he could afford a new one. Her clothes came off just as fast. Sex was the best way she knew how to calm down, and Alan was just as eager to return her to a state of tranquility as soon as possible.

Half an hour later, the two lovers were getting dressed to go out for dinner. They needed to celebrate buying the house and going public. The way they met, and fell in love was like a whirlwind. They were on the verge of becoming multi-millionaires, and even joining the billionaires club in a few more years. Life at the end of the rainbow was really good as long as the pot of gold was still there.

Since moving to Albuquerque, Cathy made changes to her looks. She altered her physical identity because The Company got her picture the previous year. She was still the fun loving woman Alan fell in love with, but now she had higher cheekbones and breast implants performed by a local plastic surgeon in town. Cathy's idea of change included physical features from top to bottom. Alan did not mind one bit.

"I'll be right out." Cathy took a few minutes longer getting ready.

"Okay, I'm ready." Cathy got in the car and kissed Alan on the cheek. "Thanks for being patient. I want to look good for us when we're out. We're about to become a large Internet company and we have to play the part." She slid into the front seat and pulled the seat belt across her. It used to be much easier when she was a 34B. Now at 36D it made getting in and out of the car a little more difficult.

"That reminds me," Alan said. "We have another meeting with an investor on Monday. I'm getting fitted for a suit tomorrow. It should be ready before the meeting. We both need to be there because you're good at talking with these people and I'm not."

"This investment thing is a no brainer, Alan. These early investors stand to make millions when we go public. The site is growing so fast even Starbucks wants in. After all, that's where the geeks mingled before this site went up."

"Really? Starbucks?" Alan asked.

"Not really. I'm just kidding." Cathy said. "But there are some coffee house owners who approached us. Since their computer clients are there anyway, sipping coffee for three hours, they might as well advertise on the site and make some money."

"Any more news about Ian?" Cathy asked.

"No, and that's fine with me. No news is good news."

"Robert doesn't think Ian has given up trying to find us, does he?" Cathy asked. "He has to be pissed off. Half of what you and Robert figured out was pure luck."

"Guys like Ian don't walk away. The last video pictures I saw of him didn't look good."

"What do you mean?" Cathy asked.

"His skin looked flushed, and rings are under his eyes indicating he hasn't slept in weeks. He's lost a lot of weight, and moves like he's really old."

"A man who knows he is going to die soon can be dangerous," Cathy added. "He's got nothing to loose trying to get back at us."

"Yeah, and in this instance it could be any of us. We know where he is. I don't see why Robert hasn't hired someone to take Ian out and be done with it. Ian will remain a thorn in our side until the day he dies."

"Well, that's Robert's problem," Cathy answered.

"It was a blast working for him and meeting you was the best part of the whole adventure," Alan said.

"Damn right it was, and I plan on never letting you forget that," Cathy said with a smile.

Alan and Cathy drove home after dinner. At the back of their minds lingered the thought of Ian and his quest for revenge. Both of them knew how dangerous the situation could be if anyone from their team was identified. Right now, they focused on their company. Hopefully, Ian and what was left of The Company was in their past.

Chapter Six

Laura still lived in New York. After rescuing Cathy from Ian's crew at *Leggs,* she stayed away from the bar for six months. A few weeks after the incident, Cathy called to tell her she was moving to Albuquerque. A week later, Laura received a bonuscheck from Robert for saving Cathy's life at Leggs.

Now she was bored and missed meeting other women with higher than average intelligence. She'd lost a friend in Cathy because of The Company and she was not getting any more work from Robert since the incident. On Friday, she decided it was safe to return to *Leggs.*

Unknown to Laura, Ian McClure hired someone to keep an eye open for the two women from the memorial service. Sera Pett, Ian's employee, only had a rough sketch of a woman and a photo of another to help identify either suspect. Sera did investigations as a side job, and visited the bar on Friday and Saturday nights, hoping to identify one of the women. For six months, no one turned up. Tonight was different.

Laura walked in around eight. She loved the energy of the women's watering hole. No heavy vibes and witty conversations used by men trying their best pickup lines. Not only did men not to go to Leggs, they weren't allowed. The 300 lb. black doorman made sure of that. He was *Mean Joe Green* in a suit, and the only male allowed in the bar.

Sera spotted her right away. Laura had changed her hairstyle but not enough to change her overall appearance. The sketch was close enough to investigate further. A large bonus was promised by Ian, to Sera, if either woman was discovered.

Laura looked around the bar and found an empty seat. She

ordered a glass of white wine and spun around on the bar stool to check out the clientele. They included professional looking females, of all varieties, coming together to meet and talk. This was their place and they planned to keep it that way.

"Hi, my name's Sera." The empty seat next to Laura was now occupied.

"Hi, Sera, I'm Sharon White." Laura used an alias when she went to public places. Conversation is what she came for. If Sera *hit on her,* she'd send her on her way.

"I've never seen you here before. Is this your first time at *Leggs?*" Sera asked.

"I used to come here a lot but work has kept me away from The Village. This is my favorite bar, and I've really missed it. Do you come here a lot?"

"Mostly on weekends. I heard it was a good place to meet women with an open mind, so I come here to talk. I do a little writing, and sometimes include some of the conversations in characters I write about."

"Really. What kind of stories do you write?"

"Fiction mostly. There are many interesting lives in this place. I doctor up the conversations, so the person I write about won't recognize themselves in the book. Most stories include women in positions of power. This place is full of them."

"No kidding. I'm afraid you might find me kind of boring compared to these other women."

"Why? What do you do?" Sera asked.

"Mostly freelance photography along with weddings. You

know, stuff like that."

"Are you single?" Sera asked.

"Last time I checked. I don't find the men in New York my type of partner material. They seem fixated on satisfying their egos. Many spend the evening talking about what they've accumulated in their lives, and it's boring as hell."

"I've had the same experiences. It's like they're cloned from a rejected Playboy magazine mold. They think the Hugh Heffner image is what women want." Sera gave a little laugh with her comment.

"I think that's why bars like *Leggs* are starting to pop up. Educated women in the workforce want to be stimulated in their brains, and not only in their 'G-spots.' By the way, are you here for a character study?"

"Yes and no. I never know who's going to walk through that door. I just talk and see where it goes."

"Have you written any books? I love mystery novels."

"Only a few articles. I'm working on a novel right now, and it should be in print next year. "

"What's it about?"

Sera thought for a moment. She wanted to see if Sharon was the woman she was looking for, so she continued to draw her out.

"Women, in positions of power, having to deal with the *good ole boys.* There're a lot who come here to talk and many have interesting lives. I just listen and take mental notes."

"Do you have a title yet? I'll look out for it."

"Working title is *Women of Wall Street.* There're a few that come here. They have to be tough to survive that business. Some of their stories are really awful and need to be told."

"I think Wall Street is man's world for sure. All the movies about that industry have only one or two women in them because a large percent of the characters are men. They're cutthroat, vain, and just full of shit."

"Yea and they usually buy their women. Don't get me started. It's all in the book."

"I wish you luck. I bet it does well," Laura said.

"Thanks. What are you drinking? White Zin?" Sera asked.

"Yes."

"Can I buy you another? I enjoy talking to you and it'll keep the lesbians away."

"Sure. I'm enjoying myself as well."

The two women spent the next hour talking about working on their own and the types of jobs they did. Laura remained on guard and kept her identity safe. She was careful not to divulge any of her work concerning Robert. When the second drinks were finished Laura said she had to go.

"I really enjoyed meeting you, Sera. Let's do this again. If I come next weekend around eight, will you be here?"

"Yes. I usually stay until ten. I don't keep late hours. I hit the gym in the mornings and take a short run afterward. How about next Friday?"

"Sounds good to me. See you then," Laura said.

*****

"Mr. McClure. This is Sera Pett. I may have something for you."

"Oh, hello, Miss Pett. I almost forgot about you. Are you still on assignment at that women's bar in The Village?"

"Yep, every Friday and Saturday night. I met a woman who fits the description of the sketch you gave me. Said she used to come to Leggs but has been busy for a while and stayed away. Her hair is shorter and a different color, but the face matches."

"What did you find out?"

"She gave me the name, Sharon White. I couldn't find a Sharon White in the local phone book so she may live further away. I'm meeting her next Friday. You may want a team outside the bar so you can find out where she lives."

"What does she do?"

"Mostly freelance photography. She says she does weddings as well. I had to play it cool so I didn't ask a lot of questions."

"What time will she be back?"

"Around eight o'clock. You should have someone get her picture leaving the bar to make sure it's her."

"Do you really think it is?"

"She's the closest to the sketch I've seen for the last six months."

Ian thought for a moment. He had to find out if this was one of the video women who identified The Company members. Maybe she'd guide him to the ringleader. All leads needed to be followed up.

"I'll have a team in place next Friday. What time will you get there?"

"Around seven. I'll arrive early and eat dinner, so we'll have a booth to talk in private."

"My crew will get a picture of her coming out of the bar. Just speed dial me when she is leaving and I'll let them know."

"Will do." Sera wanted to ask Mr. McClure why he was so interested in Sharon but decided not to. A simple paycheck is what she wanted.

"If she turns out to be who I'm looking for I'll wire you the amount we agreed upon in the deal. I will let you know either way how this plays out."

"Thank you, Mr. McClure. The money is appreciated. I can really use it," Sera said.

*****

Laura was excited about going to meet Sera at *Leggs*. With Cathy gone, Laura needed a friend she could talk to. New York was a lonely place for some, even with millions of people living there.

At 7:45, Laura walked through the door at Leggs. She thought about the false name she'd given Sera. If the friendship blossomed she'd tell Sera her real name and explain the reason for using a different one.

Sera sat in a booth in the back of the club. "Over here, Sharon. I was just having a bite to eat."

"Good to see you again. How was your week?"

"Not bad. Wrote a few more chapters and bartended at a place that uses me when someone gets sick. It pays the bills. How about you?"

"I had two wedding shoots, both high-end. It paid my rent and gave me a little spending money on the side. What are you drinking? Let me get the first round."

"Pink Lady. You should try it."

"Okay, two Pink Ladies coming up." Laura went over to the bar to give her order to the waitress. She pointed to the table where she was sitting.

"I've really looked forward to coming back here," Laura said when she returned to the table. "I love this 'woman energy'. I deal with assholes all week and I need a break."

"Some of the men in the weddings have their heads so far up their 'you know where', I'm amazed they even have a woman who'll marry them."

"I know what you mean," Sera said. "Seems the only nice men are gay. I work with a few of them on occasion and they treat me with respect."

"After a couple of drinks, we may feel better about the male population out there. What did you eat?" Laura asked.

"Some kind of fish. Halibut I think. It was their special."

The two women chatted for about an hour with mostly small talk and future plans. Sera shared more of her life and revealed she was bi- sexual. She'd been with both male and female partners and preferred women. She put Laura at ease by saying she was not hitting on her.

"I really like you, Sharon, and find our conversations interesting. I hope we can continue to meet."

"I like you too, Sera. I'd love to read what you've written so far. I do proof-reading and can help you with some of the editings."

"Agreed. I'll e-mail you what I've written so far."

"Better yet, let's meet again, and you can bring a printout of what you've written. I do better when I read something on paper." Laura was not about to give out her e-mail to someone she hardly knew.

*****

Outside the bar, Ian's team was in place. Around ten Sera called Ian.

"She is using the ladies room and about to go home. She is wearing a blue sweater and black pants. She's by herself so the picture should be easy to take."

"Good work, Miss Pett. We'll talk later." Ian hung up.

Ian called his men waiting outside the bar. Their camera was ready. As soon as Laura left the bar the shutter began to snap. A rapid-fire Cannon captured a good exposure. Laura got into her car and drove towards her apartment. Ian's men followed at a safe distance, also writing down the license plate number. This time they were not going to be seen.

About midnight Ian's phone received photos of the woman and the plate number. An address accompanied the images and it matched the address for the car. She lived close to The Village. Ian now had something to go on. A positive match by the tenants living next to the church and the cab driver that dropped her off was next on her list. After that, Ian could plan his next move.

Chapter Seven

Robert and Julia were now two weeks into their vacation. Alan and Cathy received postcards from them every other day. The cards included the palace at Lhasa, the Great Wall and a few digital prints, sent by e-mail, of monks and nuns during religious ceremonies. Neither Robert nor Julia had shaved their head so Alan knew they had not become Buddhists.

"Julia says in her e-mails she really loves being around the Tibetan people," Cathy said. "She tried meditation and thinks it's something she can continue with in her personal life."

"Really? Don't you have to be a monk or nun to practice Buddhist meditation?" Alan asked.

"Not according to Julie. She says there are many different styles of the religious practice around the world. Japan, India, Southeast Asia and Sri Lanka are just a few. Says she'll tell us more about it when she gets home."

"When's that?" Alan asked.

"Next week. We should be settled in before they land in Arizona. Any more news about Ian?" Cathy asked.

"His son is still in Ireland, learning how to make whiskey. It seems he doesn't want to be a part of the stock market business at all." Alan paused for a moment. "According to Robert, Ian has only one goal now. Revenge. Rich, crazy people are more dangerous than the average nut case."

"How do you mean?" Cathy asked.

"They have the financial means to do what they want and never answer for their crimes. They pay people off, buy judges and practically run governments from their homes. Congress is full of millionaires. How do you think they got rich? On their salaries?"

"You're starting to scare me. Do you think Ian can find us?"

"I don't know," Alan answered. "I really had to scramble to protect you and Julia from getting caught. We were lucky. Staying hidden from the McClure clan is a full-time job. Violence is a way of life for them."

"How about, Laura. Is she still safe?"

"So far. Have you contacted her in a while? Maybe you should call and make sure."

"I'll call tomorrow on the secure line. It's been a few months." Cathy jotted down on her list of things to do in the morning. *Call Laura.*

*****

"Laura, this is Cathy. How are you?"

"Wow, I've been thinking of you, Cathy. How's life in New Mexico?"

"Really good. Alan and I are moving into our new house today. The Geek Mingle site is taking off and will go public soon. How about you."

"Wow, that business is really taking off. I'm really happy for you both. I'm still doing weddings and fill in work when I get a call. I really miss working for Robert. That was a great job we did together."

"Yes, it was, and thanks again for saving my butt," Cathy added. "We got away clean. Alan helped me change my ID so I could travel again. We pop into New York every so often but only for dinner and a show."

"Tell me when you visit again. We could get a drink and talk."

"Last time we had a drink together was at *Leggs*," Cathy said.

"Funny you should mention that place. I went there the other night and may have started a friendship with someone. She's a writer and goes there to talk to women. She's writing a book titled *Women on Wall Street*. She talks to these women, gets their stories, and then puts them into a character for her book."

"Wait a minute. You say you went back to *Leggs*?"

"Yes. I figured the Company is washed up and it has been over six months since we were last there. Is anything wrong?"

"I'm not sure. All I know is Ian is still looking for a connection to anyone who had a part in taking down his family. He's probably dying and obsessed with revenge."

"Do you think I may be in danger?'

"I don't know. If he's watching the bar, you could be. I'll say something to Robert when he gets back next week. For now, I'd suggest not going there again until we can find out if it's safe."

"What about the woman I met? What should I do about her?"

"Do you have her name? We can put a trace on her and see if she checks out."

"Sera Pett. At least that's the name she gave me. Let me know right away if you find out anything."

"Will do. Just be calm. We'll handle this on our side. If Sera is clean then continue to see her, but maybe at another watering hole."

"Good idea, Cathy. Thanks. Be sure and call when you visit the City."

"We will. Love you." Cathy hung up.

"What was that all about?" Alan overheard most of the conversation, and from the tone of Cathy's voice, he could tell she was upset.

"Seems Laura thought it was safe to go back into the water. She went to *Leggs* again and met some woman. I told her we'd check her out."

"Do you think Ian still has someone keeping an eye on the bar?" Alan asked.

"Why not? It's the last place he followed me to, and he almost got me. That's not something I want to relive."

"Okay. I'll follow up on this tonight when I get my computer hooked up. Let's get to the house so we can tell the movers where we want the furniture. Most are coming from that Swedish store, IKEA, right?"

"We went together, Alan. Don't you remember that huge warehouse?"

"Yes, but you did most of the picking. I'm fine with what you got. That's not an area of interest for me at all."

"I'm glad you trust my judgment. We have to break in the new bed tonight so get ready. This is the first night in our new home. Aren't you excited?"

"Yes, but we still have lots to do before going public. After I set up the office, I'll search for Sera Pett, and see if Laura is safe. After that maybe I can relax."

*****

Alan and Cathy made the drive to the new house just as the Swedish furniture arrived. It took about three hours for the placement of all the furniture and household items. There were new pots and pans for the kitchen and a big screen TV for their evening watching pleasure. When everything was in place and all the clothes put into the closets, Cathy had early dinner ready. She'd learned to cook a few Mexican dishes while she lived with Robert and Julia after her escape from New York. Carla was a good teacher.

"While you were cooking dinner I found Sera Pett in New York. She does exist but listen to this. She's a writer but also an investigator for hire. She works for anyone who'll pay for her services."

Alan knew how to find just about anyone on the Internet. He also knew how to get into phone records to see what calls they'd made. While scanning her calls he came across one that looked familiar. It was the personal line for Ian McClure.

"This sucks. I also found out from her calls that she has been in contact with Ian. I think Laura has been compromised and could be in danger."

"Compromised? Where did you get that term? Oh, I know. From one of those detective shows you like."

"Yea, but I'm serious. Ian probably hired her to stake out *Leggs*. Laura shows up and bingo. There might have been a description of her from the people at the apartments where she took the video."

Cathy was starting to see the danger here. "Maybe. I don't think she made any big changes to her appearance. I did, but then again I was identified at the airport. I know you like some of the changes

50

I made." She grabbed her boobs and gave the larger model a lift.

"I do. I'll get to those later. I hope it isn't too late to warn Laura. She may have to disappear and obtain a new ID as well."

"What'll we do? Robert is not back for a few more days. He'd know what to do."

"Right now we should call Laura and warn her about Sera. I'll send a text message to Robert. I know he's planning on stopping by to visit William on the drive back from Phoenix."

"This may speed up his return. I'll call Laura now and give her the heads up."

Chapter Eight

"What's your name?" asked Smith.

"Laura Scott."

"It's not Sharon White?"

"No, that's my name when I don't want to use my real one."

The drug had taken effect and Smith, Ian's team leader, was taping the conversation. Ian knew he had to move on the lead from Miss Pett. The photo he had of Laura was positively identified by two of the tenants in the apartment complex next to the church where the memorial service took place. Both people said she was the one in the building carrying a camera bag.

"What do you do for work?"
"I do free-lance photography and other jobs for hire."

"Were you hired to video the memorial service for Sean McClure last year."

The truth serum was working well. There was no hesitance in her voice. The Ian team had knocked on Laura's door and stuffed the chloroform cloth over her face when she answered. No struggle or yelling involved. The team had access to the same drugs Robert used on Mark Jones.

"Yes."

"Who hired you?"

"Robert Woods."

"Where can we find this Mr. Woods?"

"I don't know where he lives. I believe Albuquerque but I don't know where."

"Were you working alone on the job at the memorial service?"

"I had a partner."

"Do you have her name?"

"Cathy Chambers"

"Where is she now?"

"Albuquerque, New Mexico."

"Does she live there?"

"She moved there last year."

"Do you know how to reach her?"

"No, she calls me.

Smith, the team leader questioning Laura, stopped and took a drink from his water bottle. He was getting nowhere as far as finding out where the ringleaders lived. He now had a name. The phone in the apartment rang.

"Let it go to the message. Just record what is said." The two men waited for the answering machine to kick in.

"Please leave a message."

"Laura, this is Cathy. We have some news for you. I need to talk to you in person so I'll call back later. Be careful. Sera is not who she says she is." Cathy hung up.

"I don't think she can give us anything else. Put her on the bed and give her the memory-loss drug. Inject it between the toes. Wipe everything down and let's go."

"What about the message on the phone? Leave it?"

"Nothing we can do about that. Not sure who Sera is anyway."

"Maybe we better call Mr. McClure. He might know who she is."

"Good idea." Smith speed dialed Ian. One ring before Ian picked up.

"Mr. McClure. We have a question." Smith repeated the phone message to Ian. Ian instructed Smith to erase the message and get out of there. Also, he instructed Smith to send the audio taping to him as soon as they cleared the building. Both men were in their car within five minutes and driving away.

Laura was not hurt. She woke up later that evening feeling like she had a hangover. The short-term memory drug wiped out any events of the afternoon.

*****

Ian received the tape over his phone. He listened to it twice. Robert Woods was the ringleader. He had to be. He was an old client who worked for the Company five or six years ago. He had disappeared and nobody knew where he was. Everything fit. The hard part was next. How do you find someone who doesn't want to be found?

*****

"She didn't answer so I left a message. I'll try again tonight," Cathy said.

"Nothing else we can do. I sent a text message to Robert and expect a call when he lands. We need to let him know what is happening right away."

Cathy was more concerned about Laura. She had befriended the woman and wanted her to be safe. Maybe she'd have to change her identity as well and move from New York. Leaving Ian alive was really starting to be a pain in the ass. This guy was never going to stop looking for them.

"Let's have lunch and take a swim in our new pool. We can't do much else until I hear from Laura or Robert. I want to show you what we can use the pool for besides swimming."

Alan was learning how to read Cathy pretty well. He knew she meant sex. This would be a first for him. Dolphins and fish did it in the water. Why not humans? He was game to try anything with his girlfriend.

"Are we expecting any more deliveries today?"

"No." Cathy was already naked and getting into the pool. Alan didn't need any prompting. Water sex. He wondered if he should blog about it on the Mingle sight? No. This was his life. He wanted to keep what he did private. The site was to find a partner. After that, what you did stayed where you were. No bragging about conquests or lewd pictures allowed.

*****

The phone rang. "Laura? This is Cathy. Did you get the message I left you?"

"Hi, Cathy. Wait a second. Let me check my answering machine. I just woke up."

Laura could see there was no flashing light on her home phone. "No, there is nothing recorded. When did you call?"

"About eleven this morning. Maybe you were asleep?"

"I must have been. I don't remember a thing. It's like the whole morning just disappeared. Even yesterday is a little fuzzy."

Cathy waited a few seconds and then gave Laura a few instructions. "Is there anything in your room out of order? I mean has anything been disturbed?"

"I don't think so. What's this all about?"

"We researched Sera. She works as a writer like you said but she's also an investigator for hire. Alan downloaded her phone records and spotted a number matching Ian McClure. We think she was hired to hang out at *Leggs* and see if you or I came back there again."

"She doesn't know where I live. I never gave out that information.

"Yea but wait. You met her more than once, right?"

"Yes."

"All she'd have to do is let Ian know you were in the bar. He could have a team follow you home. Anything unusual happen after the second meeting?"

"No, but I wasn't even looking for anything out of the ordinary. If someone followed me home they did a good job staying out of sight."

Cathy gathered her thoughts. "We left a message on your answering machine. If it's not there now then someone erased it. Is there anything else you can tell me?"

"My head hurts and so do my toes."

"Your toes? Did you look at them to see why?"

"No, I just woke up. Give me a second." Laura took off her socks and examined her right foot where the pain was coming from. A small red mark was between her big and second toe.

"Cathy, I may have been drugged. I have a puncture mark between my toes and it was not there yesterday. I cannot remember anything that happened earlier today. What's happening?"

"You're not hurt. That's the important thing. I think Ian got to you before we could warn you. Sera is working for him. You were probably given a drug to tell them what you know about Robert and the team. We have to think this through."

"Am I in danger?"

"I don't know but you are alive and that is a good thing."

"Yea, I agree with that."

"You were only working for Robert and don't know where he lives. They might still try to use you through Sera. For now, just continue like nothing happened."

"But something did happen."

"I know but we have to talk to Robert first. He'll know what to do. He's not home yet. You may be followed. Maybe we can use this as an advantage. They probably do not know we are on to them. Also, they don't know where we are."

"Should I be worried?"

"If they wanted to kill you we would not be having this conversation. Hang in there. This call cannot be traced or tapped. Alan has a system that allows us to call you but no trace can be made."

"I'm planning on meeting Sera next Friday. What should I do?"

"If you cancel they might think we're on to them. Go ahead and meet her. Keep the conversation simple but be on guard. She might try to get more out of you."

"Call me after you talk to Robert. This has really messed me up. I liked Sera."

"She may have only give Ian your identification. She may not know the history of the Company and what we did to take them down. I'm sure it was a paid job and nothing more."

"Okay, but call me after Robert has talked to you. If I am going to work for him again I want to be on the clock. This is my life we're talking about."

"I'll mention that to him. If you're going to trick Sera and Ian you need to be a part of the team. Do you own a gun?"

"No, but I know where I can get one. This is New York, remember?"

"You might want a small handgun to hide in your purse. Tell us the price and I will get Robert to pay for it. Either that or I will. I want you safe."

"Thanks, Cathy. You're a real friend. I really miss you. I so wanted to have another friend. I guess I can cross Sera off my list."

"Probably. I'll call you when we know more. Love you."

Both women hung up. Laura was still feeling a little groggy. She needed food. She ate nothing since breakfast. The Delhi down the street served takeout. She'd do nothing out of the ordinary. She was alive and that was a good thing. She was also mad as hell and would do anything to take this Ian guy out for good.

*****

Ian had someone following Laura 24/7. He also had a tracking device placed on her car after she was drugged. Smith and his team would know where she was going at all times. Ian's main focus was to find Robert Woods. He'd studied the files on Woods and came up with little information after he left the Company. He'd disappeared. What was Woods doing and why had he focused on the Company that made him wealthy?

The phone message on Laura's answering machine bothered Ian. When he had his team hack into her phone records, the calls from Cathy were untraceable. Laura said on the tape that Cathy had moved to Albuquerque. That was the last place Woods lived when he worked for the Company. An office was in that city. Spy work from New York was too difficult to manage.

"Hello, Sean. It's Ian. I think I need your help." Ian proceeded to tell Sean about the Laura incident and how the name Robert Woods popped up. He needed a couple of men, he could trust, to set up an office in New Mexico. He would pay them well and give them all the equipment to find Robert Woods. They also needed to strike quickly and get out. If he was going get revenge it needed to look like a terrorist act. No connection between himself and the death of Robert Woods.

"I have a couple of men who could do the job. When do you want them there?"

"Yesterday, but as soon as possible will do. I've rented a small office space and I'm having the equipment installed to carry out this mission. The last photographs of the women at the memorial service and Robert Woods will be in the files located at the office."

"If they find this Woods person what do you want them to do?"

Ian thought for a minute before answering. "If you were me and someone had destroyed your name and business, what would you do?"

"In Ireland, we do not mess around with courts and legal stuff. He and his family would be gone and probably any material wealth he had accumulated. We'd make the message stick in the minds of anyone who thought about crossing us."

"Now you know what I want, Sean. This is a one-time hit. If we miss, the government and other agencies will be coming after the remaining Company members. Nothing can lead back to me. Is that clear?"

"The men I send have done this type of work before. We'll set the office up to look like an investment service for Europeans wanting to buy land in the Southwest."

"Sounds good but why Europeans?"

"We don't want snoopy Americans coming into the office asking about investing. The less anyone knows what the team is doing the better."

"Sean, you are a smart man. I was right to call you. By the way, how's my son doing? Is he ready to come back here and start wholesaling your whiskey in the States?"

"He is Ian but I'm going to give you a heads up. He met an Irish lass and has fallen in love. I'll send you what I know about her family and history."

"Is it that same girl we saw him with when we visited last month?"

"Yes. They've been dating for six months."

"Is she from good stock?"

"Yes. It's all in the files. Pretty too. He has good taste."

"I trust your judgment, Sean. I'm happy he went to Ireland and didn't want to follow me in the investment world. Too many hurdles to jump on Wall Street. Whiskey's a solid business."

"Works for us. I'll send the files on my two men and we'll work out the details next week. Good luck with this Woods thing. I hope it works out."

"Me too Sean. This has taken a toll on my health. I want to live long enough to see Woods dead. After that, I can die a happy man."

Chapter Nine

The Air China plane landed in Phoenix from Hong Kong just before dark. Robert received a text message from Alan to call him when he landed. He'd call after they checked into their hotel and caught their breath. Long flights, even in first class, can wear you out.

"What do you think he wants? The text looks urgent," Robert said.

"Not sure," Julia answered. "Alan can be a little high strung. Good thing he has Cathy to help calm him down."

"I'm sure the Geek web-sight has added stress to his life. Also, they just moved. We're neighbors now."

Robert and Julia were exhausted and needed shut down for an hour before taking on the concerns of the world. Tibet, China, the Great Wall and shopping in Hong Kong wore them out. Julia had been reading about the Buddhist religion during most of the trip and wanted to practice meditation when she got home. Robert had seen a change in her and wanted to support her any way he could.

"Are we still going to visit William and Leslie in Tucson? They're expecting us aren't they?" Julia asked.

"I hope so. Depends on what Alan has to say."

"We can at least have lunch with them. Leslie really likes the student quarters in Tucson where all the ethnic dishes are served."

"We'll see. I need a shower first, and then I'll call Alan. Let's get room service for dinner. I'm shot." Robert headed towards the bathroom.

"Fine with me. I want to soak in a tub, change into pajamas and read more about the life of Buddha."

"Sounds like a plan. I'll call Alan when you're soaking."

The two travelers ordered room service and Robert made a call to Alan. Julia drew the hot water in the tub and closed the door. A glass of Pino Noir accompanied her in the bath.

"Hello, Alan. Robert here. What's up? Your message sounded urgent."

For the next twenty minutes, Alan filled Robert in with the Laura Scott drama. The possible connection with the woman, Sera, and her phone calls with Ian McClure were discussed in detail. Laura also may have been drugged and probably gave Ian all of their names. Alan came to the conclusion Laura was safe because she was still alive.

"I leave for a few weeks and the whole friggin mess starts up again. I think Ian must be dying. Why else would he risk having us send him and the rest of the Company to the cleaners?"

"Your right. I'm ready to speed up his dying process. He'll never give up as long as he is alive."

"How is Laura? Does she know she's being followed? I bet they put a tracking device on her car as well."

"I told her to go through her week as though nothing happened. Maybe we can turn this situation into an advantage."

"Good thinking, Alan. We have to play this asshole. He probably has a team looking for us right now."

"Laura is planning on seeing Sera again on Friday. She's waiting for some direction."

"Your idea of playing along is the best course to take, Alan.

Maybe we'll have her feed Sera information back to Ian. We can catch him off guard and put him where he belongs, in a deep fucking hole." Robert was pissed.

"Today is Tuesday. We're still moving in and spending a lot of time on the Mingle site. I can be of help but I've no time to come to your house. When do you plan on being home?"

"Thursday. Don't worry about the job, Alan. We have already put out job offers to replace you. We plan on visiting William on the way home. At this point, it's best not go to his house. He might be under surveillance."

"Call me when you have a plan for Laura," Alan said. "Cathy will contact her before Friday. We need a plan in place soon. I'm sure you're right about Ian sending a team to Albuquerque. We need to find them before they find us."

"Good work, Alan. I'll call you when we get home. Which house did you buy? The large stone one with the electronic gate?"

"Yes. How'd you know?"

"It was the only one on the street for sale. Good choice neighbor."

"Thanks, Robert. We want to hear about your trip as well. Hi to Julie. Cathy sends her love."

*****

"Thanks for meeting us at the restaurant you two. I'm sorry we couldn't visit your home. Ian is up to his old tricks and it may be dangerous right now."

Robert and Julie drove to Tucson and set up a lunch with Leslie and William. Making sure they were not followed was a priority.

The Rays understood.

"Will this guy ever give it a rest? William asked.

"No, I don't think so. We believe Ian is dying and has nothing to lose trying to take us out. We think he knows who I am and may have drugged our contact in New York."

"Who would that be? The one who worked with Cathy taking video of the memorial service?"

"Yes. Her name's Laura. She made a mistake and went back to the bar where she and Kathy used to meet. Ian had a spy there and evidence leans towards Laura being drugged and injected with truth serum."

"No kidding. If Ian knows your name and the city where you live, he must be looking for you right now."

"He may know about Albuquerque but not where I live. We keep a pretty tight wrap on that information."

"What's the plan now?"

"I'm working on an idea that may work. If I ever need you down the road can I count on you? It would not be in a dangerous situation."

"For sure, Robert. As long is Ian's alive there'll never be an end to this drama."

Leslie rolled her eyes. She wanted no part of the ongoing Robert investigation. At the same time, she knew Ian would never give up trying to take down the people who ruined him. Her mouth remained closed.

"I'll call on the secure line if you're needed. I have a few things to do first. Thanks again for sticking with us."

"I don't think we have a choice. We'll never be free as long as McClure keeps popping up."

During the meal, Julia told about their travels in Tibet and China. She was now interested in finding out more about Buddhism, yoga and some of the things Leslie did in her life. Leslie promised to send some vegetarian recipes to Julia and a website that talked about meditation. Julia was hooked on the eastern way and wanted to know more.

The four finished lunch and said their goodbyes. Robert and Julia left from the back of the restaurant where their car was parked. The Rays exited the front and drove home. The couples agreed to have minimal contact until Ian was out of their lives for good.

While driving home Robert and Julia discussed the plan. It involved using Laura as a person to pass on misinformation to Ian.

"We have to be careful that Laura doesn't get into any trouble. She's alone in New York and could be hung out to dry if Ian went after her," Julia said.
"Ian does not want her. He's using her to get to us. If this plan works Ian will get to us. Just not in the way he expected."

"I like the direction you're taking as long as it leads to the end of Ian. He probably has both our pictures so I plan on changing my hair again. You could use a makeover as well, Robert."

"I can't make that change yet. For the idea to work I have to look like my picture. After that, I may use a disguise. We'll see."

They arrived home at sunset. Julia called Cathy to tell them they were back. She was excited to have them as neighbors.

*****

"Hello, Laura. This is Robert." Laura had a disposable phone so the call was not traced.

"Robert. What a relief to hear your voice. I've been worried. I'm so sorry for going back to *Leggs* and getting hooked up with someone working for Ian. I thought I was in the clear after all that time passed."

"Don't worry, Laura. We may be able to turn this into our advantage. You're not in any danger or you wouldn't be talking to me right now."

"I'm glad I'm talking to you, Robert. When this is over I have a person to add to the list of people who need a lesson. Sera played me. What really pissed me off is that I liked her. I took the bait and never put up a fight. She just reeled me in."

"Don't do anything in anger, Laura. We need you to do some acting on Friday. Also, Sera may not know anything about why Ian was looking for you. He's not going to tell someone he hired, his master plan. He just got lucky and you appeared."

"Okay. I'll compose myself and do what I can to make this work. I want my life back."

"I understand. You did nothing wrong. We're going to make this right."

Chapter Ten

"Mr. McClure. Thanks for calling."

"Sera, you've done a good job finding the woman. Did you receive the check?"

"Yes, and I appreciate it a lot."

"You're meeting this Sharon person on Friday, right?"

"Yes. We seem to have hit it off. We like talking to each other."

"Don't get too attached. She's not who she says she is."

"You mean her name's not Sharon?"

"No, but that is not important. Just keep your conversation safe. No digging questions. If she feels comfortable she may reveal more information we can use."

"What should I be listening for?"

"If she ever mentions New Mexico or Albuquerque let me know. There could be another bonus check in it for you if she does."

"Should I ask her more about those places if she does mention them?"

"No. She may start getting suspicious. Let her reveal any information on her own."

"I'll call you right away if I hear anything. Thanks again for the check. It really helped."

Ian was not concerned about paying for information. Sera didn't know why he was tracking Laura or in this case Sharon. There was no reason to let Sera know anything about his investigation at all.

"Your welcome. Keep up the good work."

Ian hung up. His two men from Ireland were landing in Albuquerque today and he needed to talk to them. Where they were staying was set up and ready for occupancy. He placed a call.

"Hello, is this Michael or Clog? This is Mr. McClure."

"Oh, Mr. McClure. Michael Riley here. Clog and I were expecting your call. We just landed and didn't know where to go next." The two men traveled using false passports because of their criminal records. Clog Malloy served time for criminal activity in the 80's and Michael had been released from jail six months earlier.

"Everything is ready for you. You should have the address where you'll be staying. The two cars rented are at the airport under Avis. Drive to the address. The apartment is in the back of the office. I also sent the name of an Irish pub near you. I'll talk to you two directly from now on. Sean is out of the picture until you get the job done and are back in Ireland."

"We're both a bit confused. Neither of us have been to America before and didn't know what to expect."

"You'll get used to it. Just don't drink any of their beer. The big name brands do not know how to brew the stuff. They've got some good Irish beer at the pub. I called and checked."

"Fine. How do we get into the office?"

"Get the key from the hair salon next door. They have the names you're using. Make sure you use only the ones in your passport when you're here. Don't want anything leading back to Sean or myself."

"We should get to the office within the hour. Anything we need to do right away?" asked Michael.

Ian was being as thorough as he could with these two Irish hit men. Sean said they were professionals. He would see. The name, Michael, he understood. Good Irish name. Clog? What parent names their kid after a dance?

"Two important things. There's a file on Robert Woods in the desk drawer. We have his last residence before he disappeared. Included is the gym he went to and the restaurants he frequented. Also in the cabinet are plastic explosives. One of you is familiar with those, right."

"Yes. Clog used to blow up British tanks back in the 70's. What about personal weapons?"

"They're in the cabinet. They have silencers. We don't want to draw attention if you need to use them."

"That seems to cover us for now. Basically, you want us to do the footwork and see if anyone knows about this Woods guy. Visit his past haunts in case anyone's seen him recently, right?"

"Yes. Woods can't hide forever. I have a team to back you up if needed. They can get to New Mexico in a few hours. Just call me."

"We'll let you know if we need anything."

Ian hung up. Something would turn up. He just knew it. He needed to sit down. Shortness of breath and a fast beating heart told him the search was wearing him out. Finding Woods could be his last deed on earth. Money and power meant nothing to him now. Restoring his family honor was all that mattered.

*****

Sera was sitting in a booth and having her second drink before Laura arrived. Laura was determined to make her wait. She knew Sera would be there. After all, McClure was paying Sera to keep tabs on her.

"Sorry, I'm late. Traffic was really bad and everyone seems to be heading to the Village for the weekend. Been waiting long?"

"Just started my second drink. Wine for you?"

"Maybe something stronger. I may need it." Laura thought the extra alcohol would relax her so she wouldn't ring Sera's neck. She still could not believe this bitch had sold her out for a paycheck.

"Why, what's wrong?"

"Nothing's wrong. I need to fly to New Mexico on Wednesday for a possible job. I had to change a few things on my calendar to do this but it should be fine."

"You have to go to New Mexico for a job? What happening in Albuquerque this time of year?"

"How did you know I was going to Albuquerque? Did I mention it?"

The alcohol caused Sera to slip. She needed a fast recovery.

"I just thought there was not much else in that state other than the capital. Is that where you're going?"

"Lucky guess. Yes. I come back Friday and plan on being here around six for dinner. I'll probably come directly from the airport. I won't want to cook. Care to join me?"

"I can be here by then. I have an interview with another stock broker but it should be done by six." Sera made sure she did not pry into Sharon's job in New Mexico. She had already screwed up a moment ago and did not want to press her luck.

"I've worked for this guy before and the pay is good. I even like the area. A little hot in the summer but winters are to die for."

The rest of the evening continued without a hitch. Small talk about work love life filled the conversations. Sera was a switch hitter but leaned more towards men. Laura was sure she was never going to find a good one in the City. The best ones were married and the others were destined to be single for the rest of their lives. She was tired of the pickup lines and the crap they dished out.

Around ten Laura had to go. She had her regular schedule at the gym and a run in the morning. She needed sleep. Sera said goodbye and decided to stay a little longer. As soon as Laura was out the door she placed a call to Mr. McClure.

"Sera here Mr. McClure. Sorry, it's late but I thought you would want to know right away about Sharon and her plans."

"Yes, I would. What do you have?"

"Says she's flying to Albuquerque on Wednesday and coming back Friday. Something about a job and a person she used to work for. Didn't give me any names and I didn't press her."

"Fantastic job Sera. Another break. By the way, her real name is Laura Scott but still use the name she gave you when you're with her. Don't want her getting suspicious."
"That's all I have. I'm meeting her again when she flies back on Friday. Hope this will help you get what you want."

"You have no idea. If this pans out I will send another bonus check just like the first one. This could be invaluable information."

*****

After hanging up with Sera a call was made to Michael and Clog. The time difference was a couple of hours so the evening was just beginning in New Mexico.

"Hello, this is Ian McClure."

"Mr. McClure, this is Michael."

"Lots of noise in the background. Where are you two?"

"Barney's, the pub you told us about. Can't stand the beer anywhere else."

"We have a lead and it may cut your visit to America short," Ian said.

"Really? Clog will be happy to hear that. He's homesick already."

"The States take a little getting used to."

"I like it but then again I just got out of jail," Michael added.

"A woman we are following in New York is coming to Albuquerque on Wednesday. I need to have you two ready. We will follow her to the airport and find out what flight she's on. When we do I want you both in separate cars waiting for her. I'll fax a picture in the morning. Follow her at all times and try not to be detected."

"No problem Mr. McClure. We're on this. Call when you have her flight. Should we continue to follow up on any leads regarding Woods?"

"Yes. Don't stop what you're doing. We'll find Mr. Woods one way or another."

"We'll be waiting."

Michael hung up and repeated the message to Clog. The possibility of going home soon put a smile on his face. He didn't like America much. The Irish pub was filled with second and third generation Irishmen. None could speak Gaelic and all they were interested in was American football.

"Let's hope this woman leads us to Woods. I'm so ready to be back in Dublin with our own kind."

"Another round then back to the office. We still need to continue our research."

The two Irish hit men were more than ready to call it a night. They could catch a soccer game on the international channel back at the office and drink beer there. Wednesday was not far off and they still had a few more leads to follow up on.

*****

Laura's flight landed around noon. She only had a carry-on and clothes for two days. Robert gave her instructions and she followed them exactly. Wanting this nightmare to be over was as much a priority for her as it was for Robert.

The cab took her to the Double Tree Hilton near the Civic Plaza where she checked in. Robert had a man in place, parked across the street with a telephoto lens and a computer. The two cars that were following Laura's cab parked a block up the street. Within ten minutes Robert's man had the license plates of the cars and the photos of the two men in each car. Within an hour the Irish hit men were identified. The face recognition program, Robert owned, was worth every cent.

"Both cars were rented and billed to a Sean McClure in Ireland," Julia said. "Also the names of the men are different.

They probably used fake passports when they entered the country. It says on the printout that these two men have served time in Ireland and are employed by Sean McClure."

Julie was still reading the monitor screen and stopped. "It also says one of the men is an explosive expert and served time for blowing up English tanks during the Irish uprising."

"Which one was that?"

"The Neanderthal looking one named Clog."

Robert now had an idea as to how Ian was going to take him out. Explosives were much more efficient. Ian didn't just want him dead. He wanted to take down his whole operation in one big bang.

"I've got to hand it to Ian. He is doing his best to make sure our investigating operation never recovers after he's done."

"This is serious Robert. These two guys came all the way from Ireland and seem to be professional hit men. Now that we know who they are, do we continue with the second part of the plan or not?"

"We have to see it through. Give Laura a call and tell her everything is on schedule. She should stay near the hotel and get ready to finish this job tomorrow morning."

*****

The call was made to Laura's fourth story room overlooking the street. She was given the green light to get something to eat near her hotel and stay close. Tomorrow would be a busy day and everything was still on schedule. A car would pick her up around nine.

Laura was starving. It was *happy hour* and she was ready to unwind. Painted on jeans and a blouse that emphasized the rest of her, completed the New Mexico look. A shawl for the evening air kept her shoulders warm. The Italian bistro a block away placed her at a window seat facing the street.

Clog was on duty. He moved the car so he could watch Laura eating her dinner. Michael had gone back to the pub and purchased some Irish stew and a few beers to help Clog through the evening. They'd change shifts at midnight.

Robert's team followed Michael back to the office where the two hit men worked and lived. Woods now knew where they could find the Irish gangsters.

The information was sent to Robert and run through the system. A real estate company leased the office. Nothing led back to McClure.

*****

Laura's entrance to the bistro did not go un-noticed by the single men at the bar. After being seated she ordered wine and a gnocchi dish. She had a table looking out the window.

Clog ate his cold bowl of Irish stew in the car. This woman is good looking, he thought, but not my type. He liked his Irish girls with a little meat on them.

After dinner, Laura was about to order another glass of wine when the waiter approached.

"A gentleman at the bar wants to buy you a drink and asks if it's all right."

"Which one?" Laura asked.

"The gentleman in the green jacket."

Laura glanced in his direction and then nodded to the waiter. "Sure. Send him over. I'm ready for some conversation." Laura was not interested in going home with anyone. Any pickup lines and the meeting was over.

"Hi. My name's Jeff. I saw you come in."

"How'd I do?" Laura asked.

"If you mean were you noticed, I would say yes. I noticed you."

So far so good. He seemed nice. No creepy come-ons yet.

"Please sit down. My name is Laura." She gave him her real name.

"I've never seen you here before. You're not from New Mexico are you?"

"No, I'm from New York. Came here for a job and head back on Friday. How about you? What do you do?"

"Real estate and loans. Boring as hell but it pays the bills. I usually come in here to unwind after the day. Love the food too."

"I agree with you on that one. It was a fantastic meal."

"You said job. What exactly do you do?" Jeff asked.

"Photography mostly but I occasionally do freelance stuff and have to leave the city."
"Well, I'm glad you made it to Albuquerque."

The next two hours was spent drinking wine and going over things they had in common. Jeff was one of the nice guys and still single. No bragging about his possessions or fancy house. He like the smaller city environment of Albuquerque and the desert climate suited him well.

Laura was impressed with this guy but still was not ready to jump into the sack with someone she just met. The two exchanged cards. They would call each other if they were in the same town again. No pick up lines and attempts to take her home. Just good conversation and a few laughs.

Just as Laura was about to leave Jeff suggested another Italian restaurant two blocks the other way from her hotel. He said he would like to buy her dinner tomorrow and continue their conversation. Laura said she would call. She didn't know what her assignment entailed in the morning or how long it would take to complete. She walked the block back to the hotel. It was a fun evening.

Clog moved the car closer to the hotel and looked at his watch. In an hour he could get some sleep. Michael had the all night shift.

Chapter Eleven

The Escalante pulled up in front of the hotel around ten. Robert was driving. He made sure his face was recognized by Clog parked across the street. Clog made a call to Michael who was in his car a block away.

"It's Woods. He picked up the woman and is headed somewhere. I'll tail him. Catch up. We may have to use both cars so we won't be noticed."

"Just be careful. I'm right behind you," Michael said.

Robert drove through the streets and used a couple of maneuvers to make the two men think he was trying to avoid being followed. He pulled up at a home in a middle-class neighborhood and parked in the garage.

"They're still behind us. They need to believe I live here. We'll stay a few hours and then I'll return you to the hotel. After that, I'll play my last card."

"What do you mean your last card?"

"Tell you later. I don't know if it'll work yet. Fly home tomorrow. Cathy will call and fill you in on any further information we need to pass on to Ian through Sera."

"Am I free to have dinner with someone tonight?'

"I believe so. We've set the trap and it is now Ian's turn to make a move."

"What do you think he'll do, Robert? These guys aren't going to shoot up a neighborhood are they?"

"No. That'll draw too much attention. They still have to make their escape. I'm sure I'll find out real soon."

*****

"Mr. McClure. Michael here. We have him."

"What do you mean you have him?" Ian said. You didn't touch him did you?"

" No, we followed him. He picked up the woman at the hotel and took her to his home. They're inside now. We're calling to ask if you want us to finish the job."

Ian was given the address where the house was located.

"You need to complete this tonight," Ian said. "The woman will probably go back to her hotel. One of you needs to remain outside the house. If he leaves, follow him. Don't let him out of your sight. Make sure he returns home. The other one should pick up the explosives and return to the house tonight. I left a cell phone detonator in the same cabinet. This is it."

"I'll let Clog handle the stuff. He knows what to do. You want Woods gone tonight, right?"

"I wanted him gone six months ago. Tonight will have to do. Call me before you set off the explosives. I want to hear the blast over your phone."

"When we're done what then?"

"Get out. No need to hang around. Get the next flight back to Dublin. I'll have Sean contact you with the end result."

"Shall we burn the files you left on Woods? We should clear everything out that connects the office with any of this."

"Yes. Good thinking. I was too excited and almost forgot to

mention that. I'll be waiting for your call."

Ian hung up. He took another heart pill and something to lower his blood pressure. It was finally happening. He would live to see the day Robert Woods was gone. He could die in peace.

*****

Robert dropped Laura off at the hotel and gave her a kiss on the cheek. "You may have saved our lives. If this works we'll be forever in your debt, Laura." He handed her an envelope. "This is just a token of what you have done. Cathy will call you with the details after we know how tonight goes. We love you."

Laura was almost in tears. She was happy the job did not take all day. She could deposit the check into her account and still have dinner with Jeff. She liked the guy. Maybe this trip to New Mexico would play out well for everyone involved.

"Thank you, Robert. I really like working for you. It's always exciting and you treat me well." Laura got out of the car and return to the hotel room.

Her bank was accessible by simply taking a picture of the check and sending it to her account. Laura opened the envelope. A gasp came from her as she collapsed on the bed. $100,000 was made out to Laura Scott. She had no idea. Crap. Maybe she did save Robert's life. She could live on this check for two years. New Mexico was turning out to be a wonderful state.

Robert drove to the grocery store and then home. He was making every effort to fool the Irish gangsters into believing he lived in the home. It actually did belong to him but was used as a safe house for any clients who needed to hide out for a while. It was now being used to save his life.

*****

Laura met Jeff at the restaurant. His last name was Williamson. Was he the one? She always knew she was not going to meet the man of her dreams in New York. She didn't mind the desert that much. People got married no matter where you lived. If this worked out she could still work as a wedding photographer.

The evening went perfectly. Laura and Jeff spent the time together in pleasant conversation with no expectations of anything more. When it was time to go, Jeff drove Laura the two blocks back to her hotel. A goodnight kiss and plans on getting together in the future were made.

"Can I call you in New York, Laura? Talking with you has been such a relief. I don't meet women like you very often. I want to see if this goes anywhere."

"Just where do you want it to go?" Laura was being coy.

"You know. If this leads to something special I want to be a part of that and not think back on this night and say *what if.* I don't want you to be someone that I didn't try to see again just because we live apart from each other. It's been a wonderful night."

Laura was on the edge of inviting Jeff up to her room. She decided to play this out the old fashion way and have him pursue her a little more. After all, she was hot stuff and wanted a man to chase her. It felt good.

"You have my number. I'm usually home during the week except for Fridays when I go to a woman's bar to unwind. I enjoyed our time together as well."

Another kiss only this one lingered a little longer. Jeff returned to his car. Laura turned to watch him drive off.

*****

Clog was on duty watching Laura, while Michael was back at the house where Woods was. Clog gave Michael a call.

"She is going into her hotel now. I think they're finished being together for the night. I have the plastic explosives in the trunk of the car and the detonator. Is Woods still awake?"

"I can see the light from his TV screen flickering through the window. Not much is happening here at all. He seems to be alone. When the lights go off we should give him an hour to get to sleep before we get to work."

"Are you hungry? I am," Clog said.

"Yea. Pick up some food."

"Will do. Any more beer?" asked Clog.

"You're dealing with explosives, my friend. Not a good idea. We'll have time to celebrate back home. See you soon. I'm parked on the north side of the house. Hurry. I'm hungry."

Chapter Twelve

Forty-five minutes later Clog arrived with food. He drank the beer he bought before arriving and was chewing on a stick of gum to cover his breath. He needed alcohol to steady his hand. He knew what to do.

"Any change in the house?" Clog asked.

"What do you mean?"

"Has Woods gone to bed yet?" Clog was in the second car with Michael and watched as he devoured his fish and chips.

"The TV light is off but the bedroom light is still on. Oh, there it goes. It just went off."

"Great. Sixty minutes from now we could be finished and heading home. I hate this place."

"Why do you hate it so much?"

"The beer sucks, people mostly eat junk food and there's no rain. It's like a desert here."

"It is a desert," Michael said. "I kind of like it. The temperature is great for this time of year. The air is dry, not wet like Ireland. Not much green at all."

"That's part of it. Not green enough for me. The plants have stickers and the women are too skinny."

"You're just homesick. We need to get this job over with and get you back to Dublin," Michael said.

Both men waited patiently until they felt it was safe to set the charges. Michael kept watch from the car while Clog went to work. The house was surrounded with the plastic explosives and wired together so they would go off at the same time. Nothing would escape from the house alive. The blast should kill anything inside and the fire would burn any files or office machinery.

"I think we're ready," Clog said as he returned to the car. "Give McClure a call. He wants to hear this from his cell phone." A call was made. It only rang once.

"Hello, Mr. McClure. We're ready."

"Are you sure Woods is in the house?"

"Positive. He went inside around six and hasn't left. The TV was on for several hours but now all the lights are off. Clog placed the plastic explosives and we're ready for a countdown."

"Fine. Here it is." Ian waited a few seconds. Five, four, three, two, one."

The blast shook the car and the two men a block away. The two neighbor homes lost windows on the sides facing the Woods house but not much more. Clog used only enough explosives to take out the house and nothing more.

"Did you hear that Mr. McClure. The house is in total flames. It's gone."

"Good. Get out of there. Drive slowly so no one notices you. Take different routes to the office. Pack, clear out any papers, and take the cars back to the airport. There is a flight back to Ireland at two in the morning. Take it."

"Will do. We're ready to be home."

"I'll contact Sean after I find out what the police discover. It could take a few days."

Michael hung up. He told Clog to head back to the office a different way than he came. "Drive slowly. Don't want to get pulled over." They were going home.

*****

Laura was on the flight back to New York. She was going over in her mind how the weekend went. A huge payday plus she met a really nice guy. Her compensation would not be discussed with Sera but the new man in her life was a safe subject.

Her car was in the long-term parking. She looked in the rearview mirror and didn't see anyone following her. The evening was approaching and the sun set in the west. Laura was ready to unwind with a drink and the shrimp plate. Sera would be there so she had to put on her friendly face. The drive took longer due to Friday traffic.

"Hi, Sera. Wow, what a great time in New Mexico."

"Really? I noticed a glow on your face the moment you walked in. What happened?"

Laura told the story of meeting Jeff in the Italian Bistro and the dinner the following night. The best part of the story was that he was not out to just get laid. He was interested in her and she liked him as well.

"Maybe I should take a vacation to Albuquerque and see what I can find. How are the women there? I can go either way."

"I didn't spend any time checking out the girls. This guy came to me and I just played along. No pick up lines and all the other crap you hear from most men. It was refreshing."

"Did you sleep with him or is that too personal?"

"It is personal but no I didn't. I think he wants to know me before he takes the plunge."

"Wow, a long distant relationship. How did the job go? That was the reason you went wasn't it?"

"It went fine. Just had a short meeting to discuss plans. I think he has a job for me later and he wanted to go over it in private."

Laura was playing Sera by telling her enough to pass something onto Ian but nothing he could use. The meeting and dinner went smoothly. Sera read a chapter from her book based on an interview with a local female judge. No real names were used in the book but the stories were based on fact.

After dinner and a few more drinks and it was time for Laura to get home. She still kept her next Friday date with Sera. She liked Sera and at the same time wanted to strangle her. A dilemma for sure.

Sera remained in the bar and placed a call to Ian. "Hi, Mr. McClure, this is Sera."

"Any news from Laura?"

"Not much. She said she had a meeting and was going to be used in a future assignment. She was more excited about a man she met so the meeting was not discussed. I see you deposited another bonus check into my account. I guess the information I passed on was of some value."

"You have no idea. Just keep the Laura friendship going and report back if there is anything new."

"I will Mr. McClure and thank you again for the bonus." She hung up.

Sera had no idea what Ian was up to or what he did with the Laura information. She was starting to get suspicious and at the same time thought it best to remain in the dark. She knew Mr. McClure was a rich and powerful man. Crossing him would be a big mistake.

*****

By Monday most of the evidence had been gathered regarding the house explosion near Graton Street. Detective Joe Martin was working the case. The body of the owner, a Mr. Robert Woods, had been found in the bedroom. It was completely burnt and identification could only be made through his dental records.

Mr. Woods had no heirs. A will donated a small amount to a bank for some cancer society was discovered in a safe deposit box under his name. He seemed to be living alone. Only burnt men's clothing was found in what was left of the closets. He owned some computer equipment and their burnt remains were found in the rubble.

The more investigating Martin did the more confused he was. Robert Wood appeared out of nowhere and landed in Albuquerque seven years ago. After a year he disappeared and just now seemed to have risen from the ashes in the form of a burnt body. The corpse was found in a nice neighborhood but nobody seemed to know much about him. Woods purchased the house three years ago. Different people were seen entering and leaving it during that time.

No one saw anything but a neighbor down the street thought he heard two cars driving away after the blast. Martin sent an officer to check out car rental companies. He came up with a possible lead. Two cars were returned to Avis at the airport around one in the morning. The person who checked them in said two men were together. They sounded like they were from Ireland.

Further questioning turned up the only flight returning to Ireland at two in the morning. Surveillance cameras at the car rental provided the officer with pictures of the two men. They were on the two o'clock flight back to Ireland.

The officer had facial photographs of the two men made and headed back to the office. Detective Martin and detective Louis, his second in command, were discussing the case.

"I don't get it." Martin was going over the clues he had so far. "A house blows up, two cars pull away and they are probably linked to a couple of Irishmen who leave the country the same night."

"The names on the passports connected the men to a real estate group and some company in Dublin. The company turned out to be non-existent. The same goes with the passports. We might want the Home security team to run the pictures through their face recognition program and see what they come up with," Louis added.

"Good idea Louis. This may be more than just a gas leak explosion. Did the results regarding the cause of the blast come back yet?"

"Not yet. It might take another hour. So far the results show the blast did not come from one place in the house. There were multiple blast locations. More than likely this was a hit."

"As soon as you get the results let me know. This may be bigger than we think."

Both men went back to work follow leads and still trying to find out who this Robert Woods character was. No job or records of any kind on him. He may have lived in Albuquerque but he was able to stay out of sight almost the whole time he was here.

*****

Ian was able to see the initial report within two days of the house blowing up. The dental records, linked to Robert Woods, were enough to satisfy his desire to know more. He avenged his father's death. His family name was still in disrepair with other Company members but Ian didn't care. There was nobody looking over his shoulder and spying on him anymore.

Another heart pill and a blood pressure tab were taken with a glass of wine. Ian felt like celebrating but he had nowhere to go. His pursuit of Woods had alienated him from friends and former work colleagues. He had all his money and he felt like the loneliest man on the planet.

He hoped a call to Ireland might pick him up. "Sean. Ian here. It's over."

"Did you get your man?" Sean asked.

"I believe we did. Your two men did their job. I've sent their payment. Let them know I appreciate the work they did. They got in and got out. Just have them burn those passports in case there is any connection between them and the explosion."

"Will do. Feels good to do things the old fashion way doesn't it Ian. No courts or lawyers. If you want anything done again let me know. By the way, I think you son is going to be heading home soon with his fiancé. He wants to bring her back to the states and start the whiskey wholesale business. We'll miss him. He has a good head for booze and business. He'll do well."

"I hope so. I'm glad he has found something besides investing in the stock market. I've been out of it for a while now and don't miss it at all."

"When are you coming back for another visit? The weather here is starting to change and we should be warming up in another month."

"Soon. I need to get away for a vacation."

"Let us know when you're heading our way. I'm glad all that Company business is behind you. Maybe you can get some needed rest and take care of yourself?"

"Thanks again, Sean. Talk later." Ian hung up. He made another call to have his private jet ready by that afternoon. He knew his wife would be happy to get out of New York. She hated winter.

Chapter Thirteen

"Did you read the paper, Alan?"

"No, why?"

"It says they found a body in that house that blew up in town. They're holding the identification of the person because of an on-going investigation. It may not have been a gas leak. It looks like a murder case."

"No kidding. I thought people just shoot each other when they're ready to get rid of them. Blowing someone up takes a lot of effort."

"Have you talked to Robert in a while. I haven't heard from Julia or him since that slide show of their trip."

"All I know is Robert's been busy with this Ian case and trying to wrap it up. He hasn't told me anything about his plans or what he is doing."

"Maybe I should call Laura and see how she's doing first. I don't want to bother Robert if he's tied up with the investigation. We have our hands full with our business so I know how busy one can get."

"Good idea. Give her a call." Alan was on the computer and had to make some important changes to the site page. He needed to be focused on his work for the next hour.

"Laura, hi. This is Cathy. I'm on the secure line so our name doesn't come up."

Cathy. I'm glad you called. So much has happened, I don't know where to start."

"Try the beginning and work from there."

"Ok, let me catch my breath. First of all, I met someone."

"When? Where?"

"When I was in Albuquerque on Thursday and Friday. I flew into town to meet Robert. It was a diversion tactic he was doing with me to flush out Ian. I couldn't call or have any contact with anyone other than Robert."

"Then how did you meet someone?"

"I went to this bistro down the street and he came up to me. We had a drink together and dinner the following night."

"Did you meet Robert?"

"Yes. Whoever was following me ended up outside the hotel where I stayed. Robert was able to identify them. All I had to do was go with Robert the next morning to some house in town. We went inside for a couple of hours to make the people believe that Robert lived in the house."

"Really. I didn't know about any of this. Do you remember where the house was located?"

"Some middle-class residential neighborhood. I remember the street but not much else."

"It wasn't Graton Street was it?"

"Yes, how'd you know? You've been there?"

"Laura, a house on Graton Street blew up last Thursday night. The police are still investigating it. They found a body inside but no identification has been made public."

"What time did it happen?"

"Around eleven-thirty at night."

"I was back in the hotel, asleep. I didn't watch any local news and left the next day. You don't think it was the same house do you?"

"Laura, I haven't heard from Julia or Robert in a week. I thought to call you first to see how you were doing. We know he's really busy with the Ian case and we didn't want to bother him."

"Is there any way we can find out which house on Graton blew up? I don't remember the address. A lot of those homes in that development look a lot alike."

"Let me work on that. Would you remember the house if you saw a picture?"

"I think so," Laura answered. She now sounding frightened.

"I can get a satellite picture of it when I find out the address. I'll send it to you then. It may not be the same place so let's not get too worked up."

Cathy was doing her best not to excite Laura. She still hoped for the best but expected the worst.

"Anyway what else happened? What about this mystery person you met."

"Before I do that there was one more thing. Robert thanked me when he dropped me off and said I may have saved his life. He also gave me a check for $100,000. Kathy, that is a lot of money for just coming to New Mexico for a couple of days. Robert may be over his head on this one."

"Laura, I'll find out and let you know when I hear something.

Robert is a smart man and always seems to be one step ahead of everyone else."

"Ok, but let me know right away. I'm really worried."

"Mystery man. Tell me more." Cathy was doing her best to get Laura to stop worrying. Women, talking about their love lives, usually could do the trick. With Laura, it worked as well.

For the next thirty minutes, Laura told all the details of the two evenings with Jeff and how they planned to meet again in the future. While Laura was telling her story, Cathy was also going over in her head what might have happened to Robert. She'd have to find the address of the house that blew up. It was probably in the paper. If it turned out to be the same house, what would she do?

After Laura finished her Jeff Williamson story, Cathy reassured her she'd find out if anything happened to Robert. $100,000 was a lot of money for a meeting and a two-day trip. Then again Robert was unpredictable when it came to paying people.

"Keep seeing Sera and we'll to the bottom of this. I'll call you later."

Cathy hung up. She took a deep breath and walked over to the office where Alan was working on the Mingle site.

"How's Laura? You look like you're in shock. Something happen?"

"Did you know if Robert owned a house on Graton Street in that newer development towards the airport?"

Alan shut down his computer screen in order to give Cathy his complete attention.

"He may have. In the past, he put up women who were trying to escape abusive husbands. I think the house was a safe place for some of his clients to disappear for a while. I never went there so I'm not sure what street it's on."

"That house that blew up may have been Robert's."

"No way. Are you sure?"

"Not yet. I'm afraid to call Julia to find out. Could you call instead? I'm a little freaked."

"Were you going to find out first what the house looked like before it blew up. It might not be the same place."

"Laura went with Robert to a house on Graton Street last Thursday. She said she'd remember what it looked like. I'll Google the address and get a picture first before you call Robert."

Cathy typed in the address from the article in the paper and a picture came up. The neighborhood was photographed in 2009 so the house hadn't changed much. She then sent the picture through her phone to Laura. Ten minutes later a text message came back.

"It's the same house. Call me when you know what happened."

Cathy sat down. Alan was looking at her with a worried look.

"Laura said it was the same house. The article also says the police found a body in the charred remains of the building but no name or identification has been released because of the investigation. Alan, something bad has happened."

Alan sat in silence for a few moments. He then came over and put his arms around Cathy. We better drive down to their house and see if anyone is home. I'll get my shoes and the car. Meet you outside."

*****

Detectives Martin and Louis were about to release the name of the body found in the house. The report had come back that it was not a gas explosion at all. Six points of impact were found around the remains of the place. Someone was making sure no one could escape.

"Has the Homeland Security given you anything on those two Irishmen leaving the country on Friday? We have their passport names but nothing so far," Martin said.

Louis was the computer nerd in the office. "Homeland has given us their real names. Michael Riley and Clog Malloy. Who names their kid Clog? Isn't that some kind of Irish dance?"

"From the looks of his picture I don't think I'd say something to his face. This guy looks like the missing link. Probably not a lot of gray matter in that oversized head of his."

"Anyway Homeland was able to help but did not see the activity of blowing up houses in Albuquerque as a national threat. We're on our own with this one."

"Any trace of them in Ireland?"

"No. They seemed have covered their tracks pretty well. We don't have the funds to send anyone over there to try and catch them. We may be simply left with finding out why they blew up Robert Woods and his house. Arresting them in Ireland is out of our reach."

Martin took a sip of his coffee. He really could not give a shit about this Robert Woods guy. He'd rather make it an open and closed case but the murder aspect meant he had to see it through. "Too bad it wasn't a gas explosion. That'd be the end of it. How long were those Irish thugs in Albuquerque?" he asked.

"The airlines had them arriving three weeks ago," answered Louis.

"Do we know where they stayed? Maybe we should show their pictures around a few Irish pubs. I know those are the only places that serve warm beer. Someone could have seen them."

"I'll get on that right away," Louis said. "I'll cover the east side with officer Parson if you can check out the west. We might turn up something."

Detective Martin didn't really expect to find any hard leads. It looked like a professional hit. Someone hired Irish mobsters to do the job and then disappeared. So far they were successful.

Chapter Fourteen

"I don't see any of their cars parked out front. This is really creepy showing up here without calling first," Cathy said.

They both got out and went up to the door and rang the bell. Carla answered.

"Hola Mr. Alan. How've you been? We miss you around here."

Carla was finishing the lunch dishes and starting to prepare for Mexican night at the Woods house.

"Hi, Carla. Are Robert and Julia around? Sorry to drop in on you without calling first."

"No problem. Do you want to have dinner with us? It's Mexican night and I know that was your favorite."

"I better talk to Robert first. Is he in the office?"

"I believe so. He's been really busy. Julia is in the pool. Come in and I'll tell them you're here."

A sigh of relief came from Cathy. So far everything seemed normal as if nothing had happened.

Julia came in from the pool. She wore a bathing suit when Carla was at the house. The air was a little cool but the water was close to 90 degrees.

"Hey, neighbors. Are you all settled in yet? We're planning on dropping in on you two but thought we'd give it another week. Had our hands full with Ian."

"Julia, it is really good to see you. Is Robert okay?" Cathy gave Julia a big hug and seemed to be especially happy to see her.

"I guess you figured out who owned that house that blew up on Graton Street. How'd you do that?"

"I Googled the address and sent the picture to Laura. She said it was the same house Robert took her to last Thursday. The article also said there was a body in the ruins but no identification was released. You had us really worried."

"I think Robert needs to talk with you now. This has been a little scary for us as well but we may have pulled it off. Here he comes."

Robert entered the room from the office. Alan walked over to him and shook his hand.

"I just needed to touch you and make sure you're really here. Knowing you, there is a story, and we need to hear it."

"Your right. We didn't want to get you two involved but you are family. Let's get something to drink before I tell you the situation we're in right now."

Beers were opened. Cathy and Alan drank half the bottle in the first gulp. Ten minutes earlier they sure something awful had happened to Robert and they were just coming out of shock.

"The house blowing up had something to do with Ian, right? He discovered Albuquerque was you home. He also knew you were the one who crippled the Company and got him fired as CEO. Is that about right?" Alan asked.

"Yes, that about sums it up. I knew Ian must have a team somewhere in town trying to find me. I had to flush them out."

Alan and Cathy took another swig of their beers and drained the bottles.

"I had to make him believe he discovered and killed me. Laura was the bait and Ian took it hook, line and sinker."

"Yea but what about the house that blew up and the body they found? If that wasn't you then who was it?"

"That's the tricky part. It was me, or at least according to the police investigation it was."

"You're pretty clever Robert but this one tops the rest. How did you kill yourself?"

"You know I use different professors at the University to find computer people like you. Well, I also have friends in the medical wing that teach pre-med students. I purchased a cadaver from them and gave them enough money to buy three more."

"Do they know you as Robert Woods?"

"No, I use my alias with everyone outside my circle of close friends. Right now that circle has grown a lot smaller. The dental records came with the body. All I had to do was switch the records with the last dentist I used before I went underground six years ago."

"You mean that was a medical cadaver they found with your dental records? I know where you got this idea. You watched the last episode of *House* didn't you?"

"Guilty as charged Alan. I figured if House could get away with it then so could I."

"You are a sly SOB Robert. Who's going to claim the body? I mean if you're going to have a formal burial someone needs to come forward and finish the job."

"I had a will made with enough money in it to bury me. I've

hired a lawyer to complete the finishing touches and put me in the ground. Making Ian believe he avenged his father was my only goal at the time. It had to be convincing."

"Now what?" Do you think he will come after the rest of us?" Alan looked over at Cathy to see how she was taking the news. Color was returning to her face. The beer helped.

"I don't know but I don't think so. We've been tracking the Irish hit men and they've returned to Belfast. I'll deal with them later but first I have the Ian problem to finish up. We now have some breathing room. He thinks I'm dead and he's resting in the Cayman Islands."

"You mean this whole house business was to get Ian off your back?"

"Pretty much. He got close. He used Laura to get to me and I used her to get to him."

Cathy walked over to the kitchen to retrieve more beers for everyone. She had to say something when she heard Laura's name mentioned.

"Is Laura going to be safe? I mean will Ian try and hurt her or is she okay living in New York?"

"Right now she is the one passing on misinformation to Ian through a woman named Sera. Ian hired Sera to find me. I'm going to use Laura to confirm the belief that I'm dead. That should end the situation with Ian needing Laura anymore. There's no reason to hurt her. She gave him what he wanted."

"How are you going to take this rat bastard out? He's really impacted our lives and I'm ready to be done with him," said Cathy. She had a way with words when she wanted to express her anger.

"Right now my inner circle is you two. I may include Laura and have her go to my funeral next week. Her attending will put a seal on the case for Ian. The police don't know who Laura is. She should come to the burial as a former friend and not a former employee."

"Do you want me to tell her the whole story? I said I would let her know what happened as soon as I found out," said Cathy.

"No, not the whole story. She has to think I'm dead. Also, all conversations must be on secure lines. I can't have any contact with her until Ian is gone. He may have dropped his defenses a notch but he's still a dangerous bastard."

The second beers were finished and Alan started to get up.

"Can you two stay for dinner? It's Mexican night."

"You know how I love Carla's cooking but we have a lot to do," Alan said. "Between unpacking and working on the site, I'm a bit overwhelmed. When this is all over we'll have a house-warming party and invite Jason and Rosa down from Santa Fe. Maybe William and Leslie can drive over from Tucson?"

"I understand. Now that I'm dead I have a lot more freedom to plan an attack. I just hope Ian can stay alive long enough to get in the last punch."

"Why? Is he sick?" asked Cathy.

"His health is poor. We think his organs are shutting down. I just want to let him know that I'm still here and he lost. It's a pure ego thing on my part but this bastard's caused a lot of people pain. I guess letting him know money cannot buy him anything he wants would be my final hurrah."

"We'll keep a low profile on our part. Let us know if we can help in any way."

"Thanks for dropping by, neighbor. Talk to you later." Hugs were given. Alan and Cathy walked out to their car. There was a feeling of total relief finding Robert still alive.

Before Cathy left, Robert gave her a piece of paper with instructions as to what should be passed on to Laura. Attending the funeral would be necessary but knowing Robert was still alive could not happen. Ian had drugged her before and he could do it again. It was for her own safety.

$$*****$$

"Laura hi, it's me." Cathy was having a hard time making this call but it had to be done. The wording had to be perfect in order to pull it off.

"Cathy, I've really been worried. What'd you find out?"

"No good news so far. The house belonged to Robert. There was a body burnt beyond recognition. The police have identification but have not released it. It could be Robert."

"Nooooo! Really?" Laura was in shock. "When will they know?"

"It's a crime scene and they're waiting to find out more before names are released. They believe some outside persons may have set the explosives. It was a total loss."

"I left the house in the afternoon. Robert dropped me off at the hotel and said he was going back to the house. It had to be the people who were tailing me that blew up Robert."

Cathy was still following the script given to her by Robert. "We believe he's gone. If it is Robert, we're having a lawyer take care of the funeral arrangements and plan to bury the body next Sunday. Ian may have gotten his revenge."

"I'm in complete shock. Who's left to go after Ian?"

"Nobody. Alan and I are no longer working for Robert and Julia is alone. Do you want to come and visit next weekend? You can stay with us. By then the police will have come up with a name. Something about dental records was mentioned in the paper which will give them a positive identification."

"If the funeral is next Sunday I will be there Saturday. I'm really sorry."

"Me too. We're all in shock. Call when you have a flight. We'll have someone drive you to our house. We're still being evasive in case Ian is following you. We don't want him knowing where we live."

"I understand. I'm sick. I really am Cathy. "

"I know. See you Saturday."

Laura hung up. She had a wedding to shoot on Wednesday and a meeting with Sera on Friday. Her flight for Saturday morning was booked so she could visit before the funeral. It sounded as though Alan and Cathy were sure it was Robert's body found in the house ruins. She had to accept the fact and move on.

She called Jeff to tell him her plans. "Hi, Jeff. Sorry but I'm really bummed out. I'm flying to Albuquerque on Saturday to stay with friends and attending a funeral on Sunday."

"What?" he asked. "Who died?"

"The man I was working for was killed in a house explosion last Thursday."

"You mean the one on Graton Street. That's been in the news for several days."

"Yes, it's the same one. I was in that house just hours before it blewup."

"You're kidding me. The police are still investigating the incident. Something about plastic explosives set around the house. Whoever was inside didn't stand a chance."

"That was the man I worked for in the past. We were working on another project at the time."

"Can I accompany you to the funeral? I can give you some support."

Laura thought for a moment. Did she really want someone else involved in her work? She then realized her work with Robert was really over. She needed to move on. Allowing Jeff in her life was moving on.

"Are you sure? This is not a happy time for me."

"Laura, I like you a lot. Having a life with only happy moments is not really living. It's full of ups and downs. I want to be there for you when you are sad as well."

"Who was this guy?" Laura thought. "Some representative for the good men in the world?" Laura couldn't say no.

"You're really a sweet man, Jeff. I'll call you when I get to town and meet you at the funeral. My friends will drive me there. Maybe afterward we can eat a meal together and you can take me to the airport. I have another wedding on Tuesday. I'm looking forward to seeing you again."

"Me too, Laura. See you Sunday."

Laura still needed to protect the location of Alan and Cathy. They trusted her but Jeff a newcomer. She'd get to know him better before he could be a part of her inner circle.

*****

Friday night. Laura arrived early at Leggs. She needed a drink before meeting Sera. If Ian used Sera to find Robert, then Sera might not be alive for the rest of her natural life. Laura would do a little investigation on her own and find out how much Sera knew about Ian.

Sera came into the bar and sat down in the booth across from Laura.

"Hi, Sharon. What's the matter? You look really stressed. Men problems?"

Laura still used her fake name with Sera. It was not the right time to blow her cover.

"I've had a tragedy in the family. The guy I worked for in New Mexico was killed last week. I'm flying back to Albuquerque for his funeral on Sunday."

"What happened?" Sera started to worry about what she had done.

"The police think he was blown up in his house. All they could use to identify him was his teeth. Nothing else was left."

"You're kidding. Who would do such a thing?" Her thoughts went to Ian.

"The police have no leads at the moment. They're spending more time investigating the person in the house and finding out more about him. Not much to go on."

"You knew him? I mean the guy in the house."

"Yes but that's the problem. He was underground. His identity was a secret because he investigated bad people. Somebody from his past may have killed him. No one knows for sure."

Sera was in shock. She knew little about Ian or why he wanted her to find Laura. Ian was rich and powerful. That's all she knew. If Sera had helped lead Ian to this mystery man in New Mexico by following Laura, then she was guilty of aiding in his death. This sucked.

"I'm really sorry about all of this, Sharon." Sera knew she had to find out if Ian had something to do with the death of Sharon's ex-boss. She was hired to find someone, not to help get someone killed.

"Yea, me too. If I ever find out who did this, then another funeral will happen in the near future." Laura studied Sera's face to see if there was any reaction.

"When are you coming back from the funeral?"

"Sunday night. I plan to meet Jeff for dinner and fly out in the evening."

"Could you call me next week? I sometimes do investigations for people and I have a friend who can find out more about this incident."

"It's more than an incident. The police think it's a murder case."

"I'll see what I can do. This really sucks."

The two women ordered another drink and sat in silence for a few minutes. The conversation shifted to the book Sera was writing.

Laura watched Sera closely. So far Sera seemed to be surprised about the whole incident. She might not have known anything about Ian or his real intentions. Laura would play her cards close to her chest and see what this woman had up her sleeve.

*****

The early flight from New York to Albuquerque landed around nine. Laura kept an eye out for any cars following her to the airport. Nothing. Maybe she was no longer being followed. Robert was dead so she might be in the clear. A car was waiting for her. It was Cathy wearing sunglasses, a wig and sporting a larger bust.

"Get in and we'll talk on the way. It's really good to see you again, Laura. A lot has happened since we last saw each other."

"No kidding. I hardly recognized you. I'm really sorry about all of this. I haven't slept all week."

"We'll get through this. Alan and I have been busy with the website business. We've had little contact with Julia and Robert and now this."

Laura did not have much to say to Cathy on the way to her house. She felt responsible for the death of Robert. If she had not gone back to *Leggs* then none of this would have happened.

"What is Julia going to do? She's all alone now."

"She's underground and hidden. There is an investigation going on and she doesn't want to be connected with Robert in anyway. It's for her own safety."

"Is she going to the funeral?"

"Probably not. If Ian is still active and trying to find others involved with Robert, he may have people at the funeral taking pictures.

He may use the same ploy we did at his father's memorial service and find out who we are. Alan and I are going but we're using different names. I have gone through a few changes since living in New York."

"I noticed. There's a part of you that seems larger than when we worked together. I bet Alan's happy."

"Happy is not the word for it. He is like a kid in a candy store. What is it about men and boobs? It's a good thing I like sex so much. My body is really getting a workout."

Cathy looked in the rear view mirror. "Keep an eye out for anyone who may be following us. I have to make some driving moves just in case."

The car sped around the block and made some fast turns making sure no one was behind. Cathy then headed home. There was no mention of Robert and Julia's house just down the road.

Twenty minutes later they arrived.

"Nice place, Cathy. This Geek Mingle site must really be taking off. I'm really happy for you and Alan."

"We're going public real soon. That's why we haven't seen Julia or Robert."

"Where is Julia staying now?"

"In another house somewhere. I don't think we'll be seeing her for a while."

"Is she going to be all right?"

"Financially, yes. She's still in shock. She'll get through this and make adjustments."

Laura grabbed her suitcase and followed Cathy to the door. The bedroom with the door entrance to the pool was the room used for guest.

"Have you eaten anything?" Cathy asked. "I bet you're hungry."

"I could eat. Where's Alan?"

"He'll be back soon. He's doing some work at the office. We have about ten employees now. Between the business and what needs to be done around the house, he's slammed."

"What time is the funeral tomorrow?"

"Noon. There may be just a few of us. Robert kept a low profile. Only a few have been invited. Also, the police may be interviewing people who show up. Just be prepared."

"What do you want me to say in case I'm questioned?"

"Say you're a family friend. I don't think you want them to know you worked for Robert."

"You're right. I'd never hear the end of it."

"We all need to play it cool and get through this. I think I just heard Alan drive up."

The door opened and Alan walked in. "Laura. Hi. It's good to finally meet you. Cathy has told me so much about you."

Laura looked at Alan and was taken back at his youthful appearance. "That's right. We've only communicated by phone or computer. I've only met Robert and Cathy before."

"Julia was living here by the time we used you and Cathy at the memorial service. A lot has passed under the bridge since then."

The two shook hand. Cathy went into the kitchen to get some lunch for the trio. Alan and Laura headed out to the pool area. It was warm enough to enjoy the midday sun while they ate.

"I'm really sorry for creating this mess. I never should've returned to *Leggs*. I thought Robert was using me to draw out Ian but it looks like that rich bastard got the upper hand."

"Laura, it's not your fault. Robert was trying to draw out Ian but Ian moved too fast. This whole thing might be over for us. Ian is on vacation and you're not being followed."

"Yes, but it cost Robert his life."

"Having us all safe was his main concern."

"What about you two? What are you going to say if the cops approach you?" Laura asked.

"I set up his computers and serviced them. Cathy has an alias with no history. Her makeover changed her appearance. She looks different than her old photos. She's my girlfriend attending the service with me."

"Sounds like you have all your bases covered."

"Is anyone following up on Robert's work or is Ian home free. I don't know what's making me more pissed off? Robert's death or Ian getting away with this."

"We have to let this go, Laura. Ian seems to have stopped trying to find anyone else involved and we're too busy with our new business. Julia is going to be well taken care of."

"What about her? Is she going to be okay?"

"She'll get through this," said Alan. "Well take her under our wing and make sure she gets her life back on track. She plans on staying in New Mexico. She loves it here."

Just then Cathy arrived with lunch. The three sat out in the mid-day sun and talked about other subjects. Laura filled them both in on her new friend, Jeff. He'd meet her at the funeral and then take her to dinner. After that, he'd drop her off at the airport.

Alan was quick to remind Laura that her new boyfriend could not divulge anything to the police about knowing Robert.

"Bringing your boyfriend is fine, but if he knows you worked for Robert, he needs to keep that to himself."

"I'll let him know as soon as I call him tonight. What's the address of the cemetery?

Alan let Laura know where the body would be buried. He also knew he had apologies to make when this case was closed. Keeping the fact that Robert was alive was for her safety. It's hard to fake emotions and Laura would be in mourning. The tears would be real. Everything needed to look authentic.

Chapter Fifteen

Detective Martin had his men in place. The photographer was using a high-powered telephoto lens and standing away from those who gathered to pay their respects. The low numbers of those attending surprised Martin and at the same time, it made his job easier.

The funeral lasted half an hour. Roses were laid on the coffin and tears shed by two of the women attending, pretty much summed up the service. *'May he rest in peace'* concluded the ceremony.

Contact was made with five of the mourners and cards given to them. Martin would call them. He was not going to try and interview anyone on this sad day. He had an investigation to follow up but it could wait. He needed to find out who killed Robert Woods and why.

Laura said her goodbyes to Cathy and Alan and thanked her for their hospitality. She left with Jeff. Alan drove his usual avoidance route home making sure Ian still did not have a team following him from the service. Martin went back to the office. He was having the pictures of those attending the service sent to the main office in Albuquerque.

Jeff and Laura had time to walk around Old Town before an early dinner and then the airport. "Thanks for coming, Jeff. That really meant a lot to me."

"It meant a lot that you allowed me to be with you on this occasion. I would really like to spend some time with you and not just these quick meet-ups. Hopefully, we can plan a longer visit and get to know each other better."

"I would like that as well, Jeff. I have a flexible schedule so let's plan around your work and doing something on a weekend."

A weekend together meant romance. This included sex and she was ready to take the plunge. She liked Jeff a lot and did not get the vibe he was a player. She had her fill of those in her life.

The drive to the airport and a long kiss goodbye finished the weekend. "I'll call you when I'm home. Thanks again for being there for me."

"That's what people who care about each other do. We'll talk later. Have a good flight."

Laura took a quick look around the terminal. No one seemed to be watching them. Maybe Ian really had given up following her. Time would tell.

*****

The Cayman Islands had been just what he needed for a rest. Ian's health was still nowhere near normal. He had taken stress to a new level and some of his bodily functions were starting to shut down. Pills would keep him alive for a while longer. He didn't care. Revenge was his.

His son was arriving in a few days with his new fiancé. Ian at least looked better with a tan and a smile on his face. He'd get through this. He son getting married and carrying on the McClure name in America was important. Ian had one more trick up his sleeve before he checked out.

Only five men were left of the original 22 men in the Company. His plan was to revive the "Golden Goose" and reward these men for their faithfulness to him. Ian still had the compound that could induce the brain bleed and give a previous client the ability to see future closing stock numbers. His plan was to go out with a bang.

The research team was gone. Ian needed to find an old client who wanted to make one last journey into the world of seers and make a lot of money. With the five friends and his wealth, they could rock the stock exchange once and for all. A grand finale could put his name on the walls as one of the greatest investors who ever played in the arena of the Brass Bull.

*****

"Everything went off without a hitch, Robert. We buried you and no one seemed to question it at all," Alan said.

"What about that detective who's following up on the case? Does he suspect anything?"

"He's only calling those who attended the funeral. He wants to know what their connection is with you. So far he has little to go on. Why you were a target of Irish hit men may remain a mystery forever."

"Alan, you've been invaluable to me during this time. The cadaver

received a decent burial and I'm gone forever. Only my closest friends will know me as Robert Woods. I was thinking of changing my last name anyway."

"To what?" Alan asked.

"Julia and I discussed it and came up with the name Forester. It still has a woodsy ring to it. She thought Julia Forester would be a nice married name."

"Married? Are you two going to go all the way?"

"When Ian is gone we're getting married. We share everything together so why not share a new last name as well?"

"This is so great, Robert. Be sure to keep us up to date on the Ian investigation. What is that bastard up to now?"

Robert thought for a moment. He wished he still had Alan working for him. His new assistant was a woman in her early twenties. She was good at what she did but Robert had to keep a lot of his personal life a secret. She was still an unknown and had to earn his trust.

"Ian is back from the Caymans. He looks like he got some sun. Doesn't have that pasty white look anymore. He really thinks I'm gone and all his worries are behind him."

"Did you hire that new assistant you told me about?"

"Yes. Don't know too much about her. She's good but I have her doing basic research stuff for the few side cases I'm working on. I have to trust her more before I have her helping me with the Ian case."

"What's her name? Maybe I had a class with her?"

"Peggy Anderson. She must be Swedish. She looks a lot like that new girl on the NCIS show. You know, the one who always does her work while sitting on the floor."

"I like her. I mean the character in the show. Peggy Anderson, I also know but only from a class. She's good."

"So far. She knows her computers and the cyber world for sure."

"I'm surprised you hired a woman. Haven't all the others been men before me?"

"A single man in a house, alone with a woman assistant would not work. Talk about a possible scandal. Julia works with her mostly. I just tell Julia what I want her to do. We keep it as professional as possible."

"Good thinking, Robert. I'll do what I can if you get stuck with anything. You know where to find me. I'm at the office most of the day. We're getting close to the public date so it's just a matter of time."

"Going public seems to be a big thing, Alan. I'm sure you have a good accountant lined up. Mine is good but he may not be able to find time to deal with you. You need someone full time for sure."

"I have one. Got him through another friend who specializes in the finances for on-line companies. We are also going to follow in the footsteps of Gates and Zuckerberg and donate a lot of our income to various charities we like. I think William and Leslie did that when they started out with the Company."

"Alan, you've got a good head on your shoulders for such a young man. I respect you for your views of the world and wanting to help. Just be sure to invite us to the Who's Who dinner when they honor you at the annual Albuquerque gala."

"No problem. You may have to come in disguise. That detective called who is investigating your death. Basic questions so far. I told him I maintained your computers and did service calls. He has no idea I actually worked for you full time."

"One day I'll have to let the police know what really happened but not yet. Ian's still around and those two Irish hit men are as well. I need to tie up those loose ends before I come out in the open."

*****

Louis had some more information regarding those who attended the funeral. The person named Alan Hogan said he maintained the computers that were found in the burnt house.

"Did you find out anything more about the girlfriend of Mr. Hogan? You know, the one with the nice tits," Martin said.

"Yea, she was hot. How does a computer nerd get a girlfriend like her?" Louis asked.

Martin still had little to go on as to why Woods was killed. A few burnt computers were extracted but no information that could be retrieved. The fire had been intense and fried everything.

"How about the woman from New York? Anything on her?" Martin wanted a file on everyone at the funeral.

"Not much. Seemed to be a friend only. They connected when he flew to New York. She had a boyfriend with her. Some guy from town who sells real estate and does financing."

"What did he have to say?"

"Nothing really. He didn't even know Robert Woods. He was at the funeral to support the Laura Scott woman. The only other person there was the dentist Woods used. He provided us with the dental records."

"Either this guy had few friends or an alias. No one in the neighborhood seemed to know him at all and rarely saw him around the house. Either he was a hermit, and never came out, or he might have another residence altogether. Something's not right here."

"Do we know what he did?" Louis was just as stumped as

Martin. "He had some computers in an office but other than that we don't have much. A bank account with $126,000 and a will found in a safe deposit box. That's it."

Martin took another sip of his coffee. The case seems too neat and tidy. He couldn't find any loose ends at all. Everyone had loose ends in their lives. He just needed to find Mr. Wood's missing parts.

"We'll keep digging. We have other cases to follow up on so maybe this one will end up in the cold case file. At this point, I don't know what to do?"

*****

Friday night at *Leggs* and Sera had a couple of drinks before Laura showed up. She'd been busy and had some information. First, she needed to clear things with her. The alcohol would help.

"Hi, Sharon. How was the funeral?"

"It went smoothly. Not many people showed up. Seems my old boss was a private person and kept to himself."

"Remember I said I'd contact someone I knew in the police department to see if anything surfaced?"

"Yes." Laura was studying Sera's face.

"Well, something came up. I think I've been duped. First I have to come clean with you."

"What do you mean come clean?" Laura could tell something was bothering Sera and she was about to let it all out.

"Please let me tell my whole story first before you say anything."

"Fine. I'll shut up."

Sera filled in how she had been hired by an Ian McClure to come to *Leggs.* Her job was to see if either of two women, she had sketches of, showed up.

"I've been coming every Friday for six months before you came arrived."

Laura started to say something but decided to hold back.

"The information was passed onto Ian. I was paid a nice bonus check for identifying you and another check when I discovered you were going to New Mexico. It was all about the cash and nothing else."

"I don't know what to say, Sera?"

"I was even told your real name. It's Laura isn't it?"

"Maybe, but why are you telling me all this?"

"It's because I discovered who Mr. McClure really is. My friend found out he used to be the CEO of an investment group that did well with the stock market. The federal government investigated a few of them. Inside trading or something like that. He was fired last year and has had little to do with the NYSE since. He's a billionaire and doesn't need money."

"Did he tell you anything about me?"

"No. He gave me sketches of you and this other woman. It seems you two did something that really pissed him off."

"Are you still working for McClure now?" Laura was still being cautious and was not about to tell Sera anything that would expose those working for Robert.

"Yes and no. He pays me if I find out anything from you that will help him in any way. I have a feeling the person he may have been after was the guy blown up in that house in Albuquerque. If I had a part in that I had no idea. Mr. McClure paid me a lot of money to find you. I have been sick ever since I started putting the pieces together."

"Yes. It is the same guy. His name was Robert Woods. He's dead and Ian seems to have gotten away with murder."

"Laura. I'm going to start using your real name. I'm so sorry. I had no idea murder was his intent."

"What are you going to tell him now?"

"Nothing much to tell. You said Robert Woods is dead. If that was who he was after then the case is probably closed on Ian's end. I want to make this right. Is there anything I can do? I'm at a loss as to how I can help."

"I'm still angry with you but I see how you might have been played. I do investigation work as well and don't ask too many questions. I'll have to think about this one for a while. With Robert Woods dead the case seems to be closed. He was investigating McClure and had something to do with Ian getting in trouble with the NYSE"

"I'm really sorry about all of this. I really like you Laura and want to continue being friends."

"I like you too, Sera. I'll get over this. Maybe we can do some investigating on our own but I am not equipped to do this kind of work. I usually do the photography portion of the job. Robert did the heavy lifting."

"I'll talk to my detective friend again and see if he knows anything more about Ian. We may be at a dead end. People like

McClure use people and discard them when they're through. He also has a pretty good protection around him. He had a team that followed you from here a few weeks back. I bet they protect McClure as well."

"Let me know if you find anything from your friend in New York. I don't think there is much else we can do for now."

For the rest of the evening, the two women talked about their lives. Laura kept Alan, Cathy, and Julia to herself. Maybe they could do more through the detective friend of Sera's but then again this was not their line of work. Right now they'd keep in touch and meet at *Leggs* when they could. Laura had a weekend planned with Jeff and was looking forward to that immensely.

Chapter Sixteen

"Hello. Is this Mr. Ray?"

"Yes, it is. Whom I speaking to?"

"My name is Miss Reed. I work for Mr. Ian McClure. He represented the Company you worked for under a Mr. Jason Burns over a year ago."

William was a little taken-back. This was the last person he expected to hear from after the death of Woods.

"Oh yes. I remember Mr. Burns. How is he doing?"

"We have little contact with previous employees. All I know is that he moved to New Mexico and has taken up photography."

William knew this but wanted to make this woman think he had no contact with Jason or anyone from his past.

"What can I do for you, Miss Reed?"

"It's what we can do for you. I know the phone Jason used to contact you with is no longer in service so I am calling you on your private line. We want to make you an offer. We have the names of three previous employees who used to work for us."

"I thought the Company was shut down?"

"It has. This an independent venture. Mr. McClure knows that you were told about the drug that could re-activate the brain bleed in your head. He is contacting a few of the past employees to see if there is an interest in becoming involved in one more trade on the stock market. This is a one-time offer."

"Sounds like you're selling me something."

"Yes, it does. Mr. McClure wants to activate one of the previous clients for one last trade. I can't talk about this over the phone. If you are interested Mr. McClure will pay for you to come to New York for a meeting to discussed the details."

"Do I have to let you know right now?"

"It would be helpful. We want to get this done as soon as possible."

William thought for a moment. He had no time to call Alan or Julia. He had to stall. He could say yes and then back out. He needed to find out what McClure was up to.

"When does Mr. McClure want me in New York?"

"Next Thursday. If you're interested I'll send the information to you by e-mail and wire your ticket. Can you make it?"

"I believe I can. I'll clear my schedule and be there on Thursday. Go ahead and send me the ticket and what I'll need."

"It should be in your e-mail in an hour. Thank you, Mr. Ray, for your cooperation. This should be worth your while. Mr. McClure will be pleased."

"Thank you, Miss Reed."

William hung up. Wow. What just happened? Leslie was just coming into the room. She looked at William's face and could tell something had shaken him."

"Who was that on the phone?"

"A woman representing Ian McClure."

"What? I thought that asshole was dead by now. Wasn't he really sick?"

"Apparently he's still alive. She is calling a few past clients, who worked for the Company, to see if there is any interest in working for Ian one last time. It sounds like he is going to use the compound they developed for one last trade."

"And you said no, right?" Leslie's voice was firm.

"I said I'd fly to New York to hear what he had to say. She couldn't tell me over the phone."

"You what? Robert Woods was buried last week. What are you planning to do?"

"I don't know. I first need to call Alan and maybe talk to Julia. Someone may be still investigating this case. This might be helpful if someone is still trying to get Ian."

"Who are you?" Leslie asked. Her voice continued to get louder. "You really can't let this Company business go, can you? Doesn't playing bridge twice a week and writing your memoirs in the mornings fill your need for adventure?"

"This is more of a payback. Ian McClure probably had Robert killed. If I can help anyone take out this guy I'd sleep much better at night."

"I'd sleep better if you just forgot the whole thing," Leslie said.

"I need to call Alan and Julia. If one of them is still working on this case then I need to tell them what Ian's doing. He's paying for me to fly to New York. I haven't agreed to anything yet."

"This is it. We have to really retire William. Your 007 secret life is way past my ability to cope'"

126

"I know. I need to make the call. I fly out next Thursday."

"I'm taking mom into town to do some errands. We'll return later this evening. I plan on picking up some dinner and will bring you a doggy bag. If you mess up you need to get used to eating from one because you'll be living in the dog house for sure."

William knew Leslie was scared. He still had to make the call and find out if anyone was still going after Ian.

"I'll be fine. Just get me anything you know I'd like. I trust your judgment."

"When it comes to food you do. Not life or death situations."

"This is not a life or death situation. It is a meeting to find out what McClure wants. I'll be fine."

Leslie left with her mother. William placed a call to Alan. He had to find out if Julia was taking any calls. She could still be in mourning.

"Hello, Alan. This is William Ray."

"William. How are you? I'm at work and have a few minutes. What can I do for you?"

"It must be a sad time for everyone. We stayed away from the funeral like you suggested so we haven't talked to anyone. Is Julia seeing friends yet?"

"Yes and no. We're all trying to protect her. The loss has been terrible. Did you need to see her?"

"I think I do. Ian McClure's secretary contacted me ten minutes ago. Is anyone working on the case at all or is Ian home free on this one?"

"What do you mean contacted? Did you get a call?"

"Yes, from a Miss Reed. She made me an offer but Ian wants me to fly to New York to discuss it. Seems he is not willing to come see me like Jason did."

"What kind of offer?"
"Not exactly sure but it seems Ian has contacted several past clients and wants to use one of them again. She mentioned the compound the clinic developed. You know, the one is used to recreate the brain bleed."

"What's he going to do? Invest again?"

"I don't know. I just need to talk to Julia or someone who can direct me on this one. I have to fly to New York on Thursday for the meeting. The woman who called mentioned something about one last trade."

"One last trade. I wonder if he is going *all in* with a trade before he dies?"

"Is Julia still working the case? I really need to talk to her if she is. My meeting with Ian could bring some valuable info. I'm sure she'd love to kill the bastard if she could."

"Maybe. I'm not sure. How about I call her and give her your number. That's about all I can do. I don't work for them anymore. I think she's trying to carry on Robert's work."

"That'd be great. Have her call soon. It's been good talking to you again Alan. Your website and new business sound really exciting."

"Yea, we're both pretty happy. We may call you later regarding some of the businesses you donated money to when you worked for the Company. We have a few but may want some others to help."

"Fine. Leslie's the one who does all that research. I'm sure she has some suggestions."

*****

Alan hung up and looked over at Cathy. "I think we have to call Robert. Ian's on the move. He may be playing the stock market again using the compound with a past client."

"No shit. That was William, right?"

"Yes. He's flying to New York on Thursday to meet Ian and find out what he is planning. I better call him right now."

A call was made to Robert's phone.

"Hello," Julia answered. Robert didn't answer the phone at home because he was supposed to be dead.

"Julia, this is Alan. Something is happening and I need to speak to Robert. This is a secure line still, isn't it?"

"Yes, it is. He's right here."

"Alan, what's up?"

"I just got off the phone with William. Ian's active again. He's trying to line up an old client to use the compound on and make a final kill at the NYSE. He must think he is safe to pull this off because you're supposedly dead."

"I suspect he might try and do something like this. Did Ian contact William?

"Yes. William is flying to New York on Thursday." Alan proceeded to fill Robert in with all the information he had received minutes ago.

"William doesn't know if anyone is still investigating Ian. He's expecting a call from Julia because he wants to know what to do."

"William still doesn't know I'm alive, right?" Robert asked.

"No, he doesn't."

"Might be best to keep it that way. It's for his and Leslie's protection. She's pretty nervous anyway."

"I agree. Keeping her and William out of the loop is for their own good. If you want to direct William, you better do it through Julia."

"You're right, Alan. We could turn this into a big gain if we play it right. I'll think of something and have Julia give William a call. Thanks for the information. Talk to you later."

*****

Julia was listening to the call. "What's this about William being contacted by Ian?"

"Sounds like Ian's going to make one last investment. He is looking for a past client to use the compound on. He contacted William and a few other clients. William is flying to New York on Thursday to meet with Ian."

"What the hell can we do? This guy is right back to his old tricks."

Things were moving fast. Robert had to come up with a plan and soon. This might be the final chance to knock Ian off his pedestal.

"Call William and say you're still investigating Ian. We just need to know what Ian's up to."

"What should I tell him?"

"Just have him go to the meeting and take notes. If Ian is planning something big it'll take time and research. I don't think he'll move too quickly. Remember, he only has a small window with the compound. He has to have all his ducks in a row before activating a client."

Julia sat for a moment without saying a word. She was tired of all the work around taking out Ian. At the same time, she was still reading all the material she could on Buddhism and the Dali Lama. Killing another being was out of the question. How do you stop a person from hurting others without hurting them yourself, she thought?

"I'll call William and get this information to him. Just be sure we have nothing to do with the demise of Ian ourselves. If someone else does it, that's one thing. Just not us."

"I'm doing my best to make this work. I'm still working on a master plan but we may have to use William more than he may want us to."

"I think it is Leslie you have to worry about. She's worried all the time about William's involvement. Keeping her calm has to be a full-time job."

"Go ahead and make the call. Just have him report back to you when he returns. I think Ian is just screening old clients. He wants the right one for this move."

*****

"William, this is Julia."

"Julia, how are you doing? We're so sorry about all this. We didn't want to call you directly in case you still needed time to be by yourself."

"I'm coping. I really miss Robert. Carrying on his work is the best thing I can do to get through this."

"Good for you. So you are still going after Ian?"

"Trying to. Alan told me Ian got in touch with you. It that right?"

William spent the next twenty minutes repeating the phone call he had with Miss Reed. The compound was mentioned as well as a meeting with Ian next Thursday in New York. William was glad Julia was continuing the investigation. He just needed to know what to do.

"If Ian is screening you and other clients, he may or may not use you. Are you willing to go through with this if he hires you? He'll probably want to know first if you're in."

"Julia, this is really tough. Leslie is putting a lot of pressure on me to walk away. At the same time, I don't believe you can walk away from the McClure's of the world. They never stop until they get their way."

"You're right, William. Can I make a suggestion?"

"Sure. That's why I wanted to talk to you."

"Go to the meeting. Find out, if you can, what Ian plans are. Agree to work for him. He may choose you or one of the other clients. If he does use you then maybe we have a way in. We should have time to make our next move."

"And what would that be?" William asked.

"Let's see what Ian has planned. He still has to choose you. Is he paying you directly or basing the reward on how much he makes?"

"Not sure. Nothing's been discussed regarding pay. Only the meeting date."

"Do your best, William. We may get to Ian through you or have to try another way. Here we are again. Wait and see."

William assured Julia he would do everything he could to help her in the investigation. He and Leslie wanted to come for a visit but knew more time was needed.

Julia continued. "We," she caught herself, "I mean I, should have a plan in place after I know more. Sorry, William. I sometimes think Robert is still around."

Robert was sitting right behind Julia and put his hand over his mouth to hold back a snicker. "Good recovery," he mouthed silently.

Julia hung up. "What are you laughing at Mr. Forester? I didn't blow it completely."

"No, it was fast thinking on your part. I hope William and Leslie will forgive us when they find out I'm still alive."

"So now what. There's nothing we can do until we hear from William. Right?"

"Not really. This spy business involves a lot of patience and waiting. Ian will make a move and then we can make ours."

Chapter Seventeen

The flight touched down a little after one p.m. A car was waiting for William at the airport. He was driven to the apartment Ian used when he was in the city. Lunch was served upon arrival.

"Glad to meet you Mr. Ray. I usually don't meet any of the clients that worked for the Company. I believe Jason was your manager. Is that right?"

"Yes, he was. Good to meet you too Mr. McClure. How is Jason doing? I heard he moved to New Mexico."

"I believe so. Santa Fe. I guess the New York lifestyle was too much for him."

"I understand. I like visiting New York but prefer the quiet of Arizona."

William was finally meeting the ex-CEO of the Company that he worked for more than a year ago. Now that Robert Woods was dead, nothing stood in the way of Ian. Making one last killing on Wall Street would be his last hurrah.

"When was the period you worked for the Company? Your file says October to November of last year. Is that about right?"

"Yes, that's right. I was also used in another test the following May. A Dr. Gupta came up from Mexico and took a CAT scan of my brain in order to see why the condition lasted so long with me."

"Yes, it says here that the clinic was still looking at that test when they decided to close. Do you know what happened to the clinic and the results of the test?"

"No, I never heard. Dr. Gupta was supposed to call me to see if I'd be interested in having the condition produced again. He never called back. Eventually, the Company phone heated up and was destroyed. I assumed that meant the Company was not going to call me again."

"Where are you living now? Still in the Tucson area?"

"Yes, we moved back from Mexico that same year. Bought a house about thirty minutes from town and have been there ever since."

"Do you know any of the previous clients who used to work for the Company?

"No, Jason told me all the previous clients want to live their lives without any contact with others. I did see a woman in Tucson getting a CAT scan on the same day as me. The nurse at the hospital said Dr. Gupta brought her with him from Mexico. I assumed she was a client as well. I never had a chance to talk to her."

"Have you every heard of a Robert Woods?"

"No. Is he a client?"

"He used to be a while back."

"The reason for this meeting is to interview previous employees who worked for the Company. I'm going to activate the compound we developed in Italy and Mexico and use it one last time. I and a few previous members of the Company are doing research on a corporation about to go public."

"You mean they're going to start selling stock in their company to the public."

"Yes. We're planning on purchasing almost half their stock after it goes public. We need to know how successful they'll be because we're going to be putting in a lot of money into them. Billions to be exact."

"And you want one of the previous clients to activate in order to come up with the numbers after it goes public?"

"Basically yes. The benefit for the client we use is a guarantee of two million deposited into their account before the company goes public. No risk on their part."

"When's this going to happen?"

"Probably within the next four to six weeks. It is a firm that is involved in new ways to extract oil. They need to go public to raise funds and complete their project."

"What's the risk on your part? I mean aren't you taking a chance in buying them right after they go public?"

"Yes, but the gains could be astronomical. That's why we want the help of a previous client to make sure we're making the right move."

William was thinking that he had time before making a decision. Ian was just screening him.

"Are you asking me if I'm interested in helping with this project?"

"Yes. At the same time, I've one more client to interview. The two others I interviewed are not interested. It's between you and the woman that I talk to tomorrow."

"If I say yes, when can I expect this to happen?"

"Maybe in four weeks. I'd let you know. We'd have to have someone administer the compound."

"Would I have to fly anywhere or can I do this in Arizona?"

"You'd have to fly to New York. All we require is for you to activate and see the numbers after the company goes public. We do the rest. We wouldn't need you ever again. This is a one-time offer. Two million up front and we do all the investing."

"When would I have the name of the business to observe?"

"After we give you the injection and the compound takes effect. If you're interested I'll call you tomorrow and let you know. I'll pay you for any expenses you incurred coming here and $10,000 for taking the meeting.

"Put me on the list and call tomorrow. I'll be back in Arizona then so just use the same number your secretary dialed."

"She'll be the one calling. I'll let you know tomorrow after my last meeting. Thank you Mr. Ray for your time and effort to meet with me. I look forward to working with you if it works out. It should be well worth all our efforts to make this happen."

William could tell Ian was pleased. The two previous clients had turned him down. If he weren't helping Julia he would have turned the offer down as well. McClure was a scumbag. Taking him out was the only reason he said yes.

*****

"Julia, hi. William here."

"Hi, William. How'd the meeting go?"

"You were right. Ian is planning on using an old client for some kind of a stock market deal."

"What do you mean deal?"

"Something about purchasing stock after they go public. The person he hires will predict the numbers after the company goes public. He wants to know where the price will peak. He and the others investors sound like they're going to go all in."

"What does that mean?"

"I'm not sure. Ian mentioned the word billions. Sounds like he and his fellow investors are going to put a large hunk of cash into this final deal and let the dice roll. Ian mentioned he knows the risk. He also knows he can't lose if one of us is feeding him the closing numbers."

"Do we even know who the company is?"

"He wouldn't tell me. All he said is they are a company that discovered a new way to go deep into the earth to extract oil."

"When will you know the name of the company?"

"After someone shoots me up."

Julia thought for a moment. "So we won't know the name of the company until the client is injected? Where do they plan on doing that?"

"Ian wants it to happen in New York. I guess he feels he has more control if it's all done in his own backyard."

"What happens now? Are you staying in New York?"

"No. I'm at the airport and flying back to Tucson in half an hour. Ian's secretary will call me and let me know who is being picked tomorrow."

"How many clients are there?"

"It's between me and some woman he's interviewing in the

morning. That's all I know."

"Call when you find out who Ian's going to use. I'll start to research oil drilling companies and see if I can find one that's going public soon."

"Sounds like a plan. I'm still uneasy about having that compound in my system again. I was uncomfortable when I had the sight before. Doing it again won't be easy for me."

"I understand, William. I really do. We'll think of something. We have to make a plan and stop Ian once and for all. Having him out of our lives is the only way we'll be free to see each other again. If this trade goes through, and he makes billions, who knows what he might try next."

"You're right and it sucks. I'll call tomorrow when I hear something."

"Bye, William, and thanks. You've always been helpful in the investigation and I appreciate it. We have to keep the memory of Robert alive by taking down the man who killed him."

'That's what keeps me going. Bye, Julia."

Robert was sitting on the couch listening to the whole conversation on speakerphone. He also took notes. He was already writing a note to his new assistant to research oil-drilling companies about to go public. She should come up with something within a day.

"You heard all that, right?" Julia asked.

"Damn straight. This could be the straw that breaks Ian's back. Sounds like he and a few of his cronies are going to try and hit it big. They're taking a risk. At the same time, with a previous client, they could make a ton of money."

"What's you plan?" Julia asked.

Robert reflected for a moment before answering. "I'm working on it. We really have to see what happens tomorrow with William. If he's chosen we have a chance. If this other client is used then it becomes more difficult."

"So, to use your favorite line, we need to wait and see."

Robert smiled at Julia.

"You know me well. Investigation is a slow process. Whoever is the most patience usually wins."

"I'm going to go and practice that meditation technique, Leslie told me about it. It helped before. I need to keep doing it when I'm stressed."

*****

"Mr. Ray. Hello. This is Miss Reed. I'm calling on behalf of Mr. McClure."

"Hello, Miss Reed. How are you?"

"I'm fine. I have the decision regarding the venture you and Mr. McClure talked about. I think you are going to like the outcome."

"Really. Does that mean he wants to use me?"

"Yes, but he is also going to use the woman he interviewed. Both of you are going to be paid the set amount and make sure this investment works. Mr. McClure thinks paying double is good insurance for the business deal."

"No kidding. What happens now?"

"There is a lot of work that needs to be done on our end before we'll be ready for you and the other client. I don't expect Mr. McClure will need you for about a month. He's still working with his other investors and the company that's going public."

"Do you need me to do anything between now and then?"

"No, not really. Both you and the woman will be together in New York when you're needed. She is a student in Mexico and will be on semester break at the time of the merger. She'll have to fly up from Mexico City."

William was processing what he'd just heard from Miss Reed. Could this be the same woman he met in the hospital in Tucson when he had his CAT scan over a year ago? It sounded a lot like her description.

"Do you know the woman's name?"

"Her first name is Marie. I'm not too good at pronouncing last names in Spanish. I think it's spelled O-R-T-I-Z."

"It's pronounced Ortiz. A common name in Mexico."

"Anyway, she's more than ready to be a part of the project. It seems you and Miss Ortiz were two of the last clients used by the Company."

"This is good news. Are you going to be the one who calls me when everything's ready?"

"Probably. We don't have any more handlers like Mr. Burns. Just a research team and a few office people left."

What about the *hit squad,* thought William? I bet they're still around.

"So basically I need to make sure I'm available in the next four to six weeks and wait for your call?"

"That should cover it. Look forward to seeing you in New York. Goodbye, Mr. Ray."

William pushed the speed dial to Julie as soon as Miss Reed hung up.

"We're in."

"Is this William?"

"Yes. We're in. Ian is using the other client as well as me. He's willing to pay us each two million and be double sure the numbers are correct. He must be planning on investing a ton of money and really cashing in."

"This is good news."

"Not only that Julie, guess who the other client is?"

"Now how would I know that, William?"

"You know because you've met her."

"You're kidding. Is Ian using the woman from Mexico City with you? What was her name? Marie?"

"Yep. Marie Ortiz. She and I'll be together in New York in four to six weeks. The date depends on the moment the oil drilling company goes public."

"This is fantastic. Do we know how to get in touch with Marie?"

"I think so. She has my Mexican phone number. I think her number is still in the incoming calls section. She also may be in contact with Megan who did the CAT scan on both of us. They both seemed to hit it off in the lab."

"You know Marie came to Albuquerque and went shopping with Megan last year don't you?"

"Yes, I heard you and Robert met her."

"Robert paid for both of them to have a little vacation together and we ate lunch with them. We got the name of the new clinic director from Marie after the first director disappeared in Mexico. What was his name?"

"Mark Jones. Did the Mexican authorities ever find his body?"

"I don't think so. The Company had a way of making people disappear, no questions asked. Jones is proof of that."

"Anyway we got the name of the new director and forced him to quit the Company. It was a part of the harassment campaign Robert was using on the McClure family. I think Ian's father was the CEO at the time."

"If I can get a hold of her what do you want me to say?"

"First let me try to contact her through Megan. She knows Megan and it may be better to go through a friend first."

"Alright. Whatever you do, remember, we only have a few weeks. Miss Reed said four to six. I hope we have something in place before then."

"I'll do my best, William. Call you when I have something."

Julia hung up. Robert heard the whole conversation on the speaker. He knew they had a lot to do before William and Marie got together in New York.

"What's or next move?" Julia could see Robert going over the whole scenario in his mind. He was in deep thought so she decided to pour each of them another cup of coffee. When Robert went into these deep thought moments he couldn't respond to any questions because he was not aware of anyone else in the room.

"We've got to get Marie to help us," he finally said. "I think another shopping spree in the States with her friend Megan might do the trick. Can we pull that off?"

"I'll work on it right away. I have Megan's number. We could get her to call Marie to fly up. Paying for the whole trip should help her make the right decision."

Chapter Eighteen

It was Friday night and *Leggs* was packed. Sera was meeting Laura after fourteen days. Laura had just come back from a weekend with her new boyfriend and would fill the conversation with all the love details. Sera had information regarding Ian McClure from her detective friend. Somewhere in between these two topics, dinner and drinks would be consumed.

"Hi, Laura. How was the weekend?"

"Better than even I could have ever expected."

Laura continued to tell Sera about Jeff and where they went for a two- night outing. Silver City is a small town in New Mexico and a tourist destination. After describing all they had seen, Sera asked, "The sights sound interesting but what about the sex? It happened didn't it?"

Laura stopped for a moment and reflected on the weekend again. It was one of those magical nights. Did she want to share all the details with a friend who just a few weeks ago was paid to spy on her?

"The sex was fine. We lit candles, got into the large bathtub together and spent time exploring each other with a washcloth."

"With a washcloth? You mean you had clean sex?" Sera tried to be funny but still wanted more details.

"We dried each other off and started kissing. We made it to the bed and spent the next two hours making love before the candle finally burnt out. It was the best first night I've had with anyone."

"And the second night? More of the same?" Sera was almost as excited as Laura and she was not even in the story.

"The second night we spent experimenting. Jeff was able to get a little grass from the bartender in town. We smoked it and then decided to take our time with. Every sensory fiber on our bodies was at a new state of awareness. Touching each other took on another dimension."

"You two got high and had outrageous sex?"

"Let's put it this way. I never had multi-organisms before while making love. I would say the grass had something to do with it for sure. It was out of this world."

"Isn't grass legal in New Mexico?"

"No, but I think it is in Colorado. You should go there with someone and try it out."

"I'd like to take a couple of the woman I've met here in *Leggs* and have a go with grass and sex. I wouldn't have to go all the way to Colorado. There is plenty of ways to get high in New York."

"Your right, Sera. Anyway how about you? Anything to report on the Ian front?"

"Yes. My detective friend dug a little deeper and found out that Mr. McClure and a group of investors were probably doing some type of illegal inside trading."

"On the stock market?"

Laura was playing along. She probably knew as much about Ian as the detective did but thought maybe he could find out something she didn't know.

"Yes the NYSE. A few members of this group were investigated, lost their trading license and had to pay huge fines. It wasn't clear how the group was exposed to the authorities.

Something about a package being sent to the investigation team."

"Anything else?" Laura asked.

"Ian was let go by the group who called themselves the Company. They soon closed most of their office. Only a few of the original members stayed on. Some lost money in water treatment plants they started in Africa and Asia."

"Water treatment? What do you mean by that?"

"Desalination plants. Seems like they wanted to control parts of the world through fresh drinking water. The local countries in these areas got wind of it. With the help of the US government, the plants were nationalized and taken away from these private investors. The reasons had something to do with national security."

"That will do it. Yell national security and governments can get away with anything."

"Why wasn't Ian investigated with the others for inside trading? Wasn't he doing the same thing?"

"He might have but whoever sent the evidence to the authorities only included a few names. There was nothing to pin on McClure and most of the Company members. It seems the person or group going after the Company was selecting only a few of them."

"That sounds suspicious. Whoever did this must be holding back evidence from the government and blackmailing the remaining members." Laura knew a little about the Company and their activities but not to the extent she was hearing the story from Sera.

"Does your detective friend know who was turning in information about the Company?"

"No he doesn't but I'm starting to connect the dots. The person you worked for, Robert Woods, must have had something to do with all this. Why else would Ian risk getting caught by hiring someone to kill him? Woods must have played a part in taking down the Company."

"Your right Sera. I took pictures of Company members at a memorial service. I knew little about what Robert was doing. Killing him had to be payback."

Sera was bending over her food and speaking in a low voice. She wanted to hear everything Laura said but at the same time keep the conversation private.

"Me finding you was just a step in that process for McClure. Now that Robert Woods is gone, Ian can go back to doing what he did before being investigated. This thing is not over yet I'm afraid."

"It's over for me. I only worked for Robert. Now that he's gone I have no more connection with any of this." Laura hoped this information would get back to Ian somehow.

"There is not much we can do against Ian. I can call him but there has to be a reason. He paid me directly by depositing money in my account. Ian is not connected to me at all."

"If your detective friend finds anything else out could you let me know. I agree we're not going to be able to do much of anything."

"I still have a number I can call if I find anything else out. I could even pass on information that could damage Ian. I just don't have anything."

"Neither do I. We may be at a stand still. Let's just keep meeting here on Fridays. If either of us finds out anything then we can go from there."

"Sounds fine. I'm glad we're becoming friends. I know this has been a rocky beginning but trust me when I say I'd like to take this asshole down once and for all."

"You were just doing a job. I would have done the same thing. We didn't know what Ian planned. I just hope he's done with me."

"He must be. I've had no calls from him since the house blew up in Albuquerque. I doubt I'll hear from him unless he needs me for another job tailing someone."

"One more drink and then off to bed."

Laura and Sera finished their evening together and hugged before going their separate ways. Laura forgave Sera and hoped she could still use her to pass on information to Ian. She needed to call Cathy or Julia in the morning and see if anyone was still working on the case. With Robert gone, she expected no one was doing anything.

*****

"Louis. What are these papers on my desk?" Detective Martin hadn't had any coffee yet and was in a bad mood. "Also whose turn is it to see that the Java is made?"

"Yours actually. It's a new week and we're getting low on the beans as well. Jarvis got the donuts but we're all waiting on your coffee making skills."

"We have got to change the way we do things around here. How about the coffee guys makes it the night before and the first one in the office turns it on."

"That works for me. Go ahead and make it and I'll flip the switch."

"Funny Louis. I'll make it but first tell me about this paperwork. Who is Ian McClure?"

"McClure is a wealthy investor from New York. He got into trouble last year. A few of the men in his group were investigated and had to pay huge fines. Ian was removed as the CEO and has been inactive ever since. The report also says he is Irish with family ties to the capital. Dublin is the same town where those two hired killers flew to right after the murder of Robert Woods."

"Lots of Irish come from Dublin. Are you sure there is a connection?"

"We know he has cousins living there. Ian's son has been there for a year learning the whiskey business. Seems the McClure family used to be in the trade during prohibition and made millions. Ian's father was more interested in the stock market. Ian's son is returning to his roots. Booze."

"It also says Woods worked for the company for a short time but there's no mention what he did with them. If we don't know what Woods did with the Company, how can we make a connection with Ian?"

"We don't know yet but I think all of this is more than a coincidence. Make the coffee and I will get us a donut. I think better on caffeine."

Martin put the coffee into the pot and at the same time posted a note. *Whoever does coffee for the week, make it the night before. First one in turns on the pot.*

"Now that the coffee is brewing, tell me what we have to go on? Do you think Woods had something to do with McClure and the Company getting in trouble with the authorities?"

"It's hard to say. We don't have much on Woods at all. He

seems to be like a ghost. He moved to town when he started working for the Company as an advisor. We have no record as to where he came from. We think Robert Woods is a new identity."

"Advising? These guys were investors. What did Woods know about stocks?"

"That's just it. We have no record of him ever trading on the market. The few pictures we have of him shows that he was more like a blue-collar worker. He was fit, tan and didn't have that nerdy look of a business man. None of the photos had him dressed in a suit. Market people sleep in their suits."

"Whatever he did he must have pissed someone off really bad. No one could have survived that blast. They wanted him dead for sure."

Louis waited for a moment before continuing. He wanted the coffee to kick in as well as the sugar from his Dunkin Donuts breakfast. "I haven't found anything yet. Even if we're able to make a connection with this McClure and Woods, I doubt we'd be able to get near enough to touch him. The federal government couldn't nab him. What chance would we have?"

"Yea, but this is murder, not a stock market trading case. If we can connect McClure to the murder of Woods I would arrest him in an instant."

"Well boss, good luck. These wealthy bastards have a way of paying off people in the system and getting someone else to take the fall. I doubt we'd have much luck."

Martin didn't like the mega rich at all. They were able to buy their way out of trouble most of the time. This was not the way he had been brought up. If someone killed another person then they needed to pay for their crime.

Chapter Nineteen

Robert's investigation business was packed with new clients as well as Ian McClure. His new assistant, Peggy, was working out fine. She knew little about the McClure case and was mainly used for research. Peggy had located the two Irish men in Dublin, something the local authorities couldn't do.

"Robert, I think I have the two men in Ireland located as to where they live. I was able to tap into the phone bill of Sean McClure and found them that way. When I contacted the local authorities where they live I was told they are thugs who do strong-arm work for Sean."

"What do you mean strong-arm work? I thought the McClure's in Ireland made and sold whiskey?"

"Yes, but it seems the men are used as enforcers. The local authorities in Dublin have a file on them but no charges have been made. It seems the men make sure the liquor stores keep up their quotas. A set amount is sold to every store who deals with the McClure brand no matter if they sell their amount or not."

"This family sucks on both sides of the ocean. Basically, they're an Irish mafia that makes and sells whiskey as a front. Forcing businesses to buy their product is just what the crime bosses in the States did during prohibition."

"That seems to be the case."

"Good work, Peggy. Just leave me the addresses of the two Irish men and I'll handle the rest. I have some unfinished business with them but I have to make sure the timing is right."

Peggy was new at this computer investigation stuff. She liked working for Robert and Julia. It was paying her University expenses and she was even given a meal each day by Carla. The secrecy part of the job was explained to her in the interview. No one could know where she worked or whom she worked for. People who got caught doing evil in the world wanted to get back at those who took them down. Robert needed to remain in the shadows and not give them the opportunity.

"Is there anything else you want me to do today? I have class in an hour but could start one more project before I leave."

"No, we're good. I may have something tomorrow. If I'm not here I'll leave it on your desk. I have a few errands to do. Thanks again, Peggy."

As Peggy was leaving Julia came in the house with the shopping. She did most of the food purchasing for Carla and it gave her time away from the house.

"Hi Sweetheart," said Robert. "Good news. Peggy was able to locate where the two Irish thugs live in Dublin. When the time comes we'll use this information. Right now we have a couple of things to do before William goes back to New York."

Julia continued to put the food away as she answered Robert. "I did get a hold of Megan. I called her before I went shopping. She's more than happy to have another paid vacation in Albuquerque. She said she calls Marie every month just to talk. She'll call Marie and tell her about the paid vacation and set it up for next week."

"It has to be soon. Megan doesn't know why we want to talk to Marie does she?"

"I haven't told her anything. She eventually will know everything unless you plan to talk to Marie alone."

"What I plan on doing is to get Marie, myself and William together in the same room and create a master plan. It has to come off without a hitch. They both have to agree and be on board."

"Will I ever know what you're doing?"

"Let's find out first if they'll both agree to it. They're both getting paid before the merger happens so the money is not the issue. Marie needs to know how dangerous Ian is. Taking him out is the only way to have him out of all our lives forever."

"I should know by this evening if Marie and Megan can make the trip. We'll have to do another secret meeting and make sure Marie is not followed from the airport. I bet Ian may have her followed."

"Your right Julie. I didn't think of that. We need to have her fly from a different city under a different name. I'll get that all together in the next few days."

"You work on that and I'll make sure Megan knows a little about why we are meeting and what to expect. No surprises."

By now the number of people involved in the Ian case had grown. Robert needed to juggle them to make sure everything went smoothly. Taking down Ian meant he could not see it coming at all. In other words, it had to be a complete blindside.

"Has Cathy talked to Laura in a while? I'd like to know if she and Sera are still meeting. We might want to pass on some bit of misinformation to Ian through Sera soon."

Julia realized Cathy was busy with the website but knew she would make time for her and help out.

"I'll call her next. We need to keep them both in the loop."

Robert took a breath. Ideas were racing through his head. "We need to use all the avenues available. His guard is down right now because he thinks I'm gone. He's dying. We just need to speed up the process."

"I'll call her right after I eat something. Anything I can pass on to her that will mess Ian up?"

"Not right now. I have to see if Peggy has found out about the oil drilling company that is going public soon. Right now I need to prioritize and have her work on this one. We only have a few weeks to get ready."

"Get ready for what? Just because we have the name of the company, how does that help us get ready?"

"I can start a research on them and see if they're a viable company. I have to know if they'll be worth more or less after going public. I still know a few people who know something about the market. I'll get in touch with one of them and see if they can help me."

Julia finished her lunch and went out to the pool area to make her call to Cathy.

"Cathy, hi. It's Julia."

"Hi, Julia. You've been busy haven't you?"

"Yes, we have. I know you two are busy as well so I'll get right to the point."

"We always have time for you two."

"Thank you, sweetie. Here's where we are. Robert wants to know if you've talked to Laura recently and is she still seeing Sera?"

"No, I haven't but she needs a call. Between her work and boyfriend, she's keeping to herself right now. I believe she does visit Leggs and sees Sera but I'll ask when I call."

"Good. We may want to pass on some miss information to Ian through her but not yet. Robert is still coming up with the *'take out Ian'* plan."

Does Robert need me to call her right away? I can. Alan is at the office and I'd like to find out more about her boyfriend. You know how we women love the romantic things in life?"

Julia laughed to herself. She remembered all the effort she made to get Robert to notice her. Men were so slow in this area. "Someone has to do it. We know the men won't unless we help them along. I had to work on Robert for two years before he finally invited me to fly to New Mexico. Even then I did all the work."

"Alan wasn't that bad. He's just younger and eager to please. Taking care of me is high on his priority list and he is getting really good at it."

"Robert was a bachelor for a long time. Pretty much set in his ways. The younger ones are easier to train."

"Anyway, call when you have the misinformation to pass on. I'll call Laura now."

"Thank you, Cathy. Love you."

"Love you two. Bye"

*****

Cathy hung up and made the call to Laura. It rang three times. Laura answered. "Hey, girl. It's me, Cathy."

"Cathy. I was going to call you or Julia this morning but I had to meet with a client. You know how weddings are. When someone is getting married the whole world spins around them."

"You're right about that. No wedding bells in our future yet but we're still new at being together. This Geek Mingle site is taking all our time. Any idea of marriage will have to go on a back burner."

"How's Julia holding up? This must be a really hard time for her."

"Yes, it is. She's still working the case and that is why I called. Julia was wondering if you're still seeing Sera Pett. Isn't that her name?"

"Yes I am, and that's why I wanted to talk to you. I didn't know if anyone was still working the case but I have information," Laura said.

"We're trying to work the case on our side but we've got no experience. Sera knows a detective in New York. He gave her a lot of information regarding Ian and his possible connection with Robert."

Laura proceeded to fill Cathy in on the conversation she had with Sera. She said that Sera was livid with Ian for using her to kill Robert. Even the idea of passing misinformation to Ian was brought up. Laura said, "Sera is willing to do so without batting an eyelash."

"So you're saying her detective friend found out all this information about Ian. I guess the police know more about him than we thought they did," Kathy added. "Julia is working on a plan and may get back to you soon. Something has come up. Ian may be positioning himself for another big trade in the investment world. I don't know all the details but I'll call again. By the way how, is the new boyfriend thing working out?"

"We're doing really good together. We had a weekend in

Silverton and I am going to fly to Albuquerque in a week to visit him at his apartment."

"No hotel. That means you've become close, right?"

"If you mean did we have sex, then the answer is yes. It's not like you to beat around the bush, Cathy."

"I was just being tactful. I know you've wanted a relationship for a while. You know what this means don't you?"

"What?"

"You, me and Julie all found men in Albuquerque. What's up with that?"

"Your right. I never thought of it that way. If it wasn't so sad about Julia and Robert I would've suggested a triple date or something."

"Julia will recover and get on with her life. She's strong. We just need to keep supporting her to help take out Ian.

"Does she want to kill him?"

"I don't think so. As far as I can tell she is against killing anyone. She just wants to speed up Ian's process of leaving the earth. She doesn't know how to do that yet but I think it has something to do with his health."

"Ian's not healthy?"

"I heard he's not. I think this last year of grief and revenge has really hurt him physically as well as mentally."

"If there is anything I or Sera can do to help, let us know. We're both ready to assist."

"Alan and I are helping as much as we can. Let us know when

you visit Albuquerque. Maybe we can have dinner together?"

"That would be great. Maybe when this case is finished we can visit you and see your new home. I figure keeping your location quiet is best for now. Ian may have someone following me but Sera doesn't think so. Robert's dead and Ian doesn't need me."

"Probably not Laura, but be careful. We'll dine in some private place and make sure we're not followed."

"Call me when you hear anything more. Sera's available and that might be a big plus down the road."

"Thanks again, Laura. Love you."

Cathy called Julia back and gave her the information regarding Sera Pett. Julia thanked Cathy for her help and dialed Megan in Tucson.

"Hello, Megan. This is Julia."

"Julia?"

"Yes, Julia Larson. I was the girlfriend of Robert Woods. We met when you and Marie came to Albuquerque last year."

"Oh Julia, hi how are you? How's Robert? Haven't heard from him since that weekend with Marie."

"Robert was murdered." There was silence for a few moments before the reaction.
"What? When did this happen?"

"A few weeks ago."

"How are you doing? How did this happen? Oh Julia, I so sorry."

"I'm functioning but I need to stay busy for now. I think Ian had Robert killed and I need your help. I still have the ability to investigate the case but I need a big favor. I need to talk to Marie again. Another shopping trip to Albuquerque might be fun for both of you, all expenses paid. How does that sound?"

"Really? That last trip was fantastic. Are you sure because I'm game."

Julie then told Megan why she needed to speak to Marie. The timeline for meeting Marie was rather short. The company going public would be ready to do so in a few more weeks. If she could get Marie to fly to Tucson and then drive to Albuquerque, this would avoid any problems if Ian tracked her. Coming directly to Albuquerque would alert Ian.

"I know this is short notice, Megan but this meeting's important. We have a chance to take Ian McClure out for good. Do you think you can pull this off?"

"I'll do my best. I e-mail Marie all the time and talk on the phone once a month. Is the number you used to call me a good one?"

"Yes. It's a secure line. We can't have anyone bugging our conversations. I really appreciate this, Megan. Let me know as soon as you can."

"I will. Again I'm so sorry about Robert. I hope getting rid of this Ian character will help."

"It won't replace Robert," Julia said, "but it's a start."

"Bye for now."

****

Ian had all his ducks lined up for the big kill. This would be his last trade on the NYSE. Purchasing stock after a company went public was not unusual. Knowing what price the stock would reach was not something the common investor knew.

Everything looked good on paper. Deep Drill International represented everything Ian McClure stood for; oil exploration, using non-renewable energy sources and passing the cost onto the consumer. It was a win-win for people like him. Still, the outcome of going public was a risk. That's why he decided to use two people with the *sight* to give him the 100% edge.

"Miss Reed. How many more weeks until DDI is going public?"

"They just announced a date yesterday, Mr. McClure. One month from today. Miss Ortiz and Mr. Ray will be here two days before the public date. I have the doctor ready to administer the compound the day before."

"Be sure they're both paid before they arrive in New York. I don't want either of them to think we are not going to go through with this. Where are we putting them up?"

"The Hilton near the church where the memorial service for your father was held."

"Make sure I have enough of my heart pills in the office. When this thing goes through, my body will be going through a little strain. This is the biggest trade I've ever made. I have to purchase the stocks with my partners right after we get the closing high and after it opens."

"Are the other Company members buying the same amount?"

"Yes. We have to. It was part of the deal. Each of us is buying 1.5 billion dollars worth of stock if the numbers look good. That is an input of nine billion into DDT. If this takes off like we expect, we could make between four and five billion each. After that, I'm done with trading. My son is getting married and I plan on living out my life as a grandfather."

"Speaking of your son, he called just a few minutes ago. He said he's coming by with his future bride. What's her name?"

"Irene MacLaine. Don't let her try and fool you. She may say to you she is related to Shirley MacLaine. I researched it. No relation at all. She has a little Scottish in her but my son loves her so I'll overlook that."

"Sounds like she has a sense of humor as well."

"She does. The McClure family can use that. We're too serious."

"Do they have a wedding date?"

"Not yet. After this trade is completed I'll get to work with wedding plans. No time now."

Everything was riding on this final purchase. The other five Company members who stuck with Ian might continue to trade. They were younger and in much better health. They did not have access to the compound previously used on clients like Ian did. The only other person who had the compound was Robert Woods. McClure was sure that went up in smoke with the house explosion. Ian planned to take the formula with him to his grave.

Chapter Twenty

"Megan just called. I think we need to make a change in our plans. It seems Marie wants to fly into Phoenix and shop there instead."

Robert went over the change in his mind. Going to another city would be safer for everyone involved. "I'm fine with the change. Where should we stay?"

"Let's book everyone at the Biltmore. It's not far from the airport and there are some great shopping stores in Scottsdale. I want to go to a couple of them myself."

"When can she fly and meet Megan?" asked Robert.

"In four days. I already called William and he plans on being there as well."

"All right then. We're in count-down mode. Has Peggy found the oil company that's going public?"

"She thinks it this one called Deep Drill International. It's scheduled to list on the exchange in three weeks. It will be listed as DDI," Julia said.

"I have a friend who is pretty knowledgeable with the market. I need to give him a call and get more information."

"Robert, I have a question for you. What are we going to do? I mean we can't influence what the stock trades at. We have no idea how it will do after open trading. This looks like a crap shoot at best."

"It is a crap shoot. The only thing we can control, if they agree to it, is for William and Marie to come up with a number that does not represent the true value of the stock in the future. In other words a false closing high."

"Won't they be in danger by giving Ian the wrong closing numbers?"

"Yes and no. There is no reason they have to be around when the stock goes public. Ian just wants them for their predictions. That's how it worked when I worked for the Company."

"Big oil has got to be a risky investment, with all those accidents they keep having," Julia said.

"BP had a pretty big clean-up bill," Robert continued. "I think Ian and his investor friends are taking a risk. They could do well but they might have their lunch served to them on an oil-filled platter."

*****

Four days later the team met in Phoenix. William drove up from Tucson, Megan arrived at the airport to meet Marie and Julia flew from Albuquerque. Leslie came with William but only for the shopping. *No- business-as-usual* was her new motto.

Marie and Megan were booked into the Biltmore. William and Leslie were staying with her brother, Peter, in New River and Julia was at the Sheraton a few miles away. A meeting was planned but Julia had to make sure Marie and William weren't followed. The team met at a restaurant in the old town section of Scottsdale. A small Italian Pizza restaurant called Pablo's was located on a side street. Anyone following William or Marie would be easily spotted.

Everyone hugged and gave their greetings. William had not seen Megan or Marie since he had the CAT scan in Tucson over a year ago. Marie was not completely sure why they were meeting. Megan told her that Robert was dead. Ian McClure probably murdered him.

Marie told the group she was chosen by Ian to predict the closing merger numbers. The money was too good to pass up. She found out through Ian's secretary that William was the other client that would be used in the venture. She appreciated the chance to shop in the States again but she was not sure how she could help in the case.

Before ordering, Julie did her best to show them a plan that might work. Much of the plan's success had to do with the company they were observing.

"When does Ian want you two to be in New York? This information is important for me and my assistant."

Marie spoke first. "Miss Reed sent me a ticket to fly from Mexico City two and a half weeks from now. I think the company they want us to look at is going public several days after that."

William jumped in. "That's what I was told as well. I plan on flying by myself. Leslie will stay home with her mother. I don't think we're expected to stay after we give Ian the numbers. I think that's all we're expected to do. After that, we can leave."

"Are you both getting paid before the company goes public or after?" Julia asked.

Marie continued. "We are having the money sent to our accounts before we fly to New York."

William added. "I think Ian wants to be sure we arrive, so paying us first should guarantee that."

"Good. As soon as the compound is administered and the numbers are given to Ian, I suggest you leave New York right away."

"Why's that?" Marie's voice had a worried tone to it.

"If you're both on board with this move, the numbers given to Ian will not be the real ones. If this is going to work, the numbers from both of you have to be the same."

William asked, "What if he keeps us separate? I mean we might not be together when they inject us with the compound. Ian might want to keep us apart and make sure the numbers match. We might not be in the same building. That's what I'd do if I were Ian."

"Good point, William. You do have a knack for this detective work. Robert always said you did."

"We miss Robert too, Julia." William had a sad expression on his face when he made the comment. "Doing everything we can to help rid Ian from our lives is how I can contribute."

"Where's Leslie? I'm surprised she is not with you."

"We stayed in New River last night to visit her brother. I think she wants to shop in Scottsdale. We'll stay at the Biltmore tonight."

"Just be sure you are not seen with Marie or Megan. If Ian has a tail on either of you this could complicate things. Be careful. We flew Marie out of Mexico from a different airport," Julia said. "I'll contact you before you leave for New York. I don't expect we'll see each other again before that happens. We have to keep this quiet. Thank you for helping. I believe this is our last shot at wrapping up this case. We have to make it work."

Everyone gave each other hugs and said their goodbyes. William looked into Marie's eyes and asked her; "Are you frightened? I know I am."

"Yes but we'll do this together. After all, we are getting paid no matter what happens. Everything will be all right in the end. If it is not all right then it is not yet the end."

"You saw that movie too?

"Yes. *The Best Exotic Marigold Hotel* played in a theater in Mexico City. India is a lot like Mexico but many more people. I would like to visit that country after I finish school."

"Leslie and I want to visit as well."

"When this is over maybe we can plan a trip there together. I don't like to travel alone and we could even afford to bring Megan."

Marie looked over at Megan who was listening to the conversation and nodded her head.

"Bring me with you to India and the far east?" Megan said. "Marie you are a generous woman."

The two women left together in a cab for Scottsdale and old town. William would meet Leslie in the center near the Biltmore. She had the car so he took a cab.

Chapter

Twenty-One

Detective Martin arrived at the office early. He turned the coffee pot on and was waiting for his first cup when Louis walked in.

"You coffee idea seems to be working. Here are the donuts to go with it. I also bought a different blend of coffee yesterday instead of the Yuban crap we drink all the time. We deserve the good stuff once in a white."

"Ok Mr. Coffee, what kind did you buy? Folgers?"

"No, I got some Starbucks Special Blend. Tell me how it tastes."

Martin took a sip and waited for a moment. He took another sip and swished it around his mouth like he was wine tasting. He sat in his chair and put his legs up on the desk.

"I could get used to this stuff."

"It cost more but we're worth it."

"Works for me. Hey did you see the info we have on Ian?"

"McClure? No. What's happening in New York?"

"I have a detective friend in New York who has been doing some research on McClure. It seems an old girlfriend of his was hired by Ian to find someone. The girlfriend seems to think the woman she found for McClure was connected with the death of Woods."

"Is there any proof?"

"Not yet. The woman's name is Sera Pett. She is a writer who also does independent work such as locating people in the New York area. She told my friend that the woman she found used to work for Robert Woods. She also went to Albuquerque and was there when the explosion occurred."

"What do you mean she was there?"

"According to Sera Pett, the person she identified for Ian was named Laura. Don't have a last name. Anyway, she flew to Albuquerque to do a job for Robert Woods. She supposedly met with Woods and left on Friday. The house was blown on Thursday night. This could be a new lead."

"Her name was Laura. There was a Laura at the funeral. Laura Scott. She was interviewed and said she was a friend of Woods. She never said she worked for him."

"It gets better. Sera and Laura are now trying to conduct an investigation into Ian McClure and are using my detective friend to help them. It seems Miss. Pett is mad at McClure because he used her to help kill someone in Albuquerque."

"Does this friend have a name?" asked Martin.

"Detective John Parks. He's been on the force for over twenty years. We met on a case ten years ago and kept in touch ever since."

"This could be a break. We need to get in touch with this Laura Scott again and sit down with her and Sera Pett. If they're trying to get at Ian McClure they might need our help."

"That's what I thought, boss."

All of a sudden a voice came from the kitchen area where the coffee pot was located.

"Hey, who made the coffee?"

Louis yelled back. "Why? What's wrong?"

"Nothings wrong. This tastes like the stuff my wife gets when she meets her girlfriends. She usually brings a cup home for me."

"Do you like it?" asked Louis.

"Compared to the crap we usually drink around here, it's like day and night."

Louis had a smile on his face. "Glad we got the coffee thing figured out."

"What about McClure. Do you think we can arrange a meeting with these women and your New York friend? One of us may have to fly to the east coast. I hate big cities and Parks knows you, so maybe you should go?"

"No kidding. I'd love to visit the city. Best Pizza in the world, or so I am told."

"Make some calls and get a meeting set up. Even if he has to arrest the women, make sure they're at the meeting. Have Parks tell them we can help if this McClure character is involved in the Woods death."

"Will do boss. Wow, New York here I come."

"Don't get too excited. We only have the budget to put you up in a Travel Lodge. Hotels are expensive in that city. Get this done right away. I have a feeling we're getting close to breaking this case."

Louis went back to his desk and made the call. Martin took another sip of his coffee and went over to the kitchen. A second donut was his way of celebrating a possible break in the case. A sugar-high before nine in the morning would do the trick.

*****

Robert hung up his cell phone. He had just finished a conversation with a friend who knew about the stock market. This included companies going public and other bits of information not know by seasoned investors.

Julia came into the office. "Can we get Ian to take the bait?"

"Do you mean are we going to get him to buy in after it opens and hopefully take a bath on his investment? I have no idea. This is a close call. That was a friend on the line. He had a lot to say about this company called DDI."

"What do you mean a lot to say? Does he think it is a legit company?"

"He says they are real but the problem lies in the future. The real savvy investors are staying away from DDI. There're several reasons but the future of energy is the real one. My friend says there is a point when going deeper for oil will never overcome the cost of the endeavor. In other words, the expense of doing the deep drilling would never be recovered."

"What are the other problems?"

"Josh is my friend's name. He says he's not confident of the CEO of the company. The man lives a high-end lifestyle. Spending seems to be his goal instead of the well-being of the company. He already has several venture capitalists that have put money into the technology. They haven't seen much in the way of return yet."

"Is Ian aware of this?"

"Probably not. Josh is well informed. Other investors, like Ian, are ready to jump in and pour money into DDI. They all expect to make a killing. The stock market is not a win-win for everyone. There are losers. Josh thinks the company might not do well at all."

"No kidding. I'm amazed Ian has no clue."

"Josh feels there are too many variables working against deep oil recovery. A big problem is in the regulations that go with offshore drilling. After the Gulf disaster, a few oil-drilling companies were forced to pull out of American waters. Saudi Arabia is pouring money into solar and wind. They sell their oil but they know it will be gone one day. Not the sun. They have plenty of that in the desert."

"What are the chances the stocks could bomb after going public. What would happen to all the investors who sank money into DDI?"

"That's the game. Many do well but some do not. Josh believes the head people are painting a bright picture for the investors but it could be smoke and mirrors. There are cases of CEOs going public and cashing out. They take the millions, or in this case billions, and run."

"Run where?"

"They hide the money in documents showing it was spent. If there's no demand for deep oil exploration then it is over."

"After Ian and his partners invest, what happens then?"

"The company uses the capital in areas that they think is necessary.

"In order to financially hurt Ian all we need to do is have Maria and William come up with the same peak trading amounts after going public, right?" Julia asked.

"Yes. Here is what I plan. Josh is going to find out what the stock may open at. If we give them a number that is really high, they may stick around after they buy in. Their plan will be to sell when it reaches the high."

"Does Josh think it'll go up at all?"

"He can't predict anything but he's been doing market trading for a long time. He feels it may take a few days to see how traders feel about the stock. If there is no significant gain and they don't see any activity then it could be over quickly. Josh doesn't trust the CEO of DDI at all."

"When will Josh call you back?"

"Next week. He'll know approximately what the price may open at by then. We'll then call Marie and William with the numbers to give to Ian. If this works Ian and his fellow investors will feel the loss for sure."

"If is doesn't work what then?"

"Ian gets richer. Simple as that."

"I hope Josh knows what he is talking about. More money for Ian would really piss me off."
"Me too Julie but we have to play this out. I think we have to come up with a number that'll keep Ian and his boys interested until it is too late."

"Will Marie and William be safe?"

"That's the part of the plan I'm still working on. If the company crashes, like Josh said it might, Ian will be on the warpath. We have to get in his way somehow."

"Tell me when you have Plan B worked out. I'm going to get some lunch. Are you hungry?"

"Starving. I could really use a sandwich and a beer."

"Tuna fish and a Negra Modella coming right up."

Robert continued to think about the investment going south and Ian going crazy. He knew the health of McClure was declining. Maybe he could capitalize on that aspect of the man and use it to his advantage. Robert also knew the other Company members would not be happy with Ian if they lost a lot of money on this venture. There were several different outcome and chance was still a part of the game.

*****

Louis arrived in New York around noon. A meeting was set up for the next day with his detective friend, John, and Sera Pett. Laura promised she'd try and make the meeting but nothing was sure. She wanted to help the police take down the killer of Robert Woods. She just didn't know how her information would help.

"Hello Julia, this is Laura."

"Hi, Laura. What's going on?"

"There are several people working on the Ian case in New York. There is a meeting set up tomorrow with a detective Louis from Albuquerque, Sera Pett, myself and a local detective named Bates. He's the one Sera used to date and the one who gave her all the info."

"What do they want?'

"I don't know but they are starting to connect the dots between Ian McClure and Robert Woods. They've figured out Ian may have hired the two men from Ireland to blow up the house. Also, they feel Ian was getting back at Robert because of something he did last year that caused the downfall of the Company."

"They have started to put all that together? Wow, these detectives are better than I thought. What are you going to do?"

"That is why I'm calling you. I'm at a loss. I want to help them without exposing you."

"Thank you, Laura."

"Anyway they know I worked for Robert and visited him at the house the day it blew up. I just don't know how much I should admit to if I go to the meeting."

Robert was listening to the conversation on the speaker. He grabbed a marker pen and paper and wrote a message for Julia. It said; Tell all.

"I think we can let the detectives know your total involvement, Laura. I don't want to get you in trouble. Robert is dead. All you were doing was making a video of some men at a memorial service in New York. You were paid for the video and that's all you know."

"Should I tell them the service was for Ian's father?"

"Why not. They'll figure it out anyway. Just come clean. They seem to be working on our side. Just keep Alan and me out of the mix. If they find a way to take Ian down then it makes our job easier."

"Okay. I just wanted you to know what's happening here. I'll call you after we meet," Laura said.

"Please do. I'm doing what I can to trip up Ian. Having a detective from two different cities working on the case is a good diversion for me. It may help in the long run." Julia was pleased to have help from two different sources.

"Good. I'll call tomorrow night. Maybe meeting Sera has been a positive thing after all."

Robert had a smile on his face from ear to ear. Julia looked over at him but waited for him to say something.

"Isn't this working out better than we could have hoped for? Two different detectives are trying to pin my murder onto Ian McClure. Maybe we should just keep feeding them information as we uncover it and have them solve the case."

"Do you think they could take Ian down? Convicting him of murdering you would be amazing, to say the least. Maybe you could visit him in prison if he's sent there? That would be the cream on top of the milk bottle for sure."

"If he's convicted of killing me I'd make sure I visited him in prison. I might be wearing a disguise but just seeing his face when he realized it was me, would be worth it."

"From the health reports, he have, Ian he would not live through a trial. We have to hurt him and take him out at the same time. Visiting him in jail would be a pipe dream."

"Are you ever going to expose yourself to the world and show that you are alive?"

"Probably not. Remember he has family in Ireland. The Irish do not give up. They'd hunt me down and start all over again in this vendetta campaign. They're nuts."

"What do we have left to do? We're still waiting on your stock market friend to call us back. Laura has her meeting tomorrow. Let's go out for dinner."

"That's fine. How about a movie as well? Let's make an evening of it."

"I love you, Robert, even though you're dead."

"You need take your comedy act on the road, Julia. You could fill the theater with college kids. They'd love your humor."

"I know. I get a laugh out of it. Self-entertainment has always been a part of who I am. Get used to it. Remember, we'll be changing our names when this case is finally over. Mr. and Mrs. Forrester has a nice ring to it."

*****

They all met in the office of detective Bates. Louis introduced himself to Sera and at the same time introduced Laura to Bates. Laura remembered Louis from Robert's funeral.

"Thank you all for coming. It seems we may have a few leads that could take us somewhere in this case. Maybe everyone can update us on what they know so we will all be on the same page?"

Bates was doing his best to lead the group. He knew making a case against Ian McClure would be difficult. It was murder so he'd do what he could to see it through.

For the next thirty minutes, Laura gave her history of working for Robert Woods. This included the filming of the memorial service last year and the visit to Albuquerque on the day he died.

Next came the story of Sera and how she was hired by Ian to find a woman based on a sketch. When Laura showed up at the bar she was instructed to find out more about her.

A week later Laura went to New Mexico and Ian had a team follow her. The same day Laura met with Robert his house blew up with him in it. Coincidence?

There was still not enough evidence to make a direct connection with the two suspected men from Ireland. Even though Ian's family came from Dublin, the men seemed to have disappeared. Ian had covered his tracks and left nothing to follow.

Laura was taking mental notes to pass on to Julia later that night. If Ian could be linked to the Irish hit men then there would be a case. Maybe Julia had some evidence that could make that happen.

"Is there anything else we know regarding Ian McClure or Robert Woods that might help the case?" Louis was hoping that some of this new information might break open the investigation.

Laura still kept quiet about Cathy and Alan. Julia was also kept in the dark.

"Nothing more that I can think of," Laura said. "How about you, Sera?"

"I've told everything I know about McClure. He paid me for my services through a direct deposit. I can't trace the money back to him. I have no taped conversations and he calls me on a secure line."

"Do you have any more jobs to do for him, Miss Pett?"

"No, he seems to have cut off all interactions with me since the incident in New Mexico. The death of Robert Woods appears to be his final act."

"If you wanted to contact him, could you?"

"Possibly but I would need a good reason or something that would perk his interest. Woods might have to return from the dead before Ian needs my services again."

"If we came up with something would you be interested in getting that info to Ian?"

"Like what?"

"Don't know yet but I plan on returning to New Mexico and coming up with something. If we do, are you willing to help in any way?"

"Yes, but it has to be real and nothing that is going to endanger me. McClure takes people out that cross him. Woods seemed to be a man who stayed hidden and look what happen to him. I don't have the ability to hide. Get my drift?"

"Sounds like an old episode of *Gunsmoke*. What's a New York girl doing using terms like that?"

"Like what?"

"Get my drift."

"I do a lot of writing and read Tony Hillerman growing up. I love cowboys and western stuff."

"Well, I get your drift. We'll come up with a plan that won't get you in trouble. It may even earn you another paycheck. Can I reach you at this number?"

"Yes but give me your number as well. I'll call you back. McClure could have my number bugged. As long as he's alive I'm taking no chances."

"Good point, Sera. I'm flying back to Albuquerque in a few hours. I appreciate everything you've told me. My partner and I may piece together a strategy so please stay in touch. Call on a burner phone if you need to."

The meeting came to a close. Louis headed to the airport while Laura and Sera decided to go have a beer at their favorite watering hole. They each had a few questions and thought it best to discuss them in a safe place.

Laura had her car and drove Sera to Leggs. When they arrived the lunch crowd was gone and the Happy Hour was just starting. A couple of beers would take the edge off the visit to the police station.

"I didn't know you and that detective used to date."

"It was a while ago, Laura. We remained friends over the years. I have a comment as well. How about that Louis detective and my old boyfriend knowing each other? What are the odds of that happening?"

"In the world of crime, I bet all those cops have *Six Degrees of Separation.*"

"What does that mean, Laura?"

"It comes from a movie I saw a while back. Something to do with everyone in the world or Kevin Bacon. Not sure which. Anyway, we're somehow all connected. Everyone knows someone who can lead to anyone else in the world. Hollywood used Kevin Bacon as an example. Everyone in the movie industry can lead back to him."

"So these two detectives are connected with every detective in the country in some way?"

"Maybe but that's not something I want to lay awake at night thinking about."

"Me either. Anyway if you do find out anything more I guess we better go through either of these two crime fighters. They have more connections than we do."

"I agree. I'm heading to Albuquerque this weekend. In two weeks Jeff is flying to New York. I think he wants to see a play and visit Time Square. You know, typical tourist stuff."

"Sounds serious. Maybe I need to visit that state as well. Not much going on in this one. I do like some of the women in this bar but most are involved with someone else. Anything like this place in Albuquerque?"

"New Mexico is fairly conservative. I'm not sure but I doubt it. I'll ask Jeff when I see him."

The two women talked for an hour. Finally, Laura said she needed to go. Sera stayed to have dinner and discuss her book with a few more women. One of them was gay. Sera was attracted to her but didn't want to mix work and pleasure.

Chapter

Twenty-Two

Laura was home in thirty minutes and made a call to Julia.

"Hello, Julia. Laura."

"How are you and how'd the meeting go?"

"I found out a few things and maybe have something for you."

"Really. Let's hear it. We need something on our end."

"You keep saying *we*, Julia. Are you alone on this case or do you have someone working with you?"

"A new assistant was hired after Alan dropped out of school to work on his Geek site. It's a woman and she's really good at her job. She can get around the computer world almost as well as Alan did."

"Good. You may need her with this one. The detectives are working towards connecting Ian to the Irish men. If they can somehow match McClure with them then they may have a case against him."

"They said that?"

"Yes. They know about the two men leaving on an early flight back to Dublin. The problem is there's no trace after they landed. I think the police in Albuquerque have a file on them but where these men are now is unknown."

"We may be able to help on our end. We found out where they

Nab Yoga

live. Also, we know they were hired by Sean McClure to do his dirty work. If the police had this information then they could put pressure on Ian and maybe get an arrest warrant."

"You have that information? How come you have it and the police don't. How big was the business Robert ran? I thought everything was lost in the explosion?"

"Robert had backup computers and everything in several locations. We lost Robert but not the business. We can still access the satellites, run face recognitions and a few things the police cannot."

"You mean Robert's business is bigger than the police in New Mexico?"

"You got it. Robert's been doing this for six or seven years. He had computers, top of the line tracking devices and was always on the look out for the newest technology in the investigation business. He ran a top notch company."

"I knew he was good but I had no idea Robert was that big."
"Yes. We are getting back to full speed here and my assistant is carrying the load for sure. I talk to people but she's the one doing all the investigating."

"You think you can get this info to the police in Albuquerque?"

"I'll try. It may have to be sent to them. We have to protect ourselves. Being underground works best for us right now. The police would spend too much time asking us how we got the information instead of acting on it. Sometimes they get in their own way and forget the objective."

"And the objective is?"

"To get that asshole, Ian. Pretty straight forward to me."

183

"Well, anyway that's what I found out in the meeting. Sera used to be detective Bates' girlfriend in New York and Bates knew detective Louis from a case they worked years ago. Small world."

"No kidding. Laura thanks. This will really help. When this is over we'll get together with you and your new friend. Right now we're still underground."

"I understand, Julia. Call me if you need anything else. Sera and I can help but we are not sure what to do next. We still can feed Ian some information that could mess him up so let us know."

"I will, Laura. Right now getting this new evidence to the local police is our goal. This will come to a head soon. Ian will be livid when the police start coming after him."

"Your right. He's got nothing to loose. I heard his health is not all that good."

"Let's finish this case. I would like to get back to a normal way of living soon."

"So would we all. Thanks again Laura. You've been a great help."

Julia hung up and looked over at Robert. "Did you hear all that?"

"Pretty much. I think we need to give the police what we know about the Irish hit men. That'll keep them busy and out of our way for a while."

"What are we going to do?"

"We need to come up with the stock numbers to give Ian. I should hear from Josh any day now."

"This is really going to be an exciting ending for sure.

Tomorrow we give the police the info on Ian and the Irish mobsters. What else is there?"

"You do realize Alan and the Geek site are going public a week after DDI does? We need to finish this case one way or another so we can be free to celebrate with Alan and Cathy."

"Are we ever going to tell our friends about you still being alive?"

"Eventually but not the authorities or anyone connected with the law. Robert Woods is dead and will be rising out of the ashes as Bob Forrester."

"Bob? I'm going to marry a Bob? No way. We have to work on that one for sure."

"What's wrong with Bob? I was Bob all the way through high school."

"And that is where that name will remain. Sweetheart, I love you but calling you Bob for the rest of our lives is not going to work for me."

"Let's talk about this later. Maybe we should change both our names?"

"You don't like Julia? Who are you?"

Both Robert and Julia bantered for the next ten minutes seeing who could get the last word in. They both became heated but in a fun way. Other spats like this ended the same, in passionate love making with lots of fire.

*****

The package arrived in the mail two days later. No return address and no stamps. A courier delivered it to detective Martin in person.

"Louis. Do you know anything about this?"

"About what?"

"This. This package?"

"Maybe if you opened it we could find out what's inside," Louis said.

A file with all the information Robert and Julia had on the Irish hit men was included in the envelope. A DVD of the men going into their office that served as a front for their operation was also included. Home addresses and Google footage of the houses they lived in near Dublin were also in the package. Bank statement showing Sean McClure as their employer and the family tree connecting Sean as a cousin to Ian completed the information.

Both detectives shifted through the papers and watched the DVD on Martin's computer. After thirty minutes of processing the data, they looked at each other in complete surprise.

Martin asked, "What happened at that meeting in New York?"

"What do ya mean what happened? Everything we know about the case was presented and the Laura woman told us what she knew."

"Something must have happened because we now have proof that Ian's connected to the hit men from Ireland."

"We knew there wasn't enough evidence to connect Ian to the case. All I said in the meeting was that if a connection was made between McClure and the hit men we'd have a chance to take him down."

"Well someone heard you. It had to be either the Pett woman or

Laura. My bet is on Laura. She must know someone who gathered this information together and sent it to us."

"I think you're right, boss. This is definitely enough to bring McClure in for questioning. I think we need to get this to Bates in New York. It is his jurisdiction and he'll be the one to bring McClure in."

"Yes but the murder was in our city. We're going to have to be there as well. This is starting to look like a break in the case. Louis your trip to New York really paid off."

"Thanks, boss. Does this mean I get to go back to New York when they bring McClure in?"

"It does and I think we can upgrade a room for you to the Sheraton. This is really big. We may even make the front page in the NY Times."

"I'll fax a copy to Bates right away and send the video. We may not have jurisdiction over these two thugs from Ireland but we sure can make McClure sweat it out in this country."

"Get going on this Louis. See if Bates can reel in Ian as soon as possible. We have to see if we can make this stick. I'm sure he'll *lawyer up* right away but I believe we have enough evidence to make a case."

"We'll give it a shot boss but don't forget who we are dealing with. This is one rich bastard. Getting away with murder is something he may be used to. We'd have to extradited the suspects back to the States to stand trial as well. This could be a major case and we're in the middle of it."

"If we pull this off, Louis, you and I could get a promotion for sure. The Sheraton may be where we stay from now own. Even the Hilton."

"Okay detective, slow down. We are not there yet. We have a few steps to make before this case puts us in the Hilton. I'll fax Bates now and go from there. Get those stars out of your eyes and drink another cup of coffee. You're freaking me out."

Martin took a deep breath and seemed to come out of a trance. It was as though he had left the world and just returned from some scenario playing out in his head.

"Right Louis. I just lost it for a while. Nothing this big has hit Albuquerque in a long time. Let's get working."

Chapter

Twenty-Three

"Sean, Ian here."

"Ian. It's been a few weeks. Is everything alright?"

"No. I just got through an interrogation with my lawyer and a detective in New York. It seems the two men you sent to New Mexico have been identified by the Albuquerque police and linked to you. The fact that we're cousins has been established."

"Really. How'd they do that?"

"Someone was able to access their bank statements and you had them on your payroll. A connection has been made between myself and Robert Woods."

"This keeps getting more interesting all the time. How's Woods connected to you?"

"When the Company first started we did not have the Cayman Island accounts set up. We paid the people who worked for us through direct deposit into their accounts. Somehow it was traced back to the Company."

"Your father was the CEO back then wasn't he?"

"Yes, but I was still part of the Company. The police are saying Robert Woods was investigating the business and that's the reason the investment group dismantled last year."

"Isn't that true?"

"Yes, but how did they find this out? Someone must have sent information to the police. They're now in the process of having your two men sent back to the States for trial."

"Seriously?"

"Yes, I'm serious. Arrest warrants have been issued for Clog and Michael. It'll take a couple of days before they are picked up and handed over to the international authorities for processing and then charged with murder."

"What then?"

"They'll be flown back to New Mexico to stand trial for the murder of Robert Woods."

"Is there enough evidence to make a case?"

"Sean, there is enough evidence to connect you with the men and me with you. They flew to New Mexico using false passports. They left on an early morning flight hours after the house blew up. What do you think?"

"Who provided this info to the police. I thought you plugged the hole. Wasn't that Robert Woods?"

"I thought so too. Someone is still going after me through you. If those men get arrested and stand trial we both could be in a lot of trouble."

"What do you suggest?"

"Sean, these are your men. I'm leaving this up to you. I'm only letting you know the possible consequences. You only have a day or two to figure out something."

"This is really upsetting. I used these men for many years. They've done good work for me. Things I'd never do myself."

"They get arrested then we're both are in a precarious situation."

"I'll take care of it, Ian. I never thought the police in Albuquerque could ever find my men. Someone has the ability to find people at Federal government level."

"I trust you will do the right thing, Sean. Our family name is at stake and nothing can get in the way of tarnishing that."

"Goodbye, Ian. I need to take care of this right away."

The conversation ended. Ian was sure Sean would handle things. After all, it was their family and it needed to be protected at all cost.

*****

"Louis, when did you get back?"

"About an hour ago."

"Did the meeting with McClure and his lawyer go well?"

"Ian said little. He let his lawyer do all the talking. We showed the evidence that the Company hired Robert Woods seven years ago. The lawyer said Ian was not the CEO at the time and had no connection with Woods."

"What about the two hired Irish hit men. Their arrest for the murder of Robert Woods should be happening tomorrow. Didn't he find it interesting that these men worked for his cousin in Dublin?"

"By then the lawyer said if no charges were made then they were leaving."

"Did they leave?"

"Yes but I could tell Ian was upset. He popped a few pills during the interview. His face has little color anyway but by the time they left he was ghost white."

"So he's going to drag this out in court. If we can get these two killers to plea bargain to save their skins we may be able to take Ian down."

"Maybe. We have to get them over her first and safely behind bars. Then we have a chance."

"Who's making the arrest in Dublin?"

"Interpol. They're working with the local police in Dublin but their men are making the arrest this evening. We should be hearing from them soon."

"Let me know right away, Louis. This is exciting stuff. Albuquerque making an international arrest and trying two killers for murder!" Martin was starting to see stars again.

The afternoon went by as usual at the station. The new coffee plan was working smoothly and almost all the drinkers who enjoyed good coffee were pleased with the results.

Louis came running into Martin's office around two. He was excited and slurring his words. "They're dead!"

Martin looked up. Being a police station, the comment could refer to a number of cases happening at the time.

"What case are you talking about, Louis? Who's dead?"

"Those two hit men from Dublin. They're dead. I just got a fax from Interpol."

"When did this happen?"

"About an hour ago. Interpol went to the homes of the two men to make an arrest and no one was home. A neighbor across from the apartment of the suspect named Clog said he was picked up by a car earlier that day and never returned."

"How do you know they are dead?"

"Both bodies were found in separate locations in the woods near Dublin with a hole in the back of their heads. Execution style for sure. Hands were tied and they were just left there."

"Any leads other than one of them getting picked up?"

"None and the police don't believe anyone will come forward in this case. Both men were not liked in the community. The way they died seemed to me a message to the population to keep their mouths shut."

"It sounds like Dublin has their own little mafia working. 'Keep quiet and nothing will happen to you', seemed to be the message. Shit, we have nothing else to go on."

"Boss we have to get this story to the local paper. Someone out there sent us this information. If they find out our only lead is gone they might send us something else. We have to alert these informants that our case against Ian is dead."

"Get on this right away, Louis. There may be more info available that we don't know about. Ian probably had the men killed. No way to prove it and nothing to connect his cousin either. We need help on this one."

Both detectives were at a loss. Getting the story out to the press was their only hope at this point. Whoever sent the previous envelope might be able to give them something else.

*****

The whole story came out on the front page of the Albuquerque Tribune. The reporter, who was called in to write the story, interviewed both detectives. Connections were made between the two men, who were murdered in Dublin, to the explosion and death of Robert Woods. The detectives also made a plea to whoever sent the previous information regarding the Irish mobsters, to continue helping them. They had nothing more and were desperate.

Julia came into the bedroom. "Robert, did you read the paper yet?"

"No. Why?"

"Here. Just read it."

Twenty minutes later Robert put down the paper and shook his head.

"That son of a bitch had those men killed. Not that I'm concerned about two dead Irishmen, but now the police have nothing to go on. They're even asking for our help."

"What else do we have?"

"Nothing right now. I'm really concentrating on the DDI going public. I have the 'buy in' numbers that Ian used to invest. Josh called me yesterday."

"So right now we have nothing to send the police?"

"One thing at a time. I need to call William and Marie. They need a number to give Ian when they go to New York. It looks like Ian has gone ahead and invested and is now waiting for them to fly into New York tomorrow. "

"Does Josh have any idea how DDI will do after going public. You said he didn't feel comfortable with all the risks involved in deep oil drilling."

"He still feels the same way. It's more of a gut feeling. If he's wrong, Ian and the remaining Company members could do well.

Nothing is guaranteed."

"You better make those calls before Marie leaves for New York. I assume both of them are still on board with this idea?"

"As far as I know. I think we dodged a bullet with the Irish case. If Ian had been drawn into a trial for murder he might not have gone through with the investment. I don't know for sure but a trial would've been a lot on his plate."

"While you're making the calls I'll be working on any information we may have to send to the police. Peggy and I are trying to find out if Ian rented the office space where the two men lived and worked while they were in town."

"Make that connection and we may have another envelope to send in the mail. I might have an idea how I can take Ian over the edge. It still needs some work. Have Peggy find out which cable service Ian uses in his office. I have a feeling the network may be going down soon on the eight floor."

"What are you planning, Robert? You have that look in your eye again."

"What look?"

"The one that says 'I ate the last cookie and you can't prove it.' I've seen it before so don't try to hide it from me."

"I'm still planning this, Sweetheart. Can't tell if it'll work yet but I'll let you know when I'm ready to pull it off."

"Just don't surprise me with anything Robert. Having you die a second time would not be in my best interest, or yours."

*****

William left on an early flight from Phoenix to New York. He would meet at Ian's office the next day. He wanted to look around Time Square and take in the energy of New York.

Marie arrived in New York two days before. She brought one of her sisters with her so they could shop in the big stores and walk around the city with all the skyscrapers towering overhead. Her sister, Lupe, had never been to the states and Marie was trying to educate her with a trip.

Marie and William did not plan to meet at all before they were given the compound injection. If Ian suspected they had made any contact he might not go through with the venture. Julia had warned both of them to stay clear of each other. Also, she suggested they fly back home as soon as the business was completed and before DDI went public. If they stayed in New York they were vulnerable.

*****

While Marie and William were occupied in New York, detective Bates continued working on the murder case of Robert Woods. Yesterday he received the latest news from Louis and Martin. Another envelope had been sent to them with a video of where the Irish hit men stayed while in Albuquerque. It included the rented the office space. The real estate agent who set up the transaction said the renter paid for twelve months. The agent also said she never met the person who leased it.

The agent had more information. The voice of the person who rented the office was recorded on her answering machine. The name of the person was Mr. Watson. Louis sent a copy of the voice to Bates in New York. The lab in New York owned a voice recognition program.

Bates had a recording of Ian McClure's voice. He taped the interview with Ian and his lawyer. Both tapes were in the lab being processed. If there was a match, Ian would again be on the hot seat. He may have gotten away with murdering the two Irish hit men but now some hard evidence in the case could drag him into court. Bates knew McClure had the lawyers and money to fight anything thrown his way. It would be an uphill battle for sure.

Louis gave Bates a call to make sure the voice tape made it to his office.

"Did you get the tapes?"

"Yes, I did. The lab is processing a possible match with McClure and this Mr. Watson. It may take another day. They seem to be backed up down there and our case is not a high priority."

"Really. Another day?"

"People are getting shot and killed in New York every day. Some billionaire getting into trouble is not as important. It'll make the front page of People Magazine but that's crap news. They just want to sell copy not solve cases."

"You're right, Bates. Ian's not going anywhere. He has too much to loose and nowhere to go. Take your time with this and make sure we have a match. We need to have a rock solid case again him before we issue a warrant."

"I'll call you when I know if they are the same person. Even then we have to get a judge to sign off and talk to the DA. We've got to show him everything we have. This may take a few weeks before a warrant can be issued."

"We'll be ready. The real estate agent has signed a statement and we have her complete co-operation. She doesn't even need to be at the trial."

"That's good to know. McClure would have no problem killing her as well if it meant protecting himself. Do you have any idea who has been sending us this information?"

Louis thought for a moment before answering. "No, but we're fine keeping it that way. It seems whoever it is they want to remain anonymous. I don't plan on figuring out who they are long as they help put McClure behind bars."

"No kidding, Louis. Let's not mess with the source. They help us get McClure, they should get an award."

"Have to go Bates. Call when you have a voice match. Talk to you then."

Chapter

Twenty-Four

William arrived at the McClure office around noon. He spotted Marie going towards another elevator. He decided not to get her attention or greet her. Wanting to keep any connections with Marie a secret was the best move. Security cameras were everywhere in the building. Who knows who was watching? He took a separate elevator.

When William arrived at the eighth floor he headed down the hall towards Ian's office. The location overlooked the west end of the building. Ian occupied the whole corner of the floor. When the Company was in business he leased the whole floor. Times had changed.

Miss Reed greeted William when he entered the suite. Marie had already entered the office space and was being welcomed by Ian. The physician, who would be used to inject the compound, was also there. Ian turned to meet William and shake his hand.

"Welcome, Mr. Ray. This is Miss Ortiz and Dr. Logan. Miss Ortiz is from Mexico and was a client last year."

"Hello again, Miss Ortiz. We saw each other briefly in Tucson a year ago at the hospital. I'd just finished have a CAT scan and I believe you were going to the lab for the same procedure. Do you remember?"

"Yes, I do Mr. Ray. That was you in the hallway? I remember now."

"Did you enjoy the music they played while having the scan?"

"Not so much. I wanted some Mexican music but they only had

Beatles, Bach and some country western songs. I went with Bach and almost fell asleep."

Ian was listening to the conversation and had a look of surprise on his face. "You two have met?"

"No, we passed each other in the hospital. Miss Ortiz was with the same lab tech operating the CAT scan. The reception secretary said Dr. Gupta had another client with him from Mexico. We basically nodded at each other as we passed in the hall."

"You have a good memory, Mr. Ray."

"Only for beautiful women. Also, it was an unusual circumstance. I remember those parts of my life well."

"You flatter me, Mr. Ray. I remember you but barely. It was my first visit to America and everything was so new."

Ian spoke up. "Well, here we are again. Mr. Ray and Miss Ortiz have volunteered to participate in this venture and will be attended by Dr. Logan and his assistant. She is in the office where Mr. Ray will be. Miss Ortiz will be set up in the office next to him. We'll make this as comfortable as possible."

"We'll be in separate rooms?" Marie asked. "Fine with me. I understand it will take at least an hour for the injection to work. Is that correct?"

"I believe so. Dr. Gupta gave me instructions but I've never used the compound before. Dr. Logan has the info and is confident everything will be fine."

"I'm glad we were paid before this happens," William said. "At least our loved ones will make out financially if anything goes wrong."

"Mr. Ray, I'm 100% confident nothing will go wrong." Ian was getting a little agitated with William's comments."

"I'm sorry Mr. McClure. I'm sure we're safe. My wife was more concerned about me doing this than I am."

"We should get this started. It is supposed to last for a week and the Company you'll be observing is going public tomorrow. We won't be able to observe their numbers until after the market opens."

"So we should go back to our rooms and return tomorrow?"

"Yes, we just need you here until the blood clot has formed. The doctor and his assistant will monitor you both to make sure everything is working."

"What time do you want us to return, Mr. McClure? I have a flight back to Phoenix at noon."

"The market opens at nine-thirty. DDI is ringing the bell to open the exchange because they're trading for the first time. I don't think any numbers will come to you until then. Nine o'clock should be fine."

Marie had not said much during the conversation. She was a little nervous. Two million dollars was her motivation more than taking Ian down.

"I'm with my sister, Mr. McClure. We'll be here for one more day. How long after we see the numbers does it take for the market to reach what we see?"

"It could take a week. If the number you envision is low we'll sell right away. A high number may keep us invested for a little longer. New companies can go through a lot of changes in value in the first week. You don't have to wait in New York until the stock reaches that number."

"Thank you, Mr. McClure, for all you've done for me and my family," Marie said.

"All right then." Ian was getting nervous again. His blood pressure was starting to rise. Another pill and he'd be fine during the next few hours.

"Each of you has an office where you'll be situated. The nurse is in that room over there, Miss Ortiz. The doctor will take care of you in this office, Mr. Ray. After the compound takes effect, and it is determined you have adjusted to the injections, you're free to go. Just return by tomorrow morning before the opening bell."

Marie and William went into the offices assigned. Beds were set up.

William entered and took off his shoes. He had a headset and I-phone with two hours of music recorded for his listening pleasure. Music would pass the time waiting for the drug to take over.

Dr. Logan had the injection and amount prepared before William entered the room. The nurse, assisting the doctor, was going through the same procedure in the next office. Marie took a little longer to settle in on the bed. After ten minutes both were ready.

The only reactions that happened to previous clients who used the compound, was a slurring of words. This lasted only the first day and was gone by day two.

William wasn't worried. He was glad Leslie hadn't come to New York with him. She would have been a nervous wreck during the procedure. Keeping her in Phoenix was the best thing.

William could feel the compound enter his blood stream. After half an hour of Beatles music, he started to feel a warm feeling going up his spine. An hour later the pressure started at the base of his skull, just as it had when he was in San Diego.

"How are you feeling, Mr. Ray? You should be feeling the effects of the drug by now."

"Yes, I am. I remember this feeling and my inability to form words from my stay in the hospital in San Diego."

"I'm going to think of a number and see if you can repeat it to me. Are you ready?"

"Go ahead. I'll give it a try."

William closed his eyes and said, "48572. That's the number that came to me."

"Very good," Dr. Logan said. The compound is working. It will be full strength in about thirty minutes but I think you're able to go back to your room for the evening. I wouldn't go out and do too much. You'll be receiving thoughts from all around you and it could be over-stimulating."

"I've already visited Times Square. That's what I did first. I'll probably just head back to the hotel and rent a movie for the evening."

Marie was finished with her treatment as well. She planned on taking it easy and going to a play with her sister. After the morning session with Ian McClure and the stock market numbers, she planned on one more shopping spree in downtown Manhattan. Presents for all the family members were a must. Her sister would help decide what to buy.

Both William and Marie emerged from their makeshift doctor's offices. William looked at Marie and sent her a mental message.

"Are you good?"

Marie looked back at William and nodded. She received the message and acknowledged the drug was working. They were both free to go.

Ian McClure had already left the office. He did not want to wait while the compound took effect. He was back at his apartment letting the other five investors about the progress of the two clients and what to expect after the opening bell tomorrow.

William went back to his room and called Leslie. "Hi, Sweetheart."

"William. Is it over? When are you coming back to Phoenix?"

"Marie and I have to show up tomorrow morning and give Ian the numbers for DDI after the market opens. After that, we're free to go. I fly out around noon our time."

"I'm glad you had me stay in Arizona when you were in New York. I would've been too nervous. It's been fantastic shopping in Scottsdale. We have to go to dinner at this Pizza restaurant I found before we drive back to Tucson."

"Sounds good. A movie in my room is all I can handle right now. The pressure on my brain's working. I may watch Jeopardy and answer all the questions. That'd be a good warm-up exercise."

"So it's really working again? Is the pressure on your brain all the time?"

"Yes, so far. It takes a little getting used to. By the way, we have to send some money off to some companies again. If you could research that for me I'd appreciate it. Ian paid us two million dollars so I thought five businesses at $100,000 each should do the trick. Also, put $200,000 into the girl's trust account. They should have a decent balance after we kick the bucket."

"I'm not going to kick the bucket, William. Not until I'm at least a hundred."

"Good. I didn't want to outlive you anyway. You'll have to get the girls to spread your ashes all over Peru when they visit. Are you sure that's where you want your remains placed?"

"Very sure. And you still want yours taken to Italy?"

"You know how I loved Cinque Terra? Either you or the girls just take that hike between the five villages and sprinkle the ashes along the way. Leave most of them in Vernazza. That's my favorite town."

"Love you, William. Have a good flight. Just call when you land and I'll pick you up.

"Love you back. See you tomorrow."

William hung up and settled in for an evening movie and room service. Staying away from as much stimulus as he could was his best way to cope.

*****

Marie and William entered the office building in downtown Manhattan the same time. When someone pays you two million dollars for a job, that takes two days to complete, you don't want to be late. Both entered the elevator together and started to send mental messages to each other.

"Are you ready for this, Marie?"

"Yes, but I'm a little nervous. As long as Miss Julia is doing her part this should work. I'll be glad to be back in Mexico tomorrow. It'll be safer for me there."

Not one word was spoken between the two riding together to the eighth floor. The elevator door opened and they walked to the corner office together.

"This is it, Marie. Good luck." Miss Reed was at her desk and greeted them as they entered.

"Did you sleep well?"

"Yes. My sister and I went to see a play and had dinner in a nice restaurant. She's overwhelmed by the size of New York and all the things one can do in this city."

"You're not too tired are you?" Miss Reed asked. "We have to be sharp today."

"We're young, Miss Reed. I slept seven hours. I'm fine."

"How about you, Mr. Ray? Are you rested and ready for the morning activities?

"Went to sleep around ten and got up at seven. That's a lot of sleep for me. I stayed in my hotel room all evening."

"I bet having the sight can be a lot to handle," Miss Reed said.

William continued. "Remember that Mel Gibson movie about reading the thoughts of women. *What Women Want* I think was the title. It's kinda like that. I'm able to block out a lot of input but I still get messages I don't want to hear."

"Well, I'm told it will be gone in two or three days. I think the doctor and Mr. McClure are ready for you. Go on in and good luck. This is a special day for all of us."

Dr. Logan and Ian McClure were talking to each other near the back offices where Marie and William received the injections of the compound yesterday. The beds in the rooms were removed and computer screens were showing the podium of the NYSE. The opening bell would ring in ten minutes. The name of DDI appeared on the screen. The announcer was telling the viewing public that DDI was going public. A description of what the company did was also included in the short segment.

"Welcome, Miss Ortiz and Mr. Ray. Did you have a good night's sleep?" Ian asked.

"We're both feeling good," William said. "Marie enjoyed the city life with her sister and I watched a movie in my room. We're rested and ready to go."

"The bell is about to ring. I'll be in this room with you Mr. Ray and Dr. Logan will be with Miss Ortiz. The procedure is just the same as it was when you both worked as clients. When the market opens the numbers will appear and trading begins. We might not see too much trading with DDI because many of the investors are waiting to see what the others are going to do."

"What exactly does that mean?" William asked.

Ian answered. "Deep oil drilling is a touchy subject in the world of energy. Because of the recent accidents the government has passed regulations to protect the environment. Oil is no longer just under the surface. They have to go deeper and deeper. The risks are high and the costs are as well."

"What has your research told you regarding DDI?" William was trying to get as much information as he could out of Ian. He knew that after today he'd probably never see this man again. If McClure hit it big he'd die a very rich man. If the trade did not work out, William would not want to see Ian at all. That was the part he hoped Julia had taken care of. Safety from this mad man was his biggest concern.

"All things are leaning towards the need for deeper oil exploration. Saudi Arabia will run out eventually and we have no other choice. Alternative energy is a ways away from taking over from big oil. People will be paying $8 and $10 a gallon for gas in the States and it will be deep oil that provides that energy."

"What about the battery industry and electric cars that are taking over? Aren't they making an impact?"

"Yes but we're still in need of oil to run big business and their factories. This could be the last investment move in the area of oil. I plan to cash out on this one and walk away."

Ian looked at his watch. "It's time. The market opens in two minutes. Everyone, please be seated at your desk and let the games begin."

William looked over at Marie and sent another mental message. "Are you ready?" She nodded her head and turned to go into the office with the doctor.

Just as William sat down the opening bell was struck. It was Wednesday. Hump day. It was a day when the market usually saw plenty of action.

The opening numbers for DDI were slightly higher what Ian was told they'd open at.. He and his partners were ready to pour nine billion into the company. The CEO had a grin on his face when he struck the bell. He would make out well no matter what the stock did. William wished he could read the thought of this man and what was behind that toothy grin of his.

William already had the number he'd give Ian. Marie would give the same number to the doctor in the next room. Concentrating on the company gave William a number that the stock would eventually reach. There would be a drop in the stock price. By then he'd be back in Arizona and Marie would have returned to Mexico. Plan B would be in place and Julia would have to make sure Ian was neutralized.

Ten minutes after the opening bell William wrote down a number. "Here is what I got Mr. McClure."

McClure looked at the digits on the writing pad and dropped his pen. "Really. This is a big jump in the stock. I've got to call my team right away and give them the news."

Before making the call Ian went into the next office to compare Williams number with Marie's. They matched. He placed the call to the office of one of the investors. The other four were with him awaiting Ian's call.

After the number was passed on to them a yell could be heard coming from the cell phone on the other end. They all placed purchase orders for 1.5 billion each.

"Sounds like they are pleased with the projected high," William said. He looked at Ian and saw him start to turn a shade whiter. The excitement was too much. Ian quickly swallowed another blood pressure pill. He had just placed his order and needed to live long enough to sell when the number was reached.

"Do you have any idea how long DDI might have to wait before trading reaches that amount?" asked William.

"My research team projected that it could take weeks. DDI has to start showing some progress in their drilling ability. Results are the thing investors want to see happen."

"Good luck with you and your investment Mr. McClure. Miss Ortiz and I are happy with what you paid us. I don't think I'm interested in doing this again but I can't answer for her."

"It would be a year from now anyway. I'm the only one from the Company that has the compound and I don't expect it'll be used again."

William kept staring at Ian, trying to read his thoughts. All he could get from him was thoughts of pain. He was in bad shape and needed to get home and rest. The excitement had taken its toll.

Marie was ready to leave as well. She and her sister had more shopping. They'd fly back to Mexico City the next morning.

"Thank you again, Mr. McClure, for the opportunity to visit America again. My sister and I had a wonderful time and plan on returning again next year. I have another sister and two brothers. New York is an education and I want to give them the chance to see one of America's most exciting cities."

"You're welcome Miss Ortiz. Good to see you as well Mr. Ray. Have a safe trip back to your homes."

Marie and William left the office and walked towards the elevator. They continued to send thoughts back and forth to each other.

"What number did you really get, Marie? I actually saw only a slight gain."

"Me too. This may not turn out well for Mr. McClure."

William and Marie took the elevator to the ground floor. Marie shook hands with William and turned to the right to meet her sister for breakfast. William had his bag and caught one of those green cabs to the airport. They finished their part. The rest was up to Julia to close out the case.

Ian was done for the day as well. He gave instructions to Miss Reed and Dr. Logan. They were to take away any medical supplies and put the offices back into shape. Before the final stock high was reached Ian would deposit their bonus checks into their accounts. Two million for each of them was not much for a man about to earn billions. The amounts would also ensure their silence.

Dr. Logan planned to return to Buffalo, New York and open a clinic with his earnings. Retirement was not part of his plan.

Miss Reed felt it was time to retire. She was in her forties, single, and planned on traveling the world. She had already made an appointment for plastic surgery. A wrinkle-free complexion, bigger boobs, and a nicer butt would add to her world travel experiences. She wanted to try out some of those Italian men she'd heard about before she reached fifty. Adding some icing to her looks never hurt. She planned on having her cake and eating it too.

*****

William boarded the plane. After calling Leslie to give her his arrival time in Phoenix, he placed a call to Julia.

"We're finished. Marie and I left Ian a few hours ago. We both hope we never see him again."

"Where are you calling from?" Julia asked.

"I'm on the plane heading back to Phoenix. Marie's staying one more day with her sister and is flying back to Mexico City in the morning. How is plan B going?"

"First of all did you see the numbers the stock will reach?"

"Yes, we both did. It reached that number right after it opened. It does not look good for DDI. They could tank, especially if no one believes deep oil drilling is the answer to the energy crisis."

"We still have a few weeks to play this out. Ian and his

investors will hang on for a while expecting the stock to reach the number you gave them. We'll have the plan in place by then."

"Marie and I hope so. We don't want this crazy bastard coming after us."

"The plan is going into action right away. Is the compound still working on you and Marie?"

"Yes. We'll both be pleased when the pressure is gone. It's not that much fun reading the thoughts of others. I can't believe what the airline stewards are really thinking when they serve the passengers."

"What do you mean?"

"The ones in first class are not so bad. There are two working in the economy section. They put on a pleasant face but make animal comparisons to some of the funny looking passengers. Then they compare notes in the galley."

"Like what?"

"How about hippo woman or camel breath. There was even another one so bad I won't repeat it over the phone."

"Having the sight doesn't sound like fun at all, William. I now see why you're ready to be normal again."

"No kidding. Robert said he liked the experience. He said something about controlling others."

Julie looked over at Robert who was listening on the speakerphone and did her best to hold back a snicker. Robert rolled his eyes. He held up his finger to his mouth to try and stop Julia from laughing out loud.

"I heard that too, William. He was never able to get away with that when he tried it with me."

By now Robert was drawing his finger across his throat to tell Julia she needed to cut the conversation off. He was done hearing a joke about himself, even though he was supposed to be dead.

"I have to go now, William. Miss Anderson wants me in the office. Might have something to do with plan B. Should I call you when were ready?"

"Yes, but on my cell phone. Leslie gets too worked up about this spy stuff. It takes a long time for her to calm down after I work with you."

"I completely understand. I'll be ready for a normal life after this is finished as well."

"Talk to you later, Julia. Bye for now."

William replaced the phone on the seat in front of him. Arizona and home were next on his to-do list.

*****

"Did you have a good laugh at my expense, my dear?" Robert was not really angry with Julia but he still wanted to get the last word in.

"Wanting to control everything was too funny. I couldn't help myself."

"And you think I still do that with you?"

"No. You've learned not to. That's why we get along so well."

"You may have a point. I did like reading minds and seeing numbers. I wasn't ready for that experience to end."

"I do have one question for you, Sweetheart. Why didn't you just play the Power ball game and walk away with ten or twenty million dollars instead of working for the Company?"

"Do you realize how much attention those people get after they win? I wanted to have a life, not a tabloid existence. You see how hidden I live. Being anonymous is much more appealing. Do you think we would have ever met if I won Powerball and retired? I like working and I love being with you."

"You're just saying that because you want to have pool sex."

"Not really but if there is an offer on the table I'd be crazy not to take it."

"We can't go out there now. Peggy is still working in the office. After she leaves we have the house to ourselves."

"I've got more to work to do with plan B. I'll be in the office with Peggy for a while. When she leaves we can pick up where we left off."

"Robert, you are so romantic. I'm going to practice meditation in my office for an hour. See you later."

Julia left the living room area and headed down the hall. She had created a room for meditation equipped with special music played during the sessions. Also sitting pads helped support her legs and back. Loose fitting sweat pants a comfortable top completed her meditation attire. Her hour of going into the present moment had begun.

Chapter

Twenty-Five

"The result of the voice match between Ian McClure and whoever was on the answering machine of the real estate agent is back. Want to make a wager before I tell you the finding?"

"I bet $20 it is a match." Martin was pretty confident Ian was behind all this mess.

"You'd win. I can't believe McClure was so stupid not to use a secretary or someone else to rent the office." Louis was also ecstatic the voices had matched.

"He was probably attempting to minimize who knew about the Irish men. It's murder. Getting someone else to do the job was not a risk he wanted to take."

Martin was sure the evidence would hold up in court. He had to get a judge to sign off on an arrest warrant and give the information to the local DA. This might take a week or two but it looked like a slam-dunk. A voice match was strong evidence and could be used in the trial.

"What do we do for now? Just wait?" Louis was ready to fly back to New York and join the arresting team.

"That's about all we can do. Justice moves slowly, especially when targeting rich and powerful people. We have to have your detective friend in New York make the arrest."

"Can I be there when they put the cuffs on him?"

"I need you here, Louis. You can greet him at the airport when they fly McClure here for arraignment. Bail will be set. I don't think Ian will have a problem paying it."

"Isn't he a flight risk? That bastard can hide on some exotic island and sip frozen drinks with tiny umbrellas until he dies."

"We need to make sure the DA has Ian's passport taken away. I don't really think he'll be a flight risk. Too much is at stake. We may not see this come to trial for a year, if at all."

"Do you think he'll get off?" Louis asked.

"When you were in New York interviewing him and his lawyer I did some checking. He's in poor health. His medical records indicate his high blood pressure and heart condition may take him out before a trial does."

"Really? His medical record told you all that?"

"Yes, I have connections too, Louis. It was a bit of a hassle but I told the doctor treating McClure the information was needed in a murder case. Withholding information could result in a fine or arrest. The doctor didn't seem to have much love for McClure. I had the information sent to me before you got back from New York."

"Good job, boss. I rather have him put away but dying would save the taxpayers the expense of a trial."

"Not only that, it would close the case. He had Woods and those Irish hit men killed. He's one nasty dude for sure. I'm not picky as to how he makes his exit from the world."

"What about the person sending us the information in the case. Do we want to find out who that is or let it go?"

"Whoever is helping us doesn't want to be found out. I don't plan on killing the goose handing us the golden eggs. They seemed to be involved in the Woods case and know more than we do. Let it ride and let's take McClure out first. We can decide what to do about our secret agent later."

"Martin, I found out something else. Remember that computer geek at the funeral for Woods. The one who set up the office screens and machines for Woods."

"Yes. He had a hot girlfriend with him. Thirty-six D I believe."

That's the one. Anyway, guess who he really is?"

"What do you mean? Alan Hogan is not his real name?"

"That's his name all right but he is not just some computer geek. He's about to go public on the NYSE with a web business called Geek Mingle. He'll be our newest and youngest billionaire in Albuquerque in a matter of weeks."

"No shit. And he was working for Woods setting up computers at one time? He must be one smart nerd." Louis said.

"Yea and 36 D realizes it as well."

"What else do we have on him? Do we know where he lives?"

"He owns an office space downtown where his workers keep the site going 24/7. He's keeping his residence private. We'd have to tail him to find out where he lives," Martin added.

"Do we need to do that? Is he a person of interest?"

"Not really. He went to the university for a few years but no need for that anymore. He's smart but nothing connects him to this case. Whoever is sending us the info is computer savvy for sure. I just don't think it's this Alan character. Becoming a billionaire take a lot of your time."

"And you would know this because---?" Louis asked.

"Running a company and solving a murder? No way." Martin was sure someone else was sending them the information regarding the Woods murder.

"I wonder if he was ever involved in the past. Maybe we should put a tail on him and find out where he lives. It may be useful down the road. Want me to follow him myself? I need a break from the office."

"I need you here Louis. Get one of the rookies to do that. I don't know how it'll help but who knows?" Martin took on that look when he started to daydream.

"Wow, a billionaire computer geek right here in Albuquerque. We may make the front page in New York yet, Louis."

"Putting Ian McClure in jail would put us on the front page. Let's do that and maybe then we can do a little bragging."

"Fine. Get someone to tail Mr. Hogan and see where he lives. It shouldn't take too long. Make sure the DA has everything we know about McClure. We need to make an arrest before he dies of a heart attack."

"Got it. Want me to pick up some more donuts after I take care of all that. May need a sugar pick-me-up to get through the afternoon."

"Get some jelly-filled ones this time. I need more fruit in my diet. The raspberry ones should do the trick."

"You got it."

Louis closed Martin's door behind him as he headed across the office area. He was looking for the last rookie cop who pissed him off. Someone would get the assignment. Cold sandwiches and a soft drink for dinner put *stakeouts* at the bottom of the duty list for most cops. Louis spotted June Parsons as she walked into the department office. She'd turned him down for coffee a month ago. Payback could be a bitch.

*****

Cathy and Alan were in the last phase of work before going public on the NYSE. Both were slated to attend the opening on the day they started to trade. They'd get to ring the opening bell. Web sites were big in the market. Google, Face book and Twitter did well since they started trading. The information world was huge. Geek Mingle attracted a certain clientele but there were plenty of Nerds looking for love. The list of advertisers willing to sell their products on the site was growing.

"I think we can't do much more before going public," Alan said. "We've got plenty of office space to expand. Professor Thomas at the University gave me a list of his top computer students who want to work for us. A few are willing to start work before graduating."

Cathy added, "Now we have the top computer minds in the whole state. Let's have a party for everyone after going public. They need to know their hard work is appreciated."

"Can you set that up, Cathy? You're good at social things."

"Of course my love. I need something to keep me occupied until we go public. We should have the party right in the office so everyone can attend. I know we need a few people watching the computers at all times so we should bring the party to them."

"First thing first. I have to head back to the office and drop off some specs to Morgan. He's starting to run the place better than I can. This means I can free myself and travel with you."

"That's the way it should be. You did most of the foundation work and now the experts need to take over in the areas they're good in. Being a CEO of an internet company means hiring the right people to do most of the work."

"That's hard to do when you and I did everything in the beginning."

"Mostly you Alan. I came later. The business was up and running by the time I showed up."

"Yea but you kept me from flipping out when things got tough."

"Sex did help," Cathy answered. "We have something much bigger now and we need to make sure we don't lose ourselves. Too many people who become rich quickly forget who they are. Forgetting to do good in the world as well as making lots of money becomes their downfall."

"You're right, Cathy. This last year has been a whirlwind. We grew so fast. Who knew the Geeks of the world wanted us to make their match- making that much easier?"

"I never knew the Gay Geek community would jump on board as well. Seems they use the site as much as the straight nerds. We had to make a separate site for them so they don't start hitting on the straight community."

"It's a crazy world out there and we need to adapt to it."

"I'll be back in a few hours. Let's go out for dinner. There's a new Italian place downtown. I need a couple of glasses of wine and a good meal to help unwind."

"And then we can come back and continue with our usual way

to reduce stress. I claim on top since it was my idea."

"Looking at those beautiful breasts while having sex is fine with me sweetheart. No argument here."

"The business did pay for them and the rest of my makeover."

"The best part even if I do say to myself."

"Go to work, Alan. The fun is later."

*****

June, the rookie cop, sat outside the Geek Mingle office eating her late lunch. Corn beef and cabbage from the Irish Delhi down the street and listening to *Pink* on her earphones. What a life. Just like she envisioned on the TV shows while growing up. The man she was following had just pulled into the parking lot. He drove a Nissan Leaf. All electric. No gas. It was almost un-American.

"So this is what the newest billionaire drives?" She had a file on Alan and Geek Mingle with her. Finding out where he lived was her assignment. After that, she was promised no more stakeouts and cold sandwiches. She was ready for some real police work.

After an hour Alan returned to his car. Officer June was ready. Finding out where he lived without being seen was her only assignment.

Alan was not on his game. He usually was cautious before heading home. He always took a few trips around the block, making sure no one was following. Dinner and sex with Cathy on top was on his twenty-six- year-old mind. He was thinking through his groin and not his brain.

A phone call to let Cathy know he was on his way gave her

time to be at the door when he arrived. Officer June parked down the street and remaining hidden in her white Ford Mustang after Alan pulled into his house. A quick drive by the large house gave June the address. Most of the homes were on two-acre plots. "Lots of money out here," she thought.

Before heading back to the station officer June decided to continue through the neighborhood looking at all the upscale homes. Not bad, she thought. Maybe I should have taken more computer classes in college. Starting an Internet company seems to buy a lot of house these days.

June put in a call to detective Louis's cell. He was home.

"This is June. I've got the address. Do you want it now or wait till morning?"

"I'll get it in the morning. Good work. Your turn to get the donuts, Parsons. Make sure a couple of them are jelly filled. Detective Martin thinks he needs more fruit in his diet."

"You're kidding me, right?" June said.

"No. Why do you think that?"

"Fruit jelly in a donut is not adding anything healthy to his diet. Is detective Martin serious?"

"He's a cop. What do you think?"

"I think he needs to eat real fruit, not some donut filled with berries."

"Do you want to tell him or should I?" Louis asked.

"Not me. I'm new, remember? I don't plan on doing stakeout duty for the rest of my career."

"Good. Do you want to go for coffee sometime?" Louis asked.

"Is that why I got this duty? Because I wouldn't go to coffee with you?"

"I wouldn't say that but I can make sure you don't have that duty for a while."

"Okay. Just coffee. I don't date people I work with. Is that clear."

"Fine. Just coffee. See you in the morning."

Officer June hung up. Dialogue passed through her head like a soap opera. She thought, "That bastard put me on this job because I said no to having coffee with him? This is the 21st century, Louis. We don't get mad, we get even."

Parsons headed back home for the night. Not that she thought Louis was bad looking. She just did not want to be taken advantage of and screw her way to the top. If Louis tried to pull any shit with her while drinking coffee he would be wearing the rest of her cup on his clean uniform. They wouldn't fire her. Sexual harassment wasn't tolerated.

Chapter

Twenty-Six

Friday at Leggs and the bar was full. Sera and Laura hadn't met for two weeks. Stories of love interests and the McClure case were discussed over the Raviolis and garlic bread.

"He wants to marry you?" Sera asked. "What'd you say?"

Sera was referring to Jeff, Laura's boyfriend from Albuquerque. They had just passed the three-month period of dating.

"I wanted to say yes but decided to think it over. It's a big move for me. Moving from the city to a desert community is a total change. I could still work there. Instead of bridges and tall buildings for background wedding shots, I would use cacti and sunsets."

"Is he fine with waiting?"

"Yes. He understands how big this move is for me."

"How much time do you need?"

"I want to wait until the McClure investigation is put away. What have you found out from your detective friend?"

Sera filled Laura in on the case. The voice matched with the Albuquerque police tape and the New York police interview. Her detective friend said they were getting close to issuing an arrest warrant and send McClure to New Mexico for arraignment.

"The cops are pretty sure McClure will post bail but still have to give up his passport. This case could be a while before it even sees the inside of a courthouse. He still could walk."

"Is there no way to speed up this process?"

"The sword of justice can be slow. The DA wants a solid case before going after McClure. It would be cheaper if someone just shot the bastard and ended this once and for all."

Laura thought for a minute before speaking. She could not wait a long time before giving Jeff an answer. Maybe leaving New York and the rat race lifestyle was best.

"I may say yes to Jeff sooner than expected. Leaving this city will be hard. Rich bastards like McClure getting away with murder, just because they can buy their way out, is more than I can handle. Screw him and the rest of them."

"I totally agree, Laura. If my book sells well I may pack it in and move too."

The two women took another bite of dinner and ordered another bottle of wine. They were going to get a little drunk. This could be one of the last times they'd see each other. Laura might be moving to New Mexico and getting married sooner than expected. Sera had more research to do on her book and several more women to interview. They hoped what they contributed to the case would lead to Ian's arrest and eventual downfall. Time would tell.

*****

A week had passed. There was little change in the DDI trading numbers. Investors seemed to be holding off on a company who promised oil from deep inside the earth's crust. Fracking was popular at the present time but environmentalists were fighting this process as best they could. The energy crisis was in full swing.

Ian received phone calls from his group daily. They were getting impatient. They wanted to see the predicted high number promised by Ian and the two seers.

Robert was watching the DDI price. He was pleased so far. Wanting to see a drastic drop in the stock numbers was high on his list. Going after Ian through the courts would not work. Ian would answer to a higher court. St. Peter could hardly wait.

Josh, Roberts market friend, continued to give him information regarding DDI. His persistent doubts regarding the CEO of the company and his spending practices were starting to come true. The rumors around the exchange were that the CEO paid his founding workers huge bonuses. He could be banking much of the money for himself. After all, he was given nine billion to play with.

Attempts of DDI to gain drilling permits were put on hold. All safety measures needed to be in place. The US government was not going to let oil screw up the fishing industry again. Billions would be needed to make sure DDI would not have an accident.

By the second week, there was a change in the trading numbers. It looked like investors were not interested and the stock was heading south. Ian made phone calls to the other company members and asked them to hang in for a while longer. One member dropped out and sold. This caused another dip in the stock. One by one each member sold and took a big loss. Ian was the only one who held on. He couldn't believe it. The seers had never failed him before.

After the third week, the stock continued on its downward journey. The CEO had taken the money and hid it in paperwork and expenses. He socked away 1.1 billion for himself and was preparing to sell off the rest of his assets and pay off debts. The writing was on the wall. Deep oil drilling was becoming just like the reptiles it came from. A Dinosaur.

Robert was about to make Plan B a reality. Ian had not sold yet and was destined to lose 1.5 billion.

*****

The plane landed in New York with Robert and Julia on board. Their new identities, along with wigs and dark glasses, sped them through customs and into their hotel room two blocks away from Ian's office. The final plan was a go. Two years of going after the Company was approaching its final curtain call.

"Do we have our man ready to make a move?"   Julia was starting to get nervous.

"He's on call. He can do what we want within twenty minutes. We have to get our timing right and shut down the 8th floor when Ian's there."

"We still have an eye on him?" Roberts' voice was starting to show strain as well.

"As far as I know Peggy is keeping constant watch." Julia had Peggy on speed dial. Peggy was staying at their house 24/7 and had to be the center of the web to keep everything connected.

 Robert said, "I have the van ready to go and the uniform hanging in the closet. Timing is essential."

"Robert, we're ready. Just try and relax."

"Sweetheart this is going to be tight. Ian has lost a lot of money. He'll be going after William or Marie because of the false information. Losing is not part of his lifestyle."

"So what. He still has plenty left. He may end up being reduced to a multi-millionaire after this is through. I feel nothing for him. I want this last step to hurt him at the core."

"It probably will. Have you sent the envelopes to the other five members of the Company? Wanting to blame someone is probably high on the list. Let's make sure they go after Ian."

Robert made up packets that explained to the five men that Ian had not done enough research into DDI. The CEO of DDI had a record of dishonest spending. He probably hid what money he was given in equipment and false costs. Duping them into believing deep oil drilling would work had been his goal. If Ian had done his research he would have known.

No mention of William or Marie was made. The blame was directed to Ian only. If the investors wanted revenge then McClure is the person they should go after.

"Do you think they'll buy this and blame McClure? They've been working with him for many years."

"All five have hung on with Ian for too long. They've witnessed his downfall in the last twenty-four months. His father died as CEO and Ian was fired. They lost the desalination plants in their bid to control governments. Now they've lost most of their billion-dollar investment. They've had enough of the McClure clan for sure."

"Why not let them take him out? We could end this and walk away without getting involved."

"I'm not sure they're into murder. Ian and his father were but not all of the Company members knew about the killings in Italy and Mexico. Making money was their goal. They all have plenty of assets. Walking away from Ian would be a good move."

"I guess we are the only ones left to finish him off once and for all. Shall we get room service or go out? I'm starving."

"Let's go out. I need to walk around a bit and stretch my legs. Something simple works for me. How about you?" Robert asked.

Julia was feeling good being back in the city. She wanted to walk around as well but after dinner. There were plenty of places to eat near the hotel. New York provided more food choices than grains of sand on the Jersey shore.

"Let's go down the block."

The couple found a family owned pizza restaurant. The privately owned ones were the best according to Julia. They were seated and sipping wine within minutes of walking through the door.

"Have you spoken to Laura in a while? I'd like to know how the detectives are doing on their end of the case."

"As far as I know they are getting close to making an arrest. The voices matched but the DA in Albuquerque wants all the evidence in his hands so he can build the case. They think they have Ian but it may take a long trial to bring him down."

"Having Laura meet Sera was a stroke of luck," Robert said.

Julie was nervous. She didn't like what Robert was planning for his final act. It seemed her future husband needed to prove to the world that a crooked billionaire could fall. His plan B seemed like an extreme case of who got the last word. Robert was going to make sure it was not Ian.

"There's been a lot of luck involved," Julia added. Look how many years it took to get to this point. From now on can we just work the easy cases? Finding out who's sleeping with whom or who is stealing from a business is a walk in the park compared to this."

Robert added. "I agree. We're doing most of the investigation on our own dime. Being safe for the rest of our lives does play a part. The final reward is more than enough."

"Knowing that makes the risk worth it. Just don't tell me the ending of this final chapter. I really don't want to know how you plan to finish this."

"I'm not 100% sure myself. A lot will depend on Ian. How it ends is based on how he reacts. I have no control over that at all."

"Just be sure you walk out alive. I know you can get into the building but getting out is my concern."

"Mine too. This has been hard on you, Sweetheart. I'm sorry. I do feel we're close to finishing this debacle once and for all. I don't plan on getting involved with the mega wealthy ever again. The corrupt ones can live their lives out in their bubbles of insecurity and keep pretending the world gives a shit about them and their lifestyle."

"Not all the billionaires are corrupt. Some actually give millions away helping the world become a better place," Julia said. "I think Alan and Cathy will be ones that give back."

Dinner was finished. Robert stood up. "Let's walk for a while before heading back to the room. We may be here for a few days before we can corner Ian and finish this job."

"Fine with me. Meet you outside."

Robert waited for the bill. The couple walked around the block. A stop at a self-serving yogurt store took care of desert.

Back to the room and just in time for the Downtown Abby series on PBS. Thomas was still the asshole of the show. He played the part so well Robert gave him the nickname Ian.

After the show ended the phone rang. It was Robert's private line. Julia still used it for close friends. William Ray's name came up on the screen.

"Julia, hi."

"Hi, William. Are you home?"

"Been home for a few weeks. What have you heard regarding Ian? I see the DDI tanked."

"Yes, they aren't getting anybody to invest in deep oil drilling."

"Are you any closer to finishing the case? I keep expecting a knock on the door from one of Ian's hit men."

"Has Ian contacted you?"

"No, and that's got me worried. If he called and yelled at me I would feel better than not hearing from him at all."

"William I don't think Ian has time to go after you and Marie. As far as he knows the CEO ripped off his investment. He also is about to be faced with a criminal lawsuit."

"Regarding what?"

"The hiring of the two Irish hit men. The police have a voice match of Ian and the person who rented the office where the mobsters stayed in Albuquerque. The dots are starting to connect."

"Is that enough to take him out?"

"We're not sure yet. It'll tie him up in court for a while and tarnish his name in the papers."

"That's all fine but Marie and I stuck our necks out with those false numbers. McClure gone from the face of the earth is our only insurance he won't come after us."

"Give my team a few more days to finish this up. We are getting close. The results will be in your best interest, William. I expect this to play out real soon."

"I'm sure you and your new assistant are doing your best. I just miss Robert. He was damn good at what he did. He always seemed to have an idea or answer for every situation."

"Robert left a plan before he died. He called it plan B. It has to do with eliminating Ian. It is in action as we speak. Trust me on this, William. I will call you back as soon as it's implemented."

"I received a call from Marie yesterday. Should I call her back and tell her not to worry?"

"Just tell her what I told you."

"Thanks, Julia. I don't know what's planned and don't want to know. Call when it's over."

"I will, William. It's been a long haul. There's light at the end of the tunnel as we speak." Julia looked over at Robert who was giving her two thumbs up. The plan contained an unknown regarding what Ian would do, but even so, Robert was confident the end was near.

Julie hung up. She turned to Robert with a worried look. "William is walking on egg shells. As soon as this is over we can all take a breath. After that, we have to break the news to a few of our friends."

"What news?"

"The fact you're still alive. William and Leslie, as well as Laura, need to know. She still feels guilty she led the Irish mobsters to you and now you're dead."

"Let's limit the number to those few. The police don't have to know. Neither does the friend of Laura. Sera may have helped us but she's not part of our inner circle."

"We may have to have a small wedding if you're going to stay dead. We can't invite people who think you are gone and have you appear with me at the alter."

"By the way, what kind of wedding are we going to have? You can cross off the Mormon Church. Are we leaning towards a Buddhist marriage?"

"Not quite there yet. I love you Robert but planning a wedding and taking out a billionaire can't be done at the same time. Even multi-tasking women would find that a bit much."

"Let's see where Ian is tomorrow. If he shows up at the office we can shift to plan B. Staying at home has been his MO. I think he may be depressed and not able to show his face around work right now."

"Sleep is what we need now sweetheart. If he does show we have to be ready."

The light went out and both heads hit the pillows. Exhaustion had taken over.

*****

Ian's health took a turn for the worst. He was using a cane just to get around. Depression had set in and the drugs he was taking to function were now consumed in larger doses than a year before. How had this investment failed? Was the compound used on the two clients not working? 100% success up till now had Ian baffled. His five investment friends were not taking his calls. He was alone.

The only positive aspect of his life at the moment was the wedding of his son. The date was set for the end of the month.

Ian's wife was doing most of the arrangements due to his lack of energy and health issues.

Letting go of a number of possessions was the only way Ian could remain a billionaire. He had lost 1.5 billion and maintenance of three homes including the one in Martha's Vineyard was proving to be overwhelming. One of his houses would go as a wedding gift for his son. He would keep the Vineyard house. After all, he had to maintain the appearance of wealth to those around him. Two other homes had to be sold.

Ian was scrambling. He knew further investing in the NYSE was not a part of his recovery. Trusting the compound on more clients was no longer an option. It had failed and cost him dearly.

His personal phone rang. Markson, his lawyer, was on the line.

"Ian."

"Yes Hal, what is it now?"

"I'm afraid I've some bad news for you."

Ian reached over and grabbed his blood pressure medicine. He quickly swallowed a 20 mg pill and sat down. "Now what? I can't keep up with all this bad news for much longer."

"The DA in Albuquerque has contacted me. He says he has enough evidence to arrest you and bring you to trial. It seems they have a voice match between you at the interview with the police last month and a person leasing an office space in Albuquerque. Did you rent an office space there a few months back?"

"What? How is that possible? I've never been to Albuquerque."

"I have to know everything if I am going to represent you, Ian.

It seems the real estate person, who rented the space, recorded the conversation and kept it filed. She said the office was leased for a year and paid for."

"That sounds about right." By now Ian had nothing to hide from Hal. He knew more about Ian than his wife did. Client privilege allowed Ian to divulge everything to his lawyer. The fee he paid this man was more than 95% of what the working force in America earned in a year.

"What does that mean?" Hal asked.

"It means I may have rented the building."

"Do you also know the two Irish men suspected of blowing up the house where Robert Woods lived also stayed in that office?"

"And how does the DA know that."

"They have a videotape showing the two men going in and out of the building during the time they were in the states. This is serious business, Ian."

"Can a voice match be used as evidence in court?"

"Hell yes. It's almost as good as a fingerprint. Technology has come a long way."

"So what if I rented a building. So what if two men suspected of killing Robert Woods stayed there. Did I kill Robert Woods?"

"Ian you're not getting the picture. Robert Woods was the person spying on the Company and sending information to the authorities. That's a fact. Not proven in court yet but still evidence. He gets blown up and the two men, even though they are dead, were the #1 suspects in the case. Do you think a trial by your peers is not going to connect the facts in this case?"

"I don't know and at this time I don't much care. I've lost a great deal of money, friendships with previous Company members and have been fired as CEO. The only positive thing I have left is my son's wedding. Can you keep me out of jail until after he's married? After that, I don't give a shit."

"You mean you're prepared to go to trial?"

"I prepared to tie this up in the courts as long as it takes. My doctor says I may not have too many years left. I accomplished the one goal I set for myself. Robert Woods is dead. That's a fact. After my son is married I plan on tying up all my loose ends and disappearing until I die."

"Ian, they'll take away your passport. You're not going anywhere."

"I can always get another one, Hal. You know that. As a matter of fact, I might just go for a complete identity change and live my life out on a beach in the Caribbean."

"Who'll manage your assets? You wife doesn't know squat about your affairs. All she does is throw parties and attend social events representing the McClure family."

"I may give that responsibility to you and my account manager. You two can keep things in order and wire me money when I need it. I'm done with this crap. I won't last through a trial."

"So you're throwing in the towel?"

"That's one way of looking at it. If I disappear or even fake my death the DA will have nothing to go on. I have to think this out but I don't have much left to live for."

"Ian, you need to get some rest and think this through."

"I have, just not the details. I'm going to the office tomorrow to start clearing out files and letting people go. Miss Reed is going in for plastic surgery and wants to visit Italy and screw a lot of Italian men before she gets too old. She told me that. Can you believe it? A cougar working in my office and now she has the income to play out her fantasies."

"Too much information for me, Ian. I'm happily married. Are you sure this is what you're going to do?"

"Just keep the wolves away from me for a while longer. By the time they're ready to arrest me my son should be married and I'll have all my remaining assets in order."

"I really can't believe I'm hearing this, Ian. I have to go. If I'm going to keep the police from arresting you I need to start filing paperwork right away. Keep me up with your plans."

"Don't worry, Hal. Letting go is easier than I thought. My wife and son still have more than enough to keep them happy. Selling two homes and a couple of yachts will not be missed."

"Talk to you soon, Ian."

Ian hung up. A pending arrest was the last straw. He knew he would not survive a trial. Going to the office and giving everyone severance pay was first on the list. Clearing out files would be his final act. It had been a good run. He was tired.

*****

"Julia, Mr. McClure is going to the office tomorrow."

"Are you sure, Peggy?"

"The wiretap on his phone gave me the news." Peggy was in the office in Roberts home. She made the call as soon as Ian hung up with his lawyer.

"What did you hear?"

"McClure is wrapping up his business and may try and disappear. He just found out the news regarding the DA and pending arrest warrant. I think it put McClure over the top. He's going to the office tomorrow and shutting down. After his son is married he may leave the country. He hopes to cover up his absence with a fictitious death."

"No kidding. He's giving up. I wonder how Robert will take the news?"

"I don't know but if plan B is going to be implemented it will have to be tomorrow. Also, Ian admitted to killing Robert. We can't use that in court but we knew that anyway."

"Here comes Robert. I'll tell him. Thanks, Peggy. You're invaluable."

"No problem. Julia. This is the most exciting job I've ever done. Thanks for letting me stay at the house. I'm practically living in the office."

"If anything else come up just call, even if it is during the night. Can you stay overnight again? We still need ears on Ian."

Peggy had been sleeping in the guest room while Robert and Julia were in New York. Carla was taking a family vacation and would not be back at the house until the two returned.

"I can. This is a wonderful place to sleep. I wake up with the sun and drink coffee by the pool. I even brought my bathing suit this time."

Julie made a little chuckle to herself. "If you're alone you don't need a suit to swim. We have no neighbors who can see in our back yard. Feel free to swim *a natural.*"

"You know I just may try that. I don't like tan lines anyway. Being Swedish allows me to be freer with nudity. Nude beaches in Sweden are common."

"I'm not Swedish but I agree. I love being nude in the pool. It feels wonderful and Robert joins me all the time."

Robert was doing his finger across the throat move again trying to get Julie to cut the conversation off. Too much information for Peggy was not something he wanted to share. He did like being in the pool with Julie because he knew were it always led.

"Have to go now, Peggy. I'm getting the sign that I talk too much. Love you."

"You heard the conversation? Ian is going to the office tomorrow."

"Plan B is about to kick in. I'll call my maintenance man now and get him ready for action. It's all or nothing. Tomorrow's the big day."

*****

"What do you mean we can't issue an arrest warrant? The DA's got everything he needs to make a case. This is bull shit."

Detective Martin could not believe what Louis has just told him. Ian's lawyer had filed a motion that put the arrest warrant on hold. So many loopholes existed in the legal system that it was a wonder anyone with a good legal representative was placed under arrest at all. Poor people did not have this ability. No lawyer, chosen by the courts, was going to file motions or attempt to slow down the court system.

"I agree. Ian's lawyer knows a lot of tricks. Now that he knows we're coming after him he is pulling them out of a hat as fast as he can. He is using everything from health problems to needing time to review the evidence."

"What do we need from McClure? A verbal admission he killed Woods?"

"That might do the trick, boss. I just got this package, special delivery. We think it is from the same person providing us information on the case. The funny part is, a set of earphones came with the package."

"A set of earphones. Any message with it?"

"Yes. It says to connect them to a recording device and record anything that comes over the air. The system is really advanced. I think it's set up to receive information coming from a person wearing a wire."

"Is that legal?"

"It sure is. Whatever this person is planning it's going down tomorrow. They said to start monitoring what's coming through the earphones early in the morning."

"They give an exact time?"

"No. We better have an agent listening 24/7 and recording anything they hear."

"Fine. You get someone on this starting at seven in the morning. I hope this is another break in the case."

"I've got just the person in mind."

"Really? Is it Parsons? You've been hanging around her a lot lately."

"Maybe. I'll talk to her and get her to come in early tomorrow. She can do this job at her desk."

"Fine, just make sure she knows how to push the record button if anything comes over the air. Whoever is helping us might have a lead and help break the case wide open."

"Parsons agreed to have coffee with me. This could be a good time to follow up."

"You're such a smooth operator Louis. You need a woman in your boring bachelor life. Good luck."

Louis left the office and closed the door. Officer Parson was at her desk and saw Louis coming. "Oh crap," she thought. "I bet Louis has another assignment for me. He has that look."

"Parson, we just got a possible break in a huge case. It involves that house explosion and murder a few months back. I need to discuss it with you in private."

"How private do you want?"

"Walt's Coffee across the street. We need to go right now because the job starts tomorrow."

"I hope it's not another steak out."

Louis really wanted to take June out on a date but decided he needed to play it cool. She made it clear she didn't date people at work.

"I said before I would keep you off that duty. This is a business coffee break. I still get a social one at another time."

"Fine. I'll grab my coat and meet you there."

Louis headed across the street and found a table by the window.

June arrived three minutes later.

"What's this all about?"

Louis paused for a moment before answering. He had to keep the meeting professional. June was hot, but him feeding her pickup lines would never get him to first base.

"We're getting help on a case from an unknown source. So far we've received accurate information and are about to make an arrest."

Two Mocha Lattes, no whip arrived at the table.

"How'd you know what I drink detective Louis? Have you been spying on me?"

"I'm a detective. I know this stuff."

Officer June was impressed. She thought, "This guy actually took the time to find out what kind of coffee drink I like. Maybe I should cut him a little slack?"

"Anyway, here's the scoop," Louis said.

Parsons asked, "Do you really use that word in your work?"

"What word?"

"Scoop. It sounds like an 80's detective show on TV."

"I watched a lot of those shows. Why do you think I wanted to become a cop in the first place?"

"I didn't know. What was your favorite show?"

"Miami Vice and Hill Street Blues."

"No kidding. I bought the whole series of Miami Vice. I was in love with Don Johnson as a teenager. You could put me on a steak out with him for as long as you wanted."

"He's old now. Really. We need to discuss this case."

For the next half hour, Louis explained the package and message that came with the earphones. Making the duty sound like it could crack the case made the job of coming in to work early sound exciting.

"So all I need to do is come to work early, set up the recorder and plug in the earphones? When anyone is talking just hit the record button and tape the conversation."

"Better than being parked in some remote alley. You could call the job an office steak out. We'll get someone to relieve you so you can go on breaks but I need a reliable person on this. I thought of you right away."

June didn't answer right away. She couldn't tell if Louis was feeding her a line or being sincere. It made her feel good he thought of her first. Maybe Louis wasn't so bad after all. He didn't feed her any bullshit pick up lines and that was a plus.

"Fine. Will someone pick up the donuts for me? It's my turn again but I may not have time if I have to be here at seven."

"No problem. I'll do that for you. What kind do you like?"

"The plain ones without all the sugar. A girl has to watch her weight you know."

"I better get some of those jelly filled ones as well. Martin still thinks they're helping him supplement his diet with more fruit."

"When it's his birthday we need to chip in for a fruit basket. Maybe he'll take the hint."

"Maybe. I don't plan on breaking the diet news to him. It's his choice."

Louis and June left the coffee shop and went back to the station. The earphones were hooked up to the recorder and everything was prepared for the next day. The job might prove to be an important one in many ways. No one really knew what was going to come over the airwaves but they'd be ready.

Chapter

Twenty-Seven

Robert woke early the next morning. He placed a call to his assistant. The day had finally arrived. Plan B was about to be activated.

"George it's me."

"Robert. Is this the day?"

"It could be. I'm waiting for my assistant to tell me if McClure has left his home and heading to the office. We can't do much until then."

"It takes about twenty minutes to cut the power to the office. Will that be enough time to make your move?"

"It has to be George. Getting everyone out of his office is a must."

"I'll be in the parking lot waiting for your call. I can cut it to fifteen minutes if I'm near the building."

"Good idea. I'll call as soon as McClure is on the move."

Robert hung up. Room service had his breakfast ready at six. Julie was still asleep. He ate as much as he could. Energy was needed to get through the next few hours. He forced every bite knowing this may be the meal that got him through Plan B.

*****

Ian finished his morning breakfast of oatmeal and toast. He tried to eat healthy meals hoping for a miracle change in his body. Too many years of mistreating himself through lack of sleep and poor eating habits had taken their toll. There was no wonder drug that would reverse the body damage he'd done to himself.

Today would be the final chapter in McClure Enterprises. The office would close and all the loose ends dealt with. Most of the files were on his office computer and could easily be removed or deleted. Miss Reed and the three other staff members had already received their severance checks and needed to clear out their desks.

At nine Ian made a call to the office.

"Miss Reed. Ian here. I'll be coming in this morning to remove the office files and clear out a few things. Tell the rest of the staff they can leave. Their pay has been deposited into their accounts. Wait for me. I want to personally say goodbye."

"Thank you, Mr. McClure. I've enjoyed working for you for the past fifteen years. I didn't want to say goodbye over the phone either."

"You've done a good job working for me Miss Reed. I understand you are leaving for Europe in a few months."

"Always wanted to travel. I now have the money to do so thanks to you and the bonus check. I may retire and live there if it turns out to be as exciting as I've heard."

"We should have a glass of wine together when I get to the office. I'll pick a good one from my cellar and bring it. I may be there for the rest of the day finishing up duties. Does that work with you?"

"It'd be a privilege to share a glass of wine. I'll tell the rest of the staff goodbye for you. I think they're already clearing out their desks and getting ready to move on."

"They have three months pay to hold them over until they land something else. Make sure they all have a good reference letter from us. It's been a good run with lots of ups and downs. I got what I wanted in the end. I'm now ready to wrap up my Wall Street life."

"See you went you get here Mr. McClure. What time can I expect you?"

"Around eleven. See you then, Miss Reed."

*****

"Robert, it's me. Ian will be in the office around eleven this morning. He just got off the phone with his secretary. Only she will be there. He wants to share a glass of wine with her. After that, the office should be empty except for Ian."

"Are you sure the office will be empty?"

"He just told his secretary that he has to spend the rest of the day clearing out files. I bet he's going to download everything and take it with him. Probably doesn't want the police to find out what he has been doing for the last eight years."

"Probably right Peggy."

"Shall I call you when Ian's on the move?"

"No, I think I can handle it from her. If anything unusual comes up give Julia a call. I may be too busy to talk. She can buzz me if needed."

"Good luck Robert. It's all coming down to this final day isn't it?"

"The final day for someone. I still don't know how Ian will react but I have a feeling it should go our way in the end."

"I sent detective Parks a similar set of earphones that we sent to the police in Albuquerque. They both will have audio when this goes down."

"We still have a ten-second delay on the recording, don't we? You need to delete any reference to me if any are made. The information going to the police is riding a lot on you, Peggy."

"I'll make sure nothing gets through that involves you or any of us. Who knows what will happen but it should be interesting."

"Thanks, Peggy. Here we go. Plan B is now in play."

A call was made to George. He was waiting in his car finishing his coffee and Egg McMuffin. McDonalds was just down the street.

"George. Are you ready?"

"I can be. Is it time?"

"Think so. McClure doesn't get there until eleven. If we get this job done now the secretary will make the call to have it fixed. I'll take over from there."

"Give me one more minute to take this last bite. Twenty-minutes tops. Do you want me to hang around after I'm done?"

"No, get out of there. Don't want you getting busted and have to answer any questions."

"Fine with me. Talk to you in a few hours, Robert."

"Just make a quick call to Julia when you're done. I have to get ready as well. She'll beep me when it's time."

"Good luck. I better go. Coffee's finished and I'm ready to do this."

"Thanks again, George. See you on the other side."

George put down the empty coffee cup and took the last bite of breakfast. He had his tool box in hand and access key to the basement. He'd only need ten minutes to cut the power from the office of McClure on the eighth floor. Internet access, power and everything other than cell phone access would be shut down.

The walk to the power grid in the basement took five minutes. George worked for the company that put in the system so he knew exactly what to do. Isolating the office would not involve any of the other businesses in the building. McClure enterprise was going offline and would need someone to fix it.

*****

"Damn. My computer just shut down," Miss Reed said out loud. She'd just finished giving the three assistants their letters of recommendation. They were gone but she still talked to herself when she was alone in the office.

"I better call the repair people right away. Mr. McClure will need electricity to wrap up his business after I'm gone."

"Hello. York Tech."

"Yes, can we help you?"

"We've lost internet and power. We need a repairman right away. This is urgent."

"What name is the account under?"

"McClure Enterprises. We are located on Broadway. How soon can you get someone here?"

Julia was on the other end of the call. It had been routed to her as soon as the power went off. Robert knew the office would need someone there right away.

"We can have someone there by noon. That's the best we can do. I'm sending my closest technician in your area. Will that work?"

"Fine. I will be gone by then but Mr. McClure will be here. He has to have everything up and running. We are closing the office and it's difficult to do without power."

"I understand. I'll make sure he's there no later than twelve."

"Thank you. What a thing to happen on the last day. I have an appointment so just have the tech come into the office. 843. I'll leave the front door unlocked so he can start right away."

Julia was relieved Miss Reed would be gone. The office needed to be completely empty. Plan B depended on it.

*****

"Louis. Hi. This is Parks."

"John. I was about to call you."

"Probably for the same reason I'm calling you. Did you get an envelope from that mystery person yesterday?"

"Yes. How did you know?"

"I got one too. I figured we both received a set of earphones and a similar letter. What are you doing with yours?"

"I have an officer listening in constantly. The person who's sending us this information on McClure has been right with everything so far."

"So you are following the instructions and have a recording

device set up?"

"John, you've known me for a few years. Whoever is helping us has more information than we do. They may be the reason we wrap up this case. They want something recorded."

"I'll get someone on it right away. How do we know when this is going down?"

"We don't and neither does the mystery person. That's why they suggested we have someone listening 24/7. I have a feeling it could happen sometime today."

"Hold on a second Louis. I need to get this set up right away."

Detective Parks motioned his most reliable officer over to him and gave instructions. He needed to connect the earphones to a recorder and rotate with his partner every hour. If anything came over the airwaves the record button was to be pushed. They were to take breaks but have someone listening at all times.

"Ok, Louis we are all set here. If we get something I'll call you. This is probably going down in either your city or mine. Time will tell."

"Good. My officer is on duty right now. She's been listening since seven this morning. Nothing so far but I'll check with her right now."

"Talk later, Louis."

Louis hung up. He poured a cup of coffee for officer June and added soy creamer. Just the way she liked it. A plain donut accompanied the drink. He would keep the conversation professional but he still had his hopes up.

"Here you go, Parsons." He placed the donut and coffee on the desk and sat down in the chair next to her.

"Anything so far?"

"Nothing since I've been here. Thanks for the donut. Do you think this will happen today?"

"Don't know but I've been doing this work for a few years. I've got a feeling we're going to wrap up the McClure case."

"I need a break in about ten minutes. I'm rotating with officer Thomas. Let him know would you."

"Sure. Anything else I can get you?"

June kept watching Louis and waiting for a come on. Nothing so far. He was acting like a gentleman. She liked that.

"How about lunch. Should I rotate with Thomas at noon?"

"Sure, I'll let him know."

"Do you want to get a burger down the street?"

Louis paused. He couldn't believe what he just heard. "Are you asking me Parsons?"

"Yes. You're a nice guy. Lunch isn't a big deal."

Louis was blown away. She was asking him to go eat lunch with her. This was a big deal to him. Still, he tried to remain cool.

"I think I can get off. I'll let you know after I talk to Thomas."

June was laughing to herself. She thought, "Now he's playing hard to get. Men are so easy to read."

"You do that. I can always go with Sally if you can't make it."

"No, I'm pretty sure I can." Louis was not going to let this opportunity slip away.

"All right. Tell Thomas I need a break. He can have early lunch. I'll be ready by noon."

Louis felt ecstatic. A possible break in the case and a lunch date with officer Parson and all in the same day. The planets must be lining up in his favor.

Detective Martin arrived. He grabbed a jelly donut, coffee and headed to his office. He gave Louis a signal to join him.

"Officer Parson got anything yet?"

"Nothing. She's going to rotate with Thomas with breaks and have him take over for her at noon. We're going to get a burger down the street."

"We? You said we. Did you ask her?"

"No, she asked me. Maybe there is light at the end of the tunnel after all."

"Play it cool Louis. Several officers have tried to hook up with her. She's good looking for sure but seems to have high standards."

"You don't think I can make the cut?"

"Just don't get too aggressive. Some of the cops we have here are really full of themselves. Those are the ones who tried to take her out and got shut down. Be yourself. She might like that instead of someone trying to impress her."

"I'll take your advice. Just keep an eye on Thomas when he's listening in on the earphones. I have a feeling today's the day. Something is going down."

"Thanks for the heads up, Louis. Thomas can handle the job. Just hurry back after lunch. If this happens today I want you and officer Parson to be the ones listening in."

"No problem. We'll be back in time."

*****

Shortly after ten-thirty Ian arrived at the office. He brought with him a bottle of Petit Sarah from the Napa Valley in California. It was only an $80 dollar bottle. He left the expensive stuff in his cellar. Included were two glasses, cheese and crackers and a list of what he needed to do.

"Miss Reed. Good morning. Why is it so dark in here?"

"Mr. McClure, we seem to have a power out. Even the Internet is down. Only my cell phone works. I called and the earliest a man can be here is at noon."

"Is it down in the whole building? I saw lights on in the lobby and the elevator worked."

"Just our floor. The rest of the staff finished packing and I gave them their letters of recommendation. They left about an hour ago."

"A repair man is coming for sure? I need to download all the files from the server. I could be here till late this evening."

"The receptionists for York Tech was putting her best man on the job and guaranteed his arrival before twelve."

"Nothing to do right now. Do you have a corkscrew? I forgot to bring one."

"Mr. McClure, I'm impressed. Wine with a real cork. I'm used to opening my wine with a twist of the wrist."

"I can't believe producers are reverting to twist tops. Maybe the world is running out of cork and only the top wineries can afford it?"

"When I go to Italy I'll let you know. I think it is another cost saving method for cheaper wines. Anyway here's an opener."

Ian applied the screw into the cork and pulled. It was one of those basic openers waiters used in restaurants. Miss Reed had one in her desk in case she needed to work late on Fridays. She even stocked a bottle of Merlot in the bottom drawer so she could start with a few glasses around five. She always went out on Fridays. She needed a buzz before entering some of the bars she frequented. *So many men, so little time,* was her weekend motto. She was a cougar through and through.

"I brought some crackers and cheese. I thought you might like a snack before heading out. You've been with me for a few years Miss Reed and I've never had a drink with you."

"I appreciate the gesture, Mr. McClure. It's been a great job and now I'm really looking forward to Europe."

"My life's been packed since joining the Company. I joined when my father took over as CEO. Investing has been good to me until the recent setback. It's time to shut down and relax."

"What will you do?"

"Not sure yet. I may buy a house in Arizona for my wife to live during the winter and sell off a few of the properties around the country. Being well off is not all that it's cracked up to be. I never had the time to enjoy the money I made."

Ian poured some more wine and ate a few more crackers. He would have to get something to eat down the street in order to stay and finish everything on his list.

"What about you Miss Reed. After Europe what?"

"I may stay over there. Maybe find some village in southern Italy and learn Italian. My apartment is for sale so I am cutting all my ties with New York."

"Might as well see the world while you still can. I sometimes wish I had a simpler lifestyle and traveled more. Only short trips here and there with the family. Now my son's getting married and grandkids should be next on the list."

For the next forty-five minutes, the two chatted about future plans. Ian had never done anything like this. It felt like he had missed a part of office life by not engaging with any of the people who worked for him. *Business only* had been the creed he followed. This human side of life never surfaced. He was the carbon copy of his father when it came to living.

The wine bottle was empty. Miss Reed had only a small bag of last minute items she found in her desk. Everything was removed the day before. She got up and gave Ian a hug. That never happened the whole time she worked for him.

Ian was alone. He felt empty. Lots to do. "Where was that repair man?" he thought.

*****

Robert made a call was made to Julia. "Miss Reed just left the building. Plan B is a go."

"Be careful Robert. Are you sure you have everything you need?"

Robert was in the parking lot. He was wearing the York Tech overalls. The tool bag was over his shoulder. The dark glasses, blond wig and baseball cap completed the disguise. The security at the front desk stopped him after he entering the building.

"I'm here for McClure Enterprises. They seem to be having power and Internet problems on the eighth floor."

"Oh yes. Miss Reed called earlier and said you were coming. The elevator is behind me on your left. Office 841 on the end."

"Thank you."

Robert walked down the hall. He pushed the elevator button and waited. Two years of working on this case now came to a head. He'd be alone with Ian. Before he left the building he had a lot to get off his chest. Ian would listen. Robert wouldn't give him a choice.

*****

Alan and Cathy arrived at the NYSE an hour before the market opened. They flew in the day before. It was a whirlwind. Going public would change their lives forever. Alan had to buy a suit for the occasion. He never wore suits. None of his employees wore a tie. The four women at Geek Mingle came to work in jeans, tennis shoes and sweatshirts. Feeling comfortable at work was the new MO in the computer world.

As the two waited in the guest room drinking coffee and eating breakfast croissants, they went over what was expected of them in the next few minutes.

"Cathy, if they ask us anything you do the talking, please. You're comfortable engaging with these Suits. I'm having trouble just wearing one."

"Fine but I'm just as nervous. Did you see how many people are out there waiting for us to ring a stupid bell?"

"I know. I'll ring the bell but after that, we're out of here. We may have to shake a few hands but when that's over let's go for a walk. Are we still meeting Laura for lunch?"

"She said she's picking up Jeff at the airport and will meet us at *The Tavern on the Green.* We can walk around the park. Just keep on the suit and change into tennis shoes. That may be a good look for you."

"How about you. Are you going to change before going to the park?"

"No, I like the tennis shoe idea as well. We can keep our dress shoes in the car and put them on when we eat lunch. You are a wealthy man Alan. We at least have to dress the part when we go out in public."

"Laura's boyfriend is flying in from Albuquerque?"

"Yes. They both wanted to take us out for lunch to celebrate going public. Isn't that sweet of Laura?"

"I'm barely coping as it is Cathy. Let's just get through this and get out of here."

One of the doormen in a red coat came into the waiting room. "They are ready for you."

"This is it, Cathy. No going back now. Our lives are never going to be the same again."

"Oh stop being so dramatic. Go out there and ring that damn bell and get this show on the road. I just discovered another company who can use our help so we have a lot to do when we get home."

Cathy and Alan went out to the podium overlooking the floor of the NYSE.

"Who is going to ring the bell? You or your wife?" The man in charge did not know Alan and Cathy weren't married. He assumed they were. It was just another day for him and his job of bell-ringing duty.

"I am." Alan took the mallet from the man in charge and waited for the countdown. He and Cathy had been introduced as the founders of Geek Mingle. Their stock was projected to jump as soon as it hit the floor. The traders were getting restless. Ten, nine, eight, seven, six, five, four, three, two, one. Alan struck the bell with enough force to send the sound throughout the entire room. Another day of big money had begun.

Cathy waved at the cameras and the crowd. By now they traders were walking all over the floor with white papers in their hands. Alan was not sure if it had anything to do with his company or this was a normal day. The scene to a first timer was overwhelming.

"Are we done here?" Alan asked. He was ready to go.

"You are done. You and your wife can exit through the waiting room. Thank you for your participation. Congratulations on going public."

"Thank you. We're grateful for you having us here." Cathy was the PR person and did most of the speaking when it became time to express verbal gratitude. Alan was thankful she was in his life.

The couple made their way through the back door and out of the exchange building. The brass bull was just down the street. Cathy persuaded Alan to pose for a picture with her in front of the massive representative in the world of finance. Several shots were taken by one of the doormen who accompanied them.

They drove their car to the section of the park near the

restaurant where they would meet Laura and Jeff for lunch. Cathy and Alan took their walking shoes out of the back seat.

"That was awesome, Sweetheart," Cathy said.

"It blew me out of the water, Cathy. Thanks for getting me through the morning. Let's not do that again. Ever."

"We'll be fine. Let's put our shoes on at this park bench. We'll have coffee in an hour and lunch at half past twelve."

Alan sat down and switched shoes. He rarely wore dress shoes. They were purchased before he flew from Albuquerque. Alan didn't expect to wear them again.

Across the walkway, was another bench. A homeless man sat next to his grocery cart filled with all his earthly possessions. His long black coat had seen too many years. He was eating his breakfast of French fries purchased from a vendor in the park. Alan reached into his wallet and withdrew a hundred dollar bill. While Cathy was lacing her shoes Alan walked over to the man and handed him his shoes with the hundred- dollar bill placed in the shoelaces.

"I think these will fit you. You'll get better use out of them than I will," Alan said.

The man looked up at Alan and said nothing. His eyes started to tear. It was the look of gratitude. He was speechless. Someone had seen another being in need and did something about it.

"There's something inside the shoe to hold you over for a few days. Alan then removed his coat and handed it to the man. This should fit as well."

The man nodded his head. He had no words he could use to express his thanks. Alan turned and walked back to the bench where Cathy was watching this event unfold. She knew right then this is what she and Alan could do. Move over Buffet and Gates, a new billionaire had just joined the club.

"That was the best thing I have seen all morning. You made that man's day or even week better. Not even the event in the exchange came close to that. Thank you, Alan. I love you."

"Let walk. I have to get the kinks out of my legs." Alan was his humble self. He was young, rich and going to make a difference in the world. He didn't know how yet but he was determined to do so.

*****

Laura and Jeff arrived at the restaurant around noon. They wanted to talk to each other before Alan and Kathy arrived. They had not seen each other for over two weeks.

"This is quite the place to have lunch, Laura. Nothing like this in Albuquerque."

"I think that is why Cathy choose it. It was a big day for them both. We are having lunch with a very wealthy couple so we have to eat at a place that fits the bill."

"I just hope we can pay the bill. New York is an expensive place to live in."

"I'm covering this Jeff. Robert paid me a lot of money when I went to see him on that job. This is my way of thanking him and at the same time honoring Cathy and Alan for their success. You never had a chance to really talk to either of them."

"Funerals are not a good place to chat socially," Jeff said. "This is much better."

A little past twelve, Alan and Cathy arrived. Alan still had on his walking shoes but Kathy had replaced hers with the style suitable for a woman of her status. They found Laura and Jeff sitting by a window looking out at the park. Greeting and hugs by the women and handshakes between the men.

"How did the morning show go, Alan? Did you get to ring the bell?"

"I did but Cathy did all the waving and publicity stuff. I was ready to get out of there before I even arrived."

"That bad eh?"

"It's a bit over the top. Money can make people nuts and the exchange is no exception. The energy was too much for me."

Cathy jumped in. "I loved it. Going there every day would be too much but having the opportunity to ring the market bell is not something everyone in the world gets to do."

"How long are you two going to stay in New York? We are staying at *The Jewel* near the park. I want to show Jeff around the city. He flies back in two days."

"We head back tomorrow. This lunch and a Broadway play will about do it for us on this trip," Cathy added.

"What are you going to see?" Laura asked.

"Don't know yet. We plan to walk around and get scalped tickets. Didn't have time to call in advance and most are sold out."

"You mean you don't have any pull. You just went public on the stock market. Doesn't the world know who you are?"

"Don't be cute Laura. Alan and l like to keep a low profile. Just like Robert Woods did when he was alive."

Cathy and Alan looked at each other quickly and then back at their food. They still had to keep the fact that Robert was still alive a secret. They knew Robert and Julia were somewhere in New York trying to wrap up the Ian case but no contact could be made until it was over.

"How many countries are you expected to be in this year?" Jeff asked.

"Ten. Another six by next year. Setting up the offices with the countries of origin takes time. I have teams doing that now. Who knew Geeks were all around the world looking for love?"

Lunch arrived. The two couples halted their praises long enough to eat a few bites of salad and toast each other with beer and wine. A major accomplishment for Alan and Cathy was completed.

Laura asked, "Are you two planning on remaining in New Mexico?

"So far," Alan said. "We may have to expand and add another working space. I could never live in this city. I'm a country boy and need the open space around me."

Jeff nodded his head in agreement. "New Mexico really gives you that for sure. I hope Laura feels like giving the state a try down the road."

Laura looked over at Jeff. Jeff looked back at her. He waited for a response.

"Are you asking me something, Mr. Williamson?"

"When you feel ready to leave New York I would like you to consider us together in Albuquerque."

"Together like roommates?'

"That would only be the beginning. I want us to give us a try like what Alan and Cathy have."

Laura's face turned a little pink as she considered the question. "Are you asking me to move to Albuquerque and live with you?"

"I guess I am."

"Well just say it. I've been ready to hear that question for weeks."

"Then it's a yes?"

Laura looked over at Cathy. "What is it with men. Do we have to beat it out of them to ask the right questions?"

Cathy smiled and nodded. "I never had to hit Alan but then again I was already living in Albuquerque. I just moved in after a few weeks."

Laura looked at Jeff and blurted her response. "Of course it's a yes. I could be ready to move in two weeks. Is that too soon?"

Jeff put his arm around Laura and kissed her on the lips. "It looks like New York is losing another woman to the Southwest."

The small party finished their celebration meal. Going public and a couple's commitment, all in one day. Both agreed to meet again at Alan and Cathy's house after Laura made her transition to New Mexico.

Chapter

Twenty-Eight

The elevator bell rang as it reached the eighth floor. Robert stepped out, looking both ways before walking down the hall towards McClure Enterprises. He had been going over the plan in his head for the last hour while waiting in the parking lot.

Office suite 841. Robert entered the front office. He could see Ian seated in a chair behind the glass wall separating the receptionist desk and the main place of business. Ian looked up. He still had a wine glass in his hand. He took the last drink, emptying the contents. A short walk to the door separating the two rooms put Ian McClure and Robert Woods face to face.

"Good timing. My secretary said you would be here before noon and you are."

"What seems to be the problem?"

"Well, you can see it's dark in here. We've lost power to our Internet connection. I have to finish up some work on the computer and need access."

Robert entered the office space and placed his tool bag on the floor. He went over to the nearest computer and tried to activate the screen.

"Your right. The system is down. If I could get you to sit at your desk Mr. McClure I can proceed."

"You look familiar. Do I know you?" Ian asked.

"Maybe. Just have a seat." Robert then removed a small pistol from his tool bag and pointed it at Ian.

Ian sat back in his chair. He was sure he knew this repairman but from where? "Who are you and what do you want?"

Robert removed the baseball cap, blond wig, and dark glasses. The recognition of Robert Woods hit with a force that would have collapsed Ian had he been standing. He reached into his pocket. Blood pressure and heart pill went down before he could utter another word.

"You're dead!" Ian yelled.

"Oh, so you do recognize me."

"You're dead. I saw the police report. There was a positive match with the dental records. How can you be alive?"

"You seem to know a lot about my death, Mr. McClure. Why is that?"

"Because I had you killed." Ian was answering Roberts questions without any thought about what he was saying.

"Really? How did you do that?"

"I hired the two men and they blew you up." Ian was in shock.

"So you are saying you killed Robert Woods by hiring men to blow him up."

"Yes, but why are you referring to yourself in the third person. It's you we're talking about."

"Just answer the question."

"Yes, I did."

"The men you hired. What happened to them?" Robert was on a roll.

"Why are you asking me these questions? Why are you here?"

"I wanted to hear you one last time. It's taken me two years to get to this point. We have a few things to get off our chest and I'm giving you a chance to do that right now."

"Like what? Admit to having the hit men killed?"

"That would be a start. Did you?"

"And what if I did. I never killed anyone."

"But you had people killed."

"Fuck you. My father died and I lost my company because of you."

Robert sat down in a chair, still pointing the gun in Ian's direction. "Because of me, you lost 1.5 billion. Better add that to your sorry ass list."

"You had something to do with that?"

"How about this one. Because of me, the countries where you invested in desalination plants nationalized them. Just another item to included on your 'How Robert Woods Screwed Me' list. It could make a great book title."

Ian could not believe what he was hearing. How could this one person cause him so much financial ruin and still be alive?

"How did you do that?"

"A team effort."

"You know what. I don't give a shit what you do. Shoot me if you want. I'm dying and I know it. My wife and son have plenty to live out their lives."

"You may be right but you didn't get the one thing you really wanted before you died."

"Oh, yea? What's that?"

"Revenge. You never stopped me. I'm alive and you won't be for long."

"I was going to ask you how you pulled that off but right now I don't give a shit."

"You should because you could die in prison. I'm here to give you a choice."

"A choice? What kind of choice?"

*****

"Louis, this is Bates. Is your office picking up the conversation over the earphones? It started about ten minutes ago."

"Yes, but it is coming in segments. Whoever's talking to McClure is editing the conversation so they aren't identified. We have enough on tape to make an arrest right now."

"Well I'm in New York and you're not. I'm sending over an arrest team to the McClure office. If this is a live transmission they should be there in twenty and capture whoever is questioning McClure. I've got a feeling that person is holding a gun on him."

"Is that where you think this is going down?" Louis asked.

"It's our best guess. If someone's with McClure in another location then we're shit out of luck."

"Call me after you team gets there. I'm going back to the desk. We have the conversation on speaker."

"We do too," Bates said.

Louis went back to the work desk officer June's desk. They had just returned from having a burger together. The conversation started five minutes after June put on the earphones. As soon as the voices were heard coming over the airwaves she hit the record button.

"Anything else?" Louis asked.

"Yes but it comes in fragments. Someone is editing the conversation. We have Ian admitting to having the Irish hit men killed. Listen. There's more."

*****

"Before I tell you your options I have a few questions."

"Really? Oh, this should be interesting."

"How do you sleep at night?"

"What do you mean?" Ian asked.

"What I mean is how do you have people killed and then live with yourself. I always wondered about people like you."

Ian sat for a moment without saying anything. Right now the blood pressure drug was keeping his heart relaxed. He didn't much care if he lived. He had lost everything including his revenge on Woods. He thought he accomplished that by blowing up Robert's house. Now even that victory was gone. He was defeated in so many ways.

"Tell me one thing. Who was it in that house that blew up? The dental records said it was you."

"Switched them out with a cadaver."

"Very clever. How did you get out of the house?"

"Your two goons from Ireland never saw me slip out the back and through the fence. There's a gate and access to the block behind the house. Timers on lights and the TV shut everything down in order. I was miles away before they even set the explosives."

"Well done. You're indeed a good adversary. One more question for you. Why did you feel you needed to come after the Company after they made you wealthy?"

"You really have no idea do you, McClure?

"Not really."

"Two friends of mine died in Italy. A man, who worked for me, was killed by the Company. Street people were used as lab rats and died in the name or research. These people had lives and families and you have no idea why I needed shut you bastards down?"

"My father was the CEO then. I had nothing to do with that."

"Where you a member of the Company then?"

"Yes."

"Then you are involved. You father deserved to die. I didn't kill him. His poor health and criminal behavior killed him."

"Fuck you. He was doing what he needed to do to protect the Company. I would have done the same thing."

"That is why you and your kind are not fit to run anything. You think you are privileged. Human life means nothing to you."

"The world is a crap shoot. Someone has to step in and keep things in order. People come and people go."

Robert felt his trigger finger start to pull but he stopped. He said, "And you think your way of running the world is best? You arrogant bastard. Who in the fuck do you think you are? Because you were born into money and made a little along the way gives you the right to take away lives just to make the world see things the way you do?"

Ian sat and said nothing. In his mind, the world was in complete upheaval. The rich knew how the world should be run. The rest were in the world to help his kind get through life.

"Don't you have anything to say?"

"Not really. I know I'm right. People who get in the way or don't do their job are expendable. Mark Jones screwed up and had to be removed. We pay people well but if they can't handle the job then they can be replaced."

"You had Jones killed."

"Fuck yes. He let his guard down and my father died. He paid for that one."

*****

"How soon will the team reach the McClure office? Bates asked his team. "We now have him admitting to the deaths of a Mark Jones as well as having the Irish men killed."

"Ten more minutes. Traffic is really bad downtown."

Just then a call came in from Albuquerque. "John, are you hearing this. McClure just admitted to having another man killed. Mark Jones. Do you know him?"

"He was from New York and went missing a while back. It became a cold case."

"We have it all on tape. McClure either does not care anymore or he doesn't know he is being taped."

"I think it's both. We need to get the person who is leading this little interview. How much longer before you men get to McClure's office?"

"Ten more minutes."

"Hurry. This fucking soap opera is getting good."

*****

Julia was monitoring the conversation from her hotel room and editing the parts of the conversation sent to the two police stations. She knew Robert had less than ten minutes to finish with Ian and get out. A listening device was implanted into the earphones so she could hear them talking. She let Robert know through the earplug he had in his left ear.

"Get out Robert. The police will be there in ten."

"Ian here is your choice." Robert opened his shirt to reveal the wire he was wearing. "This whole conversation has been sent to the police. They will be here in a few minutes. They're going to arrest you for the murder of the two Irishmen you hired and Mark Jones. You can either die in prison or finish this right now."

"Shoot me. I don't give a shit."

"Your death will not be on my hands. I have written a confession for you crimes. Sign it and we're done."

"I'm not going to prison you asshole. Shoot me."

"Sign the confession and I'll give you option number two."

"And that is"

"This gun and one bullet. All you have to do is load the bullet and end your pathetic life right now. If you don't you'll rot in jail. I'll be gone before you can load the gun. Sign the paper. Last chance."

Ian was done. He knew it. He would not see his son get married. No life on a tropical island until he died. Ending this now was his only option as far as he was concerned.

"Give me a pen and I'll sign it. Just leave the gun so I can finish this before the police arrive."

"Done. Here it is."

Ian signed the confession. Robert folded it and placed it his tool bag.

"Aren't you going to leave it here?"

"So you can destroy it after I'm gone? I'm smarter than you Ian. Not rich like you but a hell of a lot smarter."

Robert pulled out another gun along with a bullet. He laid them both on the table next to him. "Just put the bullet into this chamber. Shut it like this. Then pull the trigger."

That was the only instruction Robert gave Ian. He backed out of the office still holding the original gun. The wig, dark glasses, and baseball cap were back in place. The tool bag was over his shoulder. He was again the repairman but he was now leaving the building. His gun was returned to the tool bag.

Robert walked down the hall to the elevator. Each step seemed to take an eternity. He knew it would take Ian several minutes to load the gun. He decided to take the stairs and go out the garage exit. The police would be covering anyone coming down the lift. Just as the door closed behind him a shot rang out. Robert let out a sigh of relief. The life of Ian McClure was over.

Chapter

Twenty-Nine

The newspaper headlines covered the story as best they could. Not all the facts were known because the police did not have them all. The person who was in the room with Ian McClure was gone before the police arrived. Ian McClure was found sitting in a chair holding the gun he used to put a bullet up through his chin and into his head.

The video of the York Tech repairman turned up nothing. The van used by the man posing as an employee of York was found three days later. It was wiped clean.

Miss Reed said she never saw the repairman in the office. "He must have arrived after I left," she said. "I only had a glass of wine with Mr. McClure and that was the last time I saw him."

The signed letter of confession arrived at the desk of detective Parks two days after the shooting. Signed, scaled and delivered.

"Louis. A signed confession by Ian McClure just arrived at my desk. Do you want me to read it to you?"

"Hell yes. Is it really McClure's signature?"

"So far everything checks out."

"Shoot. I mean read it. What a fucking story this has turned out to be."

Bates read the letter. "To whom it may concern. My name is Ian McClure. I am dying and want to confess my crimes against my fellow man before I meet my maker. I am responsible for the deaths of two men from Ireland. Michael Riley and Clog Malloy.

They were hired by me to kill Robert Woods from Albuquerque. Mark Jones was another person I ordered killed. He is buried somewhere in the desert of Mexico. I have no location.

My wife and son have no knowledge of my activities. I am sorry and hope they can forgive me.

May God forgive me for what I have done."

Bates sat in silence for a moment. "It's signed at the bottom. The letter was posted from New York. If Ian mailed it then he did it after he died. Someone must have put it in the mail for him."

"John, this is one of the wildest cases I've ever worked on. We're still wrapping up events in New Mexico but we can finally file the Woods case as solved."

"Are you going to pursue the alleged person who was in the room at the time of McClure's death. The partial conversations on tape gave us no clue as to their identity."

"Not from Albuquerque. If you think you need to keep the case open then be our guest. We'll help in any way we can. We think it is the same person who's been sending us information all along and who really solved the case."

"We may wrap it up here in New York as well. Let sleeping dogs lie."

"The best part about the case for me has been by love life."

"Louis, you dog. What about it."

"Officer Parsons is the person I assigned the duty to listen to the tape and record the conversation of Ian. She's gone out with me twice and seems to think I'm a nice guy. Says she's never had so much excitement working with someone on a case. We really hit it off."

"How did you make that happen, Louis?"

"I just did. Never fed her any lines and just told her I liked being around her. That's it."

"And she went for that?"

"It seemed to be enough. She seems to like me for who I am."

"Well, Louis I hope that works out for you. You deserve a good woman in your life."

"So far, so good."

"If anything else turns up on our end I'll call you. A two-city case doesn't happen that often. Did Martin make the front page of the local paper? I know he was being interviewed."

"We both did. The article comes out tomorrow morning. Martin on the front page is a life dream for him."

"You two may even make the paper here in New York. Won't be the front page but it could make page three."

"Send us a copy. I'll have it framed and give it to Martin on his birthday. It's next month. I bet he puts it on the wall in his office."

"Ok, will do. Keep in touch."

*****

Robert and Julia were home the day after Ian's suicide. To avoid detection at the airport in New York they drove to Buffalo and flew to Phoenix.

Alan and Cathy arrived the same day and were already home when their neighbors drove by.

"Did you see the paper, Alan?"

"No. Why?"

"Ian McClure is dead."

"What? When?"

"He shot himself around the time we were having lunch with Laura and Jeff. The police found his body in his office. The article says a suicide note was mailed to the police the next day. In the letter, he confessed to the murders of the two Irish hit men and Mark Jones."

"No friggin way. Do you know what this means? We're finally done having to look over our shoulders."

"Do you know where Robert and Julia are?" asked Cathy.

Alan and Cathy were involved with the NYSE and going public so they had lost track of their neighbor's activities. Robert wanted it that way. Plan B had to be accomplished by him and Julia alone. If he got caught only he would have to answer any questions the police might have for him.

"Call or better yet let's drive down. I want to see them in person."

"I'll bring the car around. I think it's charged."

Alan went out to the garage and unplugged his Prius. He purchased one after seeing William's hybrid last year. Alan decided on the all-electric version. Helping Geeks and their love life was one thing. Reducing his carbon footprint and setting an example for other billionaires was his present goal in life.

The short drive took five minutes. No car in the driveway. The doorbell rang. Carla answered.

"Mr. Alan and Miss Cathy. So good to see you. Come in. Come in."

"How have you been Carla? Are Robert and Julia around? We've been gone and just got back yesterday."

"Yes, they're eating lunch by the pool. Can I get you anything to eat or drink?"

"Two beers. I think we need to celebrate and the alcohol will help."

"You still like that Mexican beer, Negra Modella?"

"You bet. Two, please. By the way, I wanted to ask you about your cousin. You told me once she was a cook and was looking for a job."

"Yes. Carmen. She can cook a Mexican meal just like me. Everything from scratch."

"We are looking for someone full time, like you. Do you think she might be interested?"

"Que bueno. Of course she would be. I'll give her a call while you're visiting Robert and Julia."

"Thanks, Carla."

Two beers were handed to Alan and Cathy as they walked through the sliding glass door to the pool area. Robert and Julia were sunning themselves and looked up when the door opened.

"Alan and Cathy. What timing. How did the bell ringing go in New York?"

"It went great. Cathy got me through it. We met Laura and her boyfriend for lunch afterward. Guess what?"

"Don't tell me. I bet I know." Julia was intuitive about people's love lives and had a feeling Laura and Jeff were a good match. "He proposed to her."

"No, but close. He asked her to move in with him."

"What did she say? I know she said yes."

"Your right. I think we'll have another member of the team living here in Albuquerque in two weeks."

"I knew I should have bottled the air around here and sold it to the women in New York who couldn't get their boyfriends to commit."

"What the hell are you talking about Julia?" Cathy hadn't heard this story.

"Don't ask. It's old news. She's just trying to be funny." Robert blew Julia a kiss at the same time.

"You've seen the paper haven't you?"

"You mean the sports section?" Robert was trying to be a smartass.

"You know exactly what I mean. Where have you been for the last few days? Also what part did you play in this?"

"You two better sit down and have a few sips of beer. We have quite a story to tell you."

"I bet you have, Robert," Cathy said.

For the next hour, the couple filled Cathy and Alan in with the detailed account of their involvement in the demise of Ian McClure. They included their escape tactics out of Buffalo, New York and the signed confession sent to the police the day after

Ian's death. During the telling of their New York caper, Alan and Cathy sat without saying a word. They could not believe this case had finally come to an end.

"Does this mean we're all in the clear? I mean is there anyone left who would want to follow up with this McClure revenge thing?"

"Don't think so. His cousin in Ireland is under investigation for having those two thugs from Belfast in his employment. The case probably won't go far. No one says anything to the police in Ireland, especially if they want to see their next birthday."

"How about the team Ian used to go after people here?"

"Ian's gone. No more paycheck. I'm sure they are going to rent out their services to the next asshole needing some muscle. There are plenty of those around."

"Who's left?" Alan was relieved. He could now run his business and not have the feeling some hit man was following him wherever he went.

"The Company is done. The remaining five investors, who stuck with Ian, are licking their financial wounds. Peggy's been tracking their financial records and discovered they had to sell off assets to cover their losses. They still have money, just not as much."

"Poor babies." Cathy felt nothing for these rich bastards.

"We do have a few calls to make. Laura, as well as William and Leslie, still think I'm dead. They're a part of our inner circle. We have to make it up to them. Everyone had a part in bringing this case to a close. They may be mad at me for a while but it was for their own protection."

"Robert, I think they'll forgive you. Having you alive again, or in your case just alive, is all they would want. How can we do this?"

"Let's wait until Laura moves to Albuquerque. Then we can invite William and Leslie. Jason and Rosa need to be a part of this. I've not spoken to them in a long time. They have no idea what we've been doing."

"Sounds like Julia should plan another dinner. This time we don't need to keep it secret."

Julie jumped in. "I think they need to come to us, Robert. Jason and Laura have never been to our house. You are still dead in the eyes of the police. Do you want to invite them as well?"

"Are you kidding? We gave them the information to close this case. I think leaving them out of this is the best route to take. They could be useful in the future. Not knowing who we are just might help us in other cases. I have a feeling this could be a workable friendship between us and them."

Julia responded, "Really? This I have to see."

"It worked out well, in this case, didn't it? They would have arrested Ian if he didn't take his own life. We might use them again to do the dirty work in other cases. We solve them and they make the arrests."

"I'll give you that, Sweetheart. Also, we have a wedding to plan. Have you forgotten about that?"

"Are you kidding? That all I've been thinking about since we got back."

"You're so full of shit, Robert. Your cute but full of shit."

"No really. I think we should have our next get together at our house but get married at the same time. We can't invite people outside our circle who think I am dead. Let's keep the gathering small and make it a wedding at the same time."

Julia didn't answer right away. She was going over in her mind how life might be different being married. Loving Robert was not the issue. Being married and changing her name along with her identity was not a problem either. Nothing seemed to interfere. It was a go.

"Alright. Mr. Forester. We can do this."

Cathy said, "Now that we are public I have more time on my hands. I can help you plan the wedding and run any errands."

"Really. I'm going to need help. You two being so close is also handy. We should start right away. Let's shoot for next month. Laura should be in Albuquerque by then."

"We better get home. I have to drop by and crack my whip at the office. They need to see me at least once a day. I love my crew but they can get damn silly at times. You know. Geeks gone wild. We still have to be on top of our business."

"What's this I hear about you going international?"

"We already are. We have ten sites going in Europe and the Middle East is now interested. India would be the biggest fish to catch. Over a billion people in that country."

"Alan, you really amaze me. This is incredible. No, this is more than incredible. Did you have any idea this thing would take off like it has?"

"Not really. I even had a movie offer about my life. Some young director wants to call it *The Revenge of the Geeks*. I'm holding out for something more serious."

"Good for you. Don't let some asshole from Hollywood downplay your success. That Mark Zuckerberg movie was pretty good. *Social Network* or something like that. Did you see it?"

"Are you kidding? That was a Geek 'have to see' movie for sure."

"Alright then." Robert put down his drink and stood up. Hugs all around.

Alan was handed the phone number of Carmen from Carla as he walked past the kitchen. Cathy promised to give her a call. With a wedding to plan, she'd need someone right away.

*****

Laura saw on the news the story about the suicide of Ian McClure. Jeff had flown back to New Mexico. She needed to talk to someone right away. She called Sera.

"Did you see the Ian story on the news?" Laura asked.

"I did. I called detective Bates right after I saw the piece. He couldn't give me much information because they were still closing the case. He did tell me something that was off the record."

"What?" Laura asked. She was excited to hear some news.

"The day before Ian took his life, the police in New Mexico and his office received a set of earphones and instructions to listen in on them 24/7. They needed to record everything coming over the airwaves."

"Who sent the earphones?"

"John thinks it's the same person who sent the voice tape of Ian to the Albuquerque office. Whoever it is, they helped the police wrap up the case. Ian killing himself just saved the taxpayers a lot of money."

"What came over the earphones? Anything important?"

"The police were able to get a taped confession that Ian had something to do with the deaths of several people. He didn't give me any names. They're still following up on the identity of some guy from New York. He did mention the two Irish hit men and their connection with McClure's cousin in Belfast."

"No way. All that was on tape?"

"Yea, but the cruncher was a letter that arrived in the mail. Ian basically told why he was ending his life."

"Has that letter gone public?"

"John says the McClure family has stopped the police from releasing the content of the letter. Lawyers are involved so you know how that goes. Justice ends and the BS begins."

"Do you think this is finally finished?"

"It looks like it. What are you going to do?"

"I'm moving to Albuquerque."

"What? When did this happen?"

"Jeff wants us to live together and start a new life. His real estate business is there and I can take wedding pictures anywhere. I'm moving in two weeks."

"Oh, Laura. I'm happy for you and devastated at the same time. I'll miss you."

"We plan on visiting New York regularly. You should visit the Southwest. Their winter weather sure beats this cold blast we get from Canada."

"Yea but I was born here. I love the company at *Leggs* and all that information for future books coming from those women."

"Your right about that Sera. I love that bar too. Maybe I'll try and open one in Albuquerque. There are professional women living there that would love a place to go to without being hit on by every yahoo with a hard-on."

"You know you could be onto something Laura. If you do try to open a place like that and are looking for investors, call me. I have a little money set aside and I know a few others who might be interested."

Laura and Sera talked for another half hour promising to keep in touch. Sera always had a place to stay if she ever ventured out to the Wild West. Laura would send Sera her address when she was settled. Jeff was about to purchase a home with a little space for the both of them. A bachelor apartment would be too small.

Laura hung up. She was sad she was losing a friend in New York. Moving would take her two weeks. She planned to sell all her furniture and buy everything in a Southwest motif. Robert's last check covered that expense. She thought about Cathy and renewing their friendship in the same town. Change was good but sometimes difficult. New doors lead to new beginnings.

*****

Weeks passed and arrangements were made. Invitations for a celebration at the home of Julia were sent. Nothing was mentioned about a wedding or of Robert. It would be a surprise for all those attending. Laura and Jeff were settling into their new home and planned to be there. Jason and his future bride, Rosa, had the date marked on their calendar. William and Leslie were driving and bringing her mother. Doris had never visited Albuquerque.

"Have you heard from Marie and Megan? I want them to attend if they can." Robert wanted as many close friends to attend who helped with the case.

Julia answered, "Megan and Marie have a room reserved downtown in the Hilton. As far as they know we're celebrating the end of a two-year investigation. I'm throwing a party to honor all those who were involved."

"Marie could get away?"

Julia continued, "Classes are finished. She's bringing another sister with her. Her plan is to expose her family members to the US for an education."

"I'm surprised she still going to university. She does have two million bucks from Ian. That's a lot of money, even in America."

"Education is something you can't purchase at a mall. She has the finances to do what she wants. Bringing family members to the States is what she wants to do. She may never have to work but knowing about computers is the future."

"What about Megan. Is she doing ok?" Robert asked.

"She called and said she is looking forward to the party. She loves being a CAT scan tech and working full time. She may not be rich but she doesn't need a man to get her through life. Independence is what she wants."

"So next Saturday is set and they're all coming. Are we good with the way we planned this?"

"Of course. A secret wedding with no fanfare or traditional ceremony works for me. The Buddhist priest is ready and knows what to do. We'll do the ceremony around the pool. Cathy will have most of the food at her house."

"Where did you find the Buddhist priest?"

"I have to fly him in from Phoenix. I thought it best to get someone who doesn't know who you are."

"Good thinking, Sweetheart. Let's go to a movie to unwind. Saturday is going to be here real soon. This could be our last date before we have the same last name."

"What do you want to see?"

"You choose. I'm content sitting in the dark and holding your hand."

"Mushy works. I'll find a romantic comedy. There has to be one of those out there."

*****

Saturday. The weekend arrived and was different for the future Mr. and Mrs. Forrester. Robert remained hidden in the back bedroom. He wore East Indian attire including a hand-woven cotton shirt and pants. Julia greeted the guest wearing a Sari she had flown in from New Delhi. The blue and green colors worked with her complexion and highlighted her trim figure.

The Buddhist priest was introduced as a guest from Arizona. He knew the wedding was a secret and gave no indication what was going to happen in the next hour.

Megan, Marie, and her sister Penelope came together in a taxi. Jason and Rosa drove. They had never been to the home of Julia before today. Laura and Jeff also drove. Carmen, who now worked for Kathy and Alan, also came. Peggy had been in the house all morning helping Julia with last minutes duties. William, Leslie, and Doris were already sitting by the pool when the rest of the guest arrived.

When everyone was in their place and enjoying something cool to drink around the pool, Julie stood up and made an announcement. She needed to choose her words. No one knew that Robert was still alive except for Carla, Alan and Cathy and Peggy. Julie had been thinking about this moment for several days.

"I'm glad you all could come to celebrate the conclusion of a difficult investigation in which you've all participated."

Julie took a sip of her beer to clear her throat.

"What I'm going to tell you is known only by a few people. As you know there was an incident a few months back that happened in Albuquerque. A house was destroyed and the dental records of the body inside the home matched Roberts."

William started to squeeze the hand of Leslie. He could sense something was not right.

"Some of you attended the burial of Robert while others were told to stay home. There was a reason for this and it was all done for your safety. Any connection you may have had to Robert was going to be investigated by the police and maybe members of the McClure family."

Jason was starting to sense something as well. He knew Robert always had a card up his sleeve. He also thought it was unusual for Julia to be dressed in a Sari and a man from India was on the guest list.

"I'm going to get right to the point. Please forgive me and my future husband for doing this to you but it had to be done."

A gasp came from several of the women seating near the waterfall. Each guest started to look around at each other in disbelief.

"You're all really invited to attend a wedding."

This was the moment Robert was supposed to come out of the bedroom and stand at the back entrance to the patio. He arrived, right on cue, and brought everyone to their feet. They couldn't believe their eyes. Robert was alive.

"No way." William was the first to utter a sentence. It was not much of a sentence. More of an exclamation but at least it was something.

"Hi everyone." That was all he said.

"Is that really you, Robert?" Jason managed to ask before shock set in.

Robert spoke. "Please, everyone. Be seated. I don't want anyone passing out. Anyone falling into the pool is on their own. There's no lifeguard on duty."

William and Jason came over to where Robert stood. They had to touch him. Shaking his hand would work just the same.

"Julia and I had to keep this a secret and for that we're sorry. Laura, you especially were in a lot of pain. You kept thinking you were the reason for my death. Actually, you would the main reason we were able to pull this off. I have something for you and Jeff later."

Laura was in tears. They were tears of relief as well as of joy. She carried around the guilt of Robert's death with her for months.

Jeff put his arm around her. He could tell she was going through powerful emotions and would need him to help get her through.

Marie and Megan hugged each other. Their joy was evident. Marie's sister Penelope was in total confusion. She was thinking, who is this man? I thought we came here for a party and then do some shopping. I have no idea what is happening.

Marta could see Penelope didn't have a clue what was going on. She sat down next to her and explained in Spanish who the man was and why everyone was in shock. Penelope then started to understand the excitement that surrounded her. "This means we still get to go shopping, right?" she said.

"Yes, you sister will show you the city and take you where ever you want to go," Carla said.

"I was worried for a moment. So this man died and has come back to life? Like Jesus?"

"No, but most of the people here thought he was killed in an explosion. They now know he is alive."

Robert raised his arms and made a short speech. "My death was faked to draw out the Irish hit men sent by Ian. The plan worked but we had to continue the ruse. If anyone knew the truth they might have been in danger. Now that Ian is dead I can come out of the bedroom and start my life anew. You're all my closest friends and only you will know I'm alive."

William interrupted Robert. "We understand you did this for our protection. Just don't do this again. Do you see these gray hairs on the side of my head? They were not there three months ago. I owe them all to you."

Laughter and more sighs of relief. Julia was ready to start the party but the wedding had to come first.

"I have invited The Honorable Raul Sankar today because he is a Buddhist priest from Phoenix. He is going to marry Robert and me but we need your cooperation. You will be given a desert rose to hold during the ceremony. After our vows, you will each touch us on the forehead with the flower and send us good thoughts. After that, we can enjoy the food and celebrate our union."

Carla and Cathy handed each guest a red flower. The priest went to the head of the yard where statues of three eastern saints were placed. Robert and Julia brought them back from China. Everyone stood as Robert and Julia walked to their assigned spots and began to say their vows. Robert went first.

"I, Robert Forrester, pledge my life together with you, Julia Forrester. I support all that you seek in our lifetime together for your growth and well-being. May we love and share in this expression on earth."

Julie's turn. "I, Julie Forrester, pledge my life together with you, Robert Forrester. I come to you in love and will remain in that moment until we leave this plane of existence. I support you in all that you do. We remain as individuals who continue to express who we are. I love you my dearest friend."

The priest blessed the couple. He placed a white shawl around their necks and looked out at the small wedding party.

"Each of you is to hold this couple in your hearts. That is where they will remain. God lives within each of us. Namaste."

The ceremony was short and to the point. The couple turned to face their friends who had been on this journey with them for the past two years. Smiles and expressions of joy covered their faces. Leslie's mother had not said much for the past hour. She now had a question for Leslie. "I thought you said Robert died."

Leslie knew all this information was a bit much for her mother. She did her best to explain.

"He pretended to be dead for a while. Robert was working on a case and bad men were after him. The evil men are gone now and Robert does not have to pretend to be dead any longer."

"That's good. Pretending to be dead is much better than the real thing. We'll all get a chance to experience that."

Leslie looked at her mother. Doris looked back and gave a wink. She was in her 80s and moving on to eternal life was always on her mind.

Each guest touched the couple on their foreheads as they walked by.   Carla and her cousin crossed themselves just to make sure Jesus was included in the ceremony.

The food was laid out in the dining room. The rest of the afternoon was spent around the pool eating and laughing. This was a day of joy for the newlyweds.

During the celebration, Robert handed Laura an envelope. "This is for you and Jeff. It's the insurance payout for the house that blew up a few months ago. It should cover the principle of the house you two just bought. I named you as the recipient of the insurance. You saved my life, Laura. I hope this can make your move to New Mexico that much easier."

Laura didn't know what to say. Tears of joy filled her eyes. She had gone through a list of emotions in the last hour. Now this?

"Robert, you're the best. I'll recover from all this but right now I am overwhelmed. This is the best gift for us. The house was expensive. This should remove that burden. I can't thank you enough."

"Laura, you were a key to ending this case. Without drawing Ian out we would still be looking over our shoulders. Welcome to Albuquerque."

Laura and Robert embraced. Julia came up to both of them and joined in. "Laura, without you I wouldn't be getting married today. Thank you from the bottom of my heart."

Laura turned and went over to Jeff. They sat together while she told him what had just happened. Julia watched them together. She knew another wedding would be happening soon. With Jason and Rosa getting married next month the wedding bells would be ringing one after another. She needed to start bottling the New Mexico air right away.

One by one people left the home of Robert and Julia. Shopping and touring old town was on the minds of Megan and the two Mexican sisters. Laura and Jeff were taking notes and making plans for their nuptials. Carla and Carmen were busy putting the plates into the dishwasher. Cleanup didn't take long with only a handful of guests.

Finally, everyone was gone. Alan and Cathy were the last to leave. It had been difficult keeping Robert's secret hidden.

*****

As they made their way out the front door rapid sounding clicks from a camera went off. Two men were a football field length away with a powerful telephoto lense.

"Are you sure that's them?" For the past three hours the two men waited for the couple to exit the house.

"I've seen him on TV when he rang the bell at the NYSE a month ago. I'm sure it's Alan Hogan. I also remember his girlfriend. She has a rack most women would die for."

"How much did you say he might be worth?"

"Over a billion. Maybe two. He is one of the youngest billionaires in the country today."

"What's our next step?"

"I'm not sure yet. I know we can turn this into a payday. We need to plan it out."

"I wonder who lives in the house they just came out of. This guy seems loaded as well."

"Maybe but we're going after the pot of gold. No side jobs. This is the big one for us."

ABOUT THE AUTHOR

Jeff Crimmel resides in Arizona after living two years in Baja California in the town of San Felipe. After retiring from teaching in California and Flagstaff, Arizona, in 2008, he who took up writing, documenting his travels in the 70s when he journeyed around the world from 1970 to1979. He took his time. (Living Beneath the Radar).

In 2012 Jeff developed a blood clot in his leg. Treatment with a new blood thinner caused a brain bleed at the base of his skull. A week of therapy and a few interesting experiences in the hospital led him to write Brain Bleed. Ian's Revenge is the sequel in the series.

Mr. Crimmel continues to write fiction, murder mysteries as a way of expressing to the reader how he feels about certain issues in the world today. Stay tuned. There is a lot happening and more to come.